It's All About the Timing

Tom Elder

It's All About the Timing

Tom Elder
trelder48@gmail.com

It's All About the Timing

Dedicated to Mary, Alan and Jack

Any resemblance to persons living or dead is coincidental.

I

Another ugly day in Aspen. Extravagantly wealthy couples stood on sidewalks, posing in front of buildings and businesses that they might have owned. Smiling celebrities were relaxing in restaurants that they treated as personal kitchens and bars, and the City Council began its fifth decade of debate on whether the road coming into town should be two or four lanes. The simple compromise was three, but that was too easy and would have denied the Council the opportunity of continuing to serve the people in the most convoluted and expensive manner possible.

Bobby Early was having nothing to do with any of this. He was going to the beautiful part of Aspen, where his house stood. Well, actually, in comparison to the rest of the neighborhood, it was more of a shack, but as is said in the real estate world, "location, location, location."

His house stood on land where a developer planned to erect another modern day grotesque mansion that complemented the other dwellings that now surrounded his house. The developer, as well as the owners of the mansions, who lived in them about three months out of the year, considered Bobby's house an embarrassing eyesore.

It wasn't that he thought he was sitting on a gold mine. He did, however, consider it more than a possibility that his house sat above a fortune in mined silver. The trophy homes had driven land value higher than nearby Independence Pass along the Continental Divide. This was good, if he wanted to sell. He didn't. Unfortunately, this increase in real estate prices had the consequence of increasing his assessments, thereby raising his taxes. He was virtually unemployed, almost out of savings and getting, in between bouts of resentment, kind of desperate.

He wasn't shy about mentioning that there was a cache of silver buried on his property. It was a means to draw attention to what he considered to be the spoiling of Aspen as it was into what it is now. It served to remind others of the gloried past and the pricey present these Colorado mountains provided.

In a moment of desperation, thinking that if he joined the enemy he could defeat them from within, he had become a real estate broker. In Aspen, all a real estate agent type of person had to do was walk a couple of people into a bank, watch them sign some papers and then cash the check they gratefully gave you for helping each of them think they had swindled the other.

Unfortunately, for Early, he had become a real estate type of person after the recession had begun and had missed out on all those big, easy deals. He did know a lot of those types of agents, though, and didn't like any of them. He resigned after a year of no sales and at the age of sixty was thinking about what he was going to do with his life now that he had to grow up. In the meantime, he wrote weekly columns for the Aspen Chronicle, infrequently bartended, and occasionally worked the sales desk in the town's sole remaining book store. There had been six when he moved to Aspen in the early 1970's.

***

Walking on the opposite sidewalk from the wealthy couples, admiring the colorful planter boxes of pampered summer flowers on the way home with his daily newspaper, Bobby's cell phone began massaging his groin area. It kind of tickled, so Early answered the phone.

"Hello?"

"Bobby, it's Jeff." Jeff Bazzano was a younger friend who owned the restaurant in town that Bobby had to give up when the rent tripled after he'd had it for twenty years.

"I've got bad news. Tad has taken a turn for the worse. He's in the hospital now and they say he may not make it through the night."

Early had to think about this for a minute.

"Jeff, I guess this is one of those times that no matter how you say it, it just sounds like a cliché." Immediately, he regretted saying that, but, unfortunately for him, he had amassed a life-time of experience saying inappropriate comments that made him and others uncomfortable. He had become a master of taking one foot out of his mouth so that he could put the other one in.

He could hear Jeff sigh and imagined his scowl. Jeff had narrow, small eyes that squinted when he frowned and a chin that went flat. His nose looked as if all the air had been sucked through it and was held in place by an invisible nose clip that a swimmer would wear.

"You know, Bobby, that's not really the response we're looking for here."

"How 'bout 'thanks for calling and I'll see you shortly?'"

Jeff mumbled something which Early took to be a sort of acceptance and closed his phone after Jeff had disconnected.

It was only a few blocks to Early's house if he walked directly there, but he was now in more of a mood to amble. Tad had been dying in the hospital for two weeks and Early had already been up to the hospital that morning. Five or six of Tad's friends had been conducting a vigil while having coffee and pastries from the cafeteria. Generally, the only hospital food Bobby liked was Jell-O and the elderly kitchen volunteer had spent three minutes explaining that they were all out except for patient meals. She promised if he returned in a couple of hours she would have the chef make some up and asked him what flavor he preferred. He had a hard time believing that a hospital kitchen "chef" would really want to spend any portion of a morning making Jell-O, but he told her that strawberry was his favorite and to hold the little marshmallows. She had seen the movie "Five Easy Pieces" and with what she thought was a playfully seductive smile asked him where Bobby thought she should hold them. Impressed by her flagrant flirtation, Early blushed slightly and suggested she keep them in the bag. She winked and apparently thought her ancient charms were still as reliable as her white hospital sneakers.

He thought of Tad with Jell-O, a health food they both enjoyed. Then he thought of how Tad was dying from liver disease. The alcohol had found a home and then sabotaged it. Some people died from an outside cause, gun shots or car crashes, but most people, at least in Aspen and the United States, died from their own bodies. From the moment a person is born there is a time bomb ticking and Tad's was about to go off.

Bobby Early walked a few blocks east of downtown, turned south toward Aspen Mountain and began thinking of his old restaurant. Tad used to come in The Cebolla Roja for lunch sometimes, but mostly wandered in toward the end of the night when the kitchen was closed and the bar was a mix of friends and tourists. He was a handsome ski bum and construction worker who was a funny drunk and often did well with the tourist women. He was not opposed to being taken back to an older woman's hotel room and Early wondered if Tad had used his time in the hospital to visit the cafeteria ladies. As a member of the Aspen Volunteer Fire department, he had once helped successfully evacuate a senior housing center and had been rewarded by letters to the editor from elderly women with invigorated crushes on him.

The Cebolla Roja was hugely popular with all segments of locals and visitors. If the restaurant had been in Denver the prices would have been viewed as moderate. In Aspen, the prices were considered cheap, the quality consistently good and the atmosphere interesting. Next to tin types of 19th and early 20th century pugilists framed in large cases, hung mining artifacts from the 1880's and 90's that recalled Aspen's heyday of blasting and chipping silver from its mountains.

Swinging cowboy doors led through almost every passage way and into almost every conceivable accident. The swinging doors that led upstairs to the bathrooms finally had to be removed. In the cocaine days, people would park in front of them on their way back down into the bar and frustrated patrons grew anxious attempting to pass through the animated conversations lodged on the steps. When cocaine lost its cool the frustration evolved into belligerence. Oddly enough, this coincided with Aspen moving from being a playground of the rich to an exclusive domain of the absurdly wealthy. From millionaires to billionaires. This resulted in many of the middle-class and even some of the well-off moving away from Aspen to smaller towns within a fifty mile drive. As property values sky-rocketed in Aspen, so they did in these smaller towns. Many of the people that had already been living in smaller burgs did very well in selling out their property and neighborhoods, and, at the time, not many people blamed them. Eventually, of course, the "housing bubble" burst and a lot of folks got stuck in the gummy mess.

Not Bobby Early, though. He had been too smart to sell when prices were at their peak. He didn't even want to sell, though his neighborhood had sunk to the level of the rich and famous. This was his home.

***

He opened the little gate to his front walkway, stepped up to his tiny porch and found a note on the nail sticking out from his screen door. It read, "Bobby, hope you're doing great today. Call me. John."

That would be John Hamlin, Realtor for the ultra-rich and/or obviously famous. He was as wealthy now as his clients, a bit more on the nefarious side of fame, and as powerful as any agent in town. Hamlin had bought a few blocks of an old neighborhood back in the 1980's for what was then an ungodly amount of money. Bobby wondered if a godly sum of money would be evenly spread around. Nonetheless, Hamlin had relinquished and replenished his ungodly cash several times over and was apparently intent on keeping it this time. He was part of a dedicated group of greed heads whose motto was: "We got ours and are holding onto it. In fact, we're going to grab yours and hold onto it, too." That way all the money would be in one place, pretty much, and if God ever wanted the ungodly cash it would be easy to find. At least, that is what Bobby Early told Becky Hamlin, John's wife.

He would call Hamlin later. It wasn't a good time to delve back into why he didn't want to sell his home sweet shack to Hamlin and his associates. The timing was off. His interest in bantering with Hamlin just wasn't there. Tad was dying and in terms of timing it appeared Tad had less of it to play with.

***

Bobby Early had always been fascinated with and confused by the concept of timing. When he was five and a half years old his father had been killed by a shot of electricity running down a cable from a television antennae to a truck that he was leaning against. Bobby had been standing next to him, not holding his hand or touching the truck. Years later, an astrologer had questioned him about the accuracy of the information provided to draw up his chart, stating that his was the chart of a dead man. And because *he* wasn't dead, his father had died when Bobby was between five and six years old. Not that his father *might* have died, but that he did. Bobby had discussed his father's death with many people over the years and the astrologer's answer seemed to make as much sense as anyone else's. Of course, he was still waiting for God's explanation. That would be definitive. That answer, though, might not come for a while, or it might have already been given and simply not recognized. After all, maybe what it was is exactly what it was: an accident. Wasn't meant to be, but since it happened, everything gets shifted a little here and there. And the accidents keep happening just as if they were planned. Like there was a timing mechanism in people's lives, on the planet and throughout the universe that needed to be continually adjusted within each instant.

***

So, instead of calling Hamlin, Bobby stuffed his note in a pocket, went back out the walkway, got in his truck and drove up to see Jeff and the dying Tad. He almost circled the round-about at the edge of Aspen before entering Castle Creek Road. Bobby had been among those who proclaimed the removal of stop lights and construction of the round-about a silly, wasteful idea. He had broadcast his fervent opinion to customers, purveyors, friends and strangers. One week after the round-about became operational, he apologized to everyone he knew for how wrong he had been. He wrote a letter to the editor of both local papers confessing that he'd been "blinder than a miner's mule". A silver-lining to his apologia was that it put his name and that of The Cebolla Roja, of which he was still the owner at the time, in the paper and on the tongues of talkers. It also pleased the City Council people who had pushed it down through the pockets of citizens and local and state government agencies. The Council rarely received

11

laudations because it mistook them to mean further unilateral decisions were desired and warranted. Bobby soon wrote another letter of apology when the Council subsequently banned water canons, water pistols, water bottles and cups of water from the Fourth of July parade. He felt responsible for encouraging the thought that the Council thought things through.

The mile-long slightly uphill climb from the round-about to the hospital featured the sunny side of Shadow Mountain, an outcropping that plunged the town into early afternoon shade in the winter. In the silver days, so many people were in the darkness and shadows of the mines that the mountain was actually called Sunny Top because the morning light hit there first. Today, it was a shoulder of green hunched high above the town. He pulled into the parking lot and, without thinking, found himself walking toward a meditation garden instead of the front entrance. He sat on a stone bench surrounded by summer's flowers and ferns growing in the splintering, shifting sunlight and shade of aspen trees. He picked up some dirt next to a small clump of moss and rubbed it between his fingers and thumb. The dirt made him think of the Ute Indians that once lived here, which made him think of Low Dog of the Lakota Sioux who said, "This is a good day to die." Bobby had been under the misconception that Chief Joseph of the Nez Perce was the author of that statement until Tad Johnson had cheerfully corrected Bobby and everyone else in The Cebolla Roja one evening. Tad's major in college had been Native American Studies until he changed it to drinking.

Chief Joseph had said, "I will fight no more forever." Either way, Bobby thought, both were probably true of Tad.

Tad was surrounded by his friends when Bobby came into the hospital room. Within a minute a nurse entered and ushered everyone out. Bobby gave the young friends of Tad hugs and then noticed an older woman sitting by herself. She looked as if she had been crying and that she could only glance at Tad's friends momentarily before crying again. Bobby walked over to her.

"Are you a friend of Tad Johnson?"

The woman looked up silently, shifted her watery gaze to the floor and nodded.

"I'm his aunt." She rose from the chair, extended her hand and introduced herself as Donna Deerfield.

"I'm sorry, but a handshake just won't do. You need a hug, Aunt Donna." Bobby smiled and gave her a brief hug which Donna returned.

"You can just call me Donna." She gave a slight pursed smile, but her soft brown eyes lit up a little and she asked him who he was.

"My name is Bobby Early. Tad has been a friend the last few years. Well, actually, his friends have been friends more than he has and I guess I'm up here to see them as much as I am him."

She gave Bobby a questioning look that seemed to ask, at the same time, are you really that insensitive and that honest?

"That's very kind of you," Donna said, instead.

He realized that his reply had been open to an unflattering interpretation, but he wasn't interested in flattering himself. No, and could he really be thinking of flattering the Aunt of the dying nephew?

"Well, if I was as kind as you are attractive, I probably wouldn't have just said that."

Bobby smiled and lifted his palms up while slightly shrugging his shoulders. Donna just stared at him.

"Do you know Jeff Bazzano?" he asked.

"Sure. He's been so helpful to me and Tad's mother."

13

"Well, I need to step over and speak with him for a minute. Will you still be…"

Suddenly, there was a disruption at Tad's door. One of Tad's friends, Tracy, was being escorted out of the room by the nurse, who said, "There will be no hot stones placed on his forehead or anywhere else without his doctor's permission. Please respect privacy here and remain outside of the room."

Tracy explained how the stones weren't hot, only warm, and had been gathered from the sacred mountains of New Mexico, a known source of healing energy formations that were one day going to bring peace to all mankind. As she finished speaking to the nurse, gradually bringing her voice from a calm, soothing tone to a paint-peeling, shrill, accusatory, finger-waving, condemnation enunciation, a priest approached. The diminutive priest explained that God made the world and the world made stone, so he would be honored to be presented with a stone that he would keep with him as he visited with Tad Johnson in a few minutes. First, he said, he needed to meet with the woman in the next room. She, too, was dying. Bobby thought about the holy woman he had known when he was much younger. Those who had gathered around her as she passed had remarked that they could have used sunglasses because her soul was so bright. Bobby had ever since been concerned that anyone attending his death would probably need night vision goggles. He hoped that was an exaggeration, but he also feared it was only a weak attempt at humility.

The priest returned from the next room as Donna was telling Bobby that she had thought Bobby was at the hospital to visit the dying woman instead of her dying nephew dying.

"Because I am closer to her age than Tad's?" asked Bobby.

He hadn't seen the woman, but had noticed previous visitors to her room and they seemed to be about his age. Once people reached their sixties they joined the generation of old folks. Much of the subtle differentiations came down to make-up and being physically fit. Bobby didn't wear make-up and both Donna and he were in good shape.

"Yes," Donna said. "Frankly, I haven't seen her, but almost all her visitors seem to be, well, our age. If I'm not being too presumptuous, I think we might be about the same 'up there in years'."

Bobby grinned and replied, "I do believe that it would be presumptuous for *me* to assume we're about equal age, Donna. You are undoubtedly younger than I."

"Well, of course, I am, even if I'm not."

They stopped the world for a few seconds and actually looked each other in the eyes and let those stranger eyes become familiar. The faintest of closed-lips smiles accompanied the acquaintance.

The priest walked over to them and asked if Donna was a relation to Tad. She nodded, introduced herself, and with a backward glance at Bobby joined the priest as he approached Tad's door. Inside, Donna watched the priest take the stone he had received from Tracy, rub it in his hands and place it on the area of Tad's solar plexus.

"You never know," said the priest. He had travelled throughout the Southwest and had great respect for Native American's traditions and beliefs. He wasn't too crazy about Tracy, but there was no reason to discard the message, throw out the stone with the bearer or let Tad's fading body be denied a last touch of the planet.

The door opened and the doctor came in. She was a very pretty woman in her early thirties who looked ten years younger. Perhaps it was the freckled face. If she was an older woman, those complexion signatures would be called liver spots and would help her appear ten years older than she really was. Either way, it was just another reminder to Donna that it's too easy to misinterpret a person's age by their appearance. And, in Bobby's case, maybe she had done that. Maybe he was younger than she. He didn't really look like he was her age, the same as hers, but then she didn't either. Neither one of them acted like they thought sixty year old people were supposed to act, but nobody seemed to know anymore how that age group, bordering on the ever-shifting definitions of senior citizen, were acting these days. And that age group was so self-absorbed they weren't aware how other age groups were defining themselves. Oh, well, Donna thought. She would get back to that later.

"Donna Deerfield? Hello, I'm Dr. Lacey and I'm covering for Dr. Monk. He was called Downvalley for surgery. Unfortunately, he doesn't think he'll be back in time. Do you understand what I'm saying?"

Donna reached for the metal arms of a chair and slid into its seat. "Yes, I do." She turned to the priest and asked him to give Tad the Last Rites.

Bobby was talking with Jeff Bazzano when Donna emerged with Dr. Lacey from Tad's room. They ceased conversing when the women approached, giving Donna the distinct and uncomfortable impression that they were talking about her. Jeff leaned into her with a firm hug while Bobby Early introduced himself to Dr. Lacey.

"Are you a friend of Donna?"

"No, I'm just a friend of Tad Johnson." He looked around and added, "And these kids here." He was glad that the "kids," all in their thirties, hadn't heard him. He wondered if he should continue his conversation with Jeff now or wait until this evening. They had been reviewing plans for Tad's memorial when Bobby had insinuated Donna's attractiveness into the conversation. Jeff offered

Bobby a furrowed, squinty-eyed stare and Bobby returned a look of resignation. Neither one of them could believe Bobby was considering flirting with Donna while her nephew lay dying a few feet away. But he was.

"You have my sympathies," Dr. Lacey offered and walked over to Tad's friends. Bobby watched her as she spoke to each one of the twelve and took their hand or touched their shoulder. After she finished, Bobby turned back to Donna and Jeff. They both had tears in their eyes and their arms around each other.

Donna repeated for Bobby's benefit that the Last Rites had been administered and that she was staying at the hospital, hoping that Tad's mother would arrive in time from New Orleans. The flight was due in a couple of hours and Dr. Lacey had said that Tad might make it until then. Tad was unconscious, but Jeff and Donna both expressed hope that Tad's mom would at least be able to spend a few minutes with him before he died. Jeff told Bobby that he had mentioned to Donna about the possible memorial for Tad which he and Bobby had been discussing when she and Dr. Lacey approached them a few minutes before.

"I know we will want to do something here in Aspen," said Donna. "After all, he's spent most of his adult life here and it's amazing how many people he knows." In addition to the fire department, Tad volunteered with the search and rescue teams specializing in saving people from themselves. The teams were fraternal groups whose expertise and friendly influence spanned the valley communities. Tad often remarked whenever these teams saved a life, that it was astounding to him how many folks he suddenly knew. People appeared from everywhere to thank him.

***

The working class of the town was very close knit, young and old, newcomers and veterans, ski bums and

17

bank tellers, bartenders and bus drivers. They all had one thing in common that overrode any distinction of educational or geographical origin. They all had to work at least one job, often two or three, to have any chance of staying from one season to the next. Spring and fall were lean times, so the bonanza bucks of summer and winter needed to be flittered away on fun in a discriminating fashion. Enough for rent, and possibly food, must be saved until the next wave of tourists came cashing through. In the case of those who had year-round jobs those positions were subject to lay-offs and cut-backs after the visitors left.

One of the exceptions to the rule was Jeff Bazzano. He was a trust-funder. Parents with fortunes gave large sums to their children to help them purchase businesses and residences. Most of them were young, some were idealistic and a few were creative. Jeff was all of these.

II

John Hamlin's real estate company was named House and Home. Hamlin was about the same age as Bobby and had made a fortune twenty years earlier. While the fortune had been made, Hamlin began making over himself. Bobby first noticed it one day while skiing during Christmas week. Hamlin was in a short lift line with some other skiers. All of them were dressed in outfits that spoke of a trip to the most expensive section of the store that very morning. Hamlin's had a fur collar to match his clientele's. This from a man who just weeks before, on Thanksgiving's opening day of the season, wore blue jeans and a faded lime green parka. Three days after Bobby saw him in Thanksgiving's lift line, Hamlin had been assigned to answering phones at the real estate office where he had only recently been employed. It was a rookie's job, working on a Sunday morning. After answering one phone call, he was showing a wealthy Arab a mansion on the mountain. Within ten days the deal was done and Hamlin joined a new social and financial circle. The day Early and Hamlin encountered each other in the lift line with Hamlin's entourage, Hamlin didn't return Bobby's greeting.

The office of House and Home was on the brick mall downtown that opened up to Wagner Park, a large playing field that hosted rugby games, dogs chasing Frisbees and the annual Food and Wine Festival featuring thousand dollar-a-day tickets. Before Hamlin opened his office, he bought out a t-shirt shop owned by Freddie Finker, an eighty-year-old former jazz trombone player now retired to Phoenix, Arizona, and suffering from what

19

was later diagnosed as Alzheimer's disease. Some people thought Hamlin had taken an unfair advantage in the transaction.

Clients entered through two oversized wood and glass doors. The wood was mahogany and the glass was etched with sketches of Aspen Mountain in winter and summer. The left door featured white outlines of skiers descending through the steeps and slopes. When the door opened, what had been a fuzzy light gray brush stroke in the middle of the design revealed itself to be the line of gondolas taking the skiers up to the top of the mountain. The right door suggested an iridescent green with fields of red and gold wild flowers that shimmered when the door opened and closed.

Once inside, the scene was more like what someone had imagined a venerated English library would be if it had been set inside a Persian palace. Beautiful Middle-Eastern rugs alternated with dark cherry wood desks. Intricate tapestries serving as wall hangings separated gorgeous artist renderings of expensive Aspen area houses. SOLD was stamped in red ink across the drawings and pictures. Several of these were of houses in Bobby's neighborhood. Plaques and certificates of awards and recognition, most mentioning Hamlin's name, were prominent throughout the room, on desks, bookcases, shelves and walls.

Becky Hamlin leaned over the receptionist's desk, stiff-arming her hands on two stacks of folders.

"If you can't get it done, I'll have to do it myself. And if I have to do it myself, someone else will be doing it next time so I don't have to. Do you understand, Melissa?"

The pretty young blonde understood that no matter how much or how hard she tried someone else would be doing it the next time. Melissa pushed herself away from the desk, stood and leaned on it in the same manner as Becky.

"Fuck you and the man you rode in on," said Melissa with just enough volume for the entire room to hear. It was possible that people in offices with doors not completely shut also might have heard. She pulled open the center drawer of the desk, removed some personal belongings, chiefly a cigarette pack and breath mints, and calmly slid the chair back underneath the desk.

"Aspen's full of pretty young women, Melissa, and not all of them are as empty of brains as you." Becky turned, walked to the summer door and opened it as Melissa smiled at her on her way out. Becky marched through the maze of desks and into John Hamlin's large office at the rear of the room.

John sat in the red leather chair behind his broad oak desk. His thin-lipped smile suited his too-tight tie and jacket. Becky slammed the door behind her and laughed. She cocked her head, put her fingertips behind her left ear and said, "Like 'em?"

"They're beautiful, just like you. New?"

"Of course. Got 'em from Joan at Sunrise Jewels. Talked her down $500."

"That sounds about right. I guess you needed new earrings."

"Right now what we need is a goddamn new receptionist."

"So I heard."

Rarely did John Hamlin hear what was going on between Becky and the staff so quickly. He let her rant some about how irresponsible and ungrateful Melissa had been, anyway, before Becky finally got around to her solution for a replacement.

"Hell, maybe I'll just do it myself," she said.

Hamlin knew this wasn't a good idea. She had played receptionist once after they had married. If John really loved her, he would open his books to her and let her

21

see how much money *they* now had. Instead of being in awe and realizing she had hit the mother lode, Becky saw where John could save some money and, at the same time, she could keep a closer eye on the employees. She was convinced that not all the profits due House and Home were necessarily finding their way into Mr. and Mrs. Hamlin's personal house and home.

Real estate transactions are not always about making the seller of a home and the buyer of a house happy. Sometimes, it turns out, they are also about the agents making some extra money above their usual commission percentage. There had been some unproven rumors that Hamlin's agents worked both sides of transactions to their own personal benefit and had actually accepted surreptitious payments to raise or lower buying and selling prices. This, of course, is illegal and unethical. Becky wanted a part of that.

She also had an aggravating tendency to violate one of the prime tenets of the business: if the wife likes the house the deal is more than half way there. Exhibiting coarse proclivities of the nouveau rich, Becky had been overheard commenting deprecatingly about wives and girlfriends' taste in clothing and accessories. Occasionally, there had been nasty opinions expressed about one wife to another that, unexpectedly, were relayed. And, of course, the interior decorating choices of clients were always brought into question.

However, Becky's crowning achievement hadn't been so much with the clients as with the staff. A rather shady practice among some agents was stealing clients from other agents. Becky encouraged this, thinking it made the agents tougher and sharper. Unbeknownst to Becky or John, however, several of their agents suffered extended bouts of attacks from the loyalty and integrity portions of their character. When this was exposed, accusations of not playing by the rules were leveled at these agents. Two of them were fired and two resigned. All four filed charges with the local board governing Realtor ethics and behavior. This made for some salacious headlines in the town's newspapers, as well as for some interesting lunches between other Realtors and their clients. The Gang of Four, as they became known, was welcomed in other offices where they adopted some of the tactics *against* House and Home that they wouldn't do *for* it. John didn't appreciate the notoriety and Becky didn't appreciate John's attitude that, not necessarily, was any press good press. The local board allowed enough time for the press and gossip to fade away, then dismissed the charges. The president of the board had given John his first job and, among other considerations, didn't desire his former student to suffer sanctions. There had been a late night meeting between the two in an expensive restaurant just before the board's decision.

Still, Becky resigned as the Office Manager during the episode and the remaining staff threw her an expensive going away party on the company business account.

"Honey, I'm not sure that is the best answer to this situation."

"I straightened 'em up once before and I can do it again, John."

"You're the best person for the job, no doubt about that, sweetie. But it may be a little too soon after your going away party and, besides, we need you to break Bobby."

It was true that it had only been six months since the "House and Home Agents on the Street" headline in the Aspen Chronicle. And also true that John thought Becky was the key to convincing Bobby to sell his bungalow.

"Besides," John added, "I think Casey is ready for the job and I think she would be a good fit."

"Oh, I'm sure you do. She'd be a good fit for your prick is what you mean, John."

"Well, she might, but I'll never find out."

Becky looked at him and the anger quickly left her eyes and she smiled. "No, you won't, will you?"

"I don't bring up your past with Bobby and you don't bring up my past with you." John had propositioned Becky at a Halloween party a month before they were married. Unfortunately, for John, he didn't know it was Becky. He thought Becky was out of town and a last fling with a woman dressed as a hooker cum laude would be a harmless secret. John's costume consisted of twenty dollar bills coming out of his pants, shirt and coat. He claimed to be a Realtor, Banker and Lawyer. There were a few members of each profession at the party and each thought it a cheap and accurate shot at the others. Becky thought she would surprise John at the party in her fabulously trashy hooker costume. Her fake French accent was so phony it was charming. She wore a mask that completely disguised her facial features. Certainly, she was offended that John had tried to pick her up, but even more so that he hadn't recognized the beauty spot above her left nipple. She took all his money that night and thereby began the tradition that continued to this very morning.

"Well, let's get Casey started," Becky said as they walked hand in hand, exchanging trademark looks of love. They approached Casey, a tall brunette wearing a short navy blue dress and high heels. Everyone clapped and rushed to congratulate Casey after Becky made the announcement. Casey was so excited she excused herself to the restroom to dry her eyes. There, she said to the mirror, "Great, now I'm next. Thanks, Melissa!"

God wasn't too happy with conditions at House and Home, but he'd seen worse.

III

Jeff Bazzano carried two plates on his left arm and another in his right hand as he approached a small booth in The Cebolla Roja. He saw Melissa enter through the cowboy swinging doors at the front of the restaurant and marveled at how she always seemed to be beaming. "I'm beaming for you, baby," she would say to Jeff in the mornings and then to the sun as she pulled up the wooden slat shades.

She stood near the far end of the bar while Jeff served the patrons, two electricians and a City Parks irrigation worker. They were regulars that were almost always there for Thanksgiving dinner on a Wednesday. Roast turkey, mashed potatoes, gravy, green beans and cranberry relish. A different lunch special was set for Monday through Friday and the roast turkey on Wednesdays had become even more popular since Jeff began advertising it as Thanksgiving Dinner. This confused some patrons because they had difficulty with the concept of dinner at lunch time. Also, every Thanksgiving, a few customers complained that it had ruined their traditional Thanksgiving feast the next day.

Jeff and Melissa met halfway down the bar and she excitedly told him about the incident at House and Home. He picked her up, pirouetted her around and put her back down with a laugh.

"For a girl that doesn't swear, that was quite an exclamation point you slapped her with."

Melissa's last boyfriend had been the kind of guy whose first reaction would have been to threaten to go tell Becky what a bitch she was and challenge John to a fight.

Jeff was delighted in what he saw was yet another demonstration of Melissa's surging confidence. Or, was he to be concerned that she just gave up a well paid job with benefits and probably should not be expecting a positive letter of reference? By the time he finished kissing her and ordering her a glass of wine he knew he was going to be both delighted and concerned. Perhaps, even more so when she told him she was ready to work at The Cebello Roja. Jeff was going to put off that moment as long as possible, though he knew it was coming as sure as the afternoon thunderstorm brewing outside.

The Cebello Roja was positioned halfway down a bricked mall facing south toward Aspen Mountain. The mountain's peak could barely be seen these days, buildings across the mall blocking off the "back in the old days'" view of hikers on the green summer slope and skiers barreling down the afternoon's last white winter run. The view west, however, was still largely open and that's the direction from which most storms struck town.

On early August afternoons like this, a thirty-minute thunderstorm usually kicked through about 2:45 on the mining era miniature grandfather clock high on the wall behind the bar. It was more like a grandson clock and the hands of it were fashioned from silver in the shapes of a pick and an axe. The clock struck 2:30 with a soft single chime and the wind began to whip through the cottonwood, spruce and aspen trees planted along by narrow little streams meandering through the mall. A little early today, thought Jeff. He paused for a minute, wondering if Bobby Early was still at the hospital, before leaving Melissa at the bar.

The servers and bussers were already asking customers seated in the outdoor patio area to be prepared to move inside as they cleared the other tables so the settings wouldn't get wet from the coming rain. Visitors looked questioningly at the sky, didn't feel any rain and wondered if these scurrying staffers weren't over reacting. Locals were gathering their plates and drinks and heading inside. Jeff saw the band of heavy shaded gray Downvalley growing taller, took in the sign asking patrons to please wait to be seated on the patio and looked throughout the restaurant for open tables. Sometimes people from the outside joined customer's tables inside, and sometimes they stood until the fast-moving storms passed. Today, there was room for everyone to sit, if they came in now.

Once the ordained downpour arrived, strollers on the mall rushed into any store or restaurant they could find to escape the rain. Many shops did their best business during these summer squalls, having a captive clientele. The few restaurants that weren't normally busy prayed for rain. The single dive bar remaining in town, seedier than a community garden watermelon, poured its only daylight drinks during this precious half hour.

Within five minutes thunder, lightening and horizontal rain slammed through Aspen. Jeff and Melissa went upstairs through some cowboy swinging doors and into his office.

"Honey, I'm proud of you," Jeff started, but was interrupted.

"God, it's been half an hour and I'm already looking back on the last six months working for them and wondering what the hell was I thinking."

God didn't really seem to mind having his name used this way and was often encouraged when people thought of hell at all. It didn't happen as much as it used to in the good old Biblical days. Though, he admitted, all this sensational talk about the Mayan Calendar running out of time, every other Hollywood movie depicting the end of the world and, in fact, some serious discussion on the actual End Times had made hell popular again.

"Sweetie, I know you are excited, as you should be, and I'm excited for you, for us," Jeff said, hoping to finish his thought before she bubbled over again. "But, right now, I need to get back downstairs and help out on the floor."

These possibly chaotic times in the restaurant were Jeff's forte. He thrived on situations that were barely under control. Melissa knew and appreciated this, but still had to tuck her tongue behind her lower teeth so she didn't contest it. Instead, she moved next to him and pressed her body against his.

"We're standing on a floor right here. And there are other things we can do besides stand on it."

Jeff smiled and parts of his body became more sensitive. It wouldn't be long before his mind ceased to function coherently. In a last gasp, he whispered, "I love you more than The Cebolla Roja," backed away slowly, opened the door behind him without looking and laughed as he bounced down the stairs and through the cowboy swinging doors. Her naked body danced in his mind, smooth and silhouetted, as he slid through the crowd of customers and staff and into the kitchen.

IV

Square sections of strawberry Jello-O jiggled as the cork surface of the tray kept the small bowl secure. Bobby was carrying the tray at an angle while watching the hard rain turn into a minute of hail. It was another reminder why he didn't miss owning The Cebolla Roja all that much. He could envision the busyness moving from the patio to the inside and thought of Jeff working the crowd, pleasing everybody all the time, just as Abraham Lincoln wanted to do but knew he couldn't. Of course, it wouldn't last for Jeff, either. The kitchen would get behind, the bartender would stop making drinks to answer the phone, a server would take the wrong plate to a table, a keg would blow, the lights would flicker and the power would go out. Almost every day during the summer this, or a variation of it, would happen when the afternoon storm came through. But Jeff would keep a juggling act going, just as Bobby had, until the crisis mode and mood passed. As the customers dispersed outside again, the staff would gather together and cheer with a shot of their favorite liquor unless they were on the shot wagon again. Someone was always trying to recover or begin a new lifestyle.

"I've never been to a hospital that didn't serve Jell-O," said Donna. "I've also never been to a hospital that *did* serve alcohol." Bobby opened the miniature plastic bottle of chardonnay for Donna and sat down opposite her at a small table against the wall where the hail was turning back into rain. "If we're lucky, we'll see a rainbow," said Bobby nodding to the light graying of the Downvalley sky.

"If we're lucky, my sister will make it here in time," replied Donna.

29

Bobby poured the small bottle of wine into a paper cup and handed it to Donna. He placed the bottle on its side on his Jell-O tray and began spinning it with his right thumb and forefinger.   Absentmindedly, his left hand moved up behind his left ear and began to comb through his blond and graying hair. Thinning on top, he had let the sides and back grow out, though it seemed to him that at a certain length his hair just quit growing. He hoped he hadn't reached that point, yet, but he also knew there was nothing to be done about it. He could always cut it short again and mark time by how long it took to grow back. Though, the gray could do that for him, too.

Equally absentmindedly, Donna rotated the paper cup of wine as they both continued to stare out the window at the quickly clearing storm. Donna felt comfortable in the silence, but Bobby felt as if he were intruding on her contemplation of Tad and her sister.

"My sister's name is Laura and she hates the name Laurie. Have you ever met her?" No, Bobby thought, but I was just thinking of her. By this time in his life, Bobby was never surprised or startled when so-called coincidences such as this occurred. Most of the time, though he noticed them, he didn't mention it. He thought God was just checking to see if he was paying attention.

"No, I haven't. I was just thinking that you might want to have some time alone to think about things and prepare to see her."

"Yes, you know, I probably would."

The moment the words left her mouth she wished she could retract them. All she had thought about since this morning had been Tad and Laura. She had been at an old boyfriend's house in Denver when Jeff Bazzano had called her with the news that Tad had only another day or so to live. When Donna had seen Tad just a couple of days ago he hadn't looked well, but he was more active and upbeat than he had been during the previous few visits she had made.

She hadn't felt like spending last night alone and had met her old boyfriend at a downtown restaurant. One glass led to another and they had left to spend the night together at his place. He passed out naked in bed and Donna remembered again one of the many reasons they were no longer a couple.

She was still dressed in her clothes from last night when the cell phone rang with Jeff's call. She went home, changed, packed and drove back to Aspen. As she was leaving Denver, the old boyfriend called and thanked her for the evening. He didn't remember the love-making, he said, but he was sure it was good. If only, Donna thought. Ever.

She drove past Vail and headed south to Leadville, an old Victorian town with a checkered and prosperous mining history at 10,000 feet elevation. Leadville had dominated Aspen in the early days of the silver boom, but had no skiing to offer and not many people wanted to live in the thin air and brutal winter cold. In the summer, Leadville was host to endurance races on foot and bicycle and offered access to those who wanted to climb "Fourteeners" – mountains with peaks 14,000 feet or more – and also were thirsty for white water rafting. She ate chicken enchiladas for an early lunch in a small, colorful and noisy Mexican restaurant, chatted with the Latinos in impeccable Spanish and drove off toward Independence Pass.

She pulled her VW bug off the road several times to look at small herds of deer and elk. She walked along a creek in between wild flowers and memories of Tad Johnson. Indian Paintbrush for the time they painted flowers on Laura's garage door while Tad's mother was on a house-hunting trip in another part of town. When Laura returned and saw the wild splash of color she decided against moving. Penstemon for the Roman Candles the three of them would fire off during July Fourth celebrations on the driveway in front of that garage door. Columbines for the way Tad spread out with his 6'5" frame and easy smile, his head bobbing from his long neck. Primrose for the path he didn't take, mountain bluebells and purple beardtounge that matched Tad's eyes and aura, and white bittercress that reminded her why she was on her way back to Aspen.

Donna stopped again at the top of the pass before the descent into town. Snow was still packed in spots and had no plans of moving, global warming or no. The Earth's rising temperature was bringing more moisture to the top of the Rocky Mountains which meant a couple more degrees of heat had to melt another twenty feet of snow. Boulders had been parked by glacial forces between where the cars had pulled in and the peaks to the north. Hikers with small backpacks, frisky dogs and families with protesting children wearing Disneyworld hats dotted the landscape. Tad would never again see this Continental Divide panorama that stretched east to the Atlantic and west to the Pacific. She took another picture in each direction between wiping tears, acknowledged with a self-conscious smile the concerned looks from an elderly couple carrying cameras and canes, slid back into her bug and crept back out onto the highway.

She made a final stop near a series of waterfalls and walked above them into a grove of aspens. White-barked, with shimmering green leaves (they didn't begin their quaking until autumn was awakening), she noticed that she could see the forest because of the trees. They were so close and she was too near to miss them. By looking at one she saw them all. She was overwhelmed by this gift of nature that she stood in and above. She would be grateful for this when she stood beside Tad's bed.

***

Now, here she was in the hospital cafeteria telling Bobby Early she wanted to be alone. All she had been was alone, even with Tad's friends eager to spend time with her and their common sorrows. Yet, it was true. She did want to be alone. She actually wanted to be alone and alone with him at the same time, but they didn't know each other that way.

Donna was tired of one-week stands with old boyfriends that only reinforced the reasons why those relationships had failed. She had also chosen to believe that the frogs had absconded princes and that if they ever escaped she'd be paying attention. She knew she might meet him in a library, coffee shop, grocery store or car accident. She didn't think she'd encounter him in a bar or a hospital. Bobby Early looked like he might have been a frog at one time. There was only one way to find out, but this wasn't the time.

"No, wait. Finish your Jell-O, at least."

"I see. Interested in my nutritional needs, are you?"

"If I was interested in you I would be. Now I'm also thinking that you are wondering what kind of wacko woman would say something like that at a time like this."

"I'm thinking the kind of wacko woman that can have her head and heart in more than one place at a time." Bobby looked carefully at Donna and saw her blush just for an instant. There was something about her that spoke of worldly wise and childish innocence playing and working together. Her blonde hair maybe wasn't really so blonde, but it didn't appear that it was supposed to be. Her brown eyes weren't pools to fall in to, but they were warm and their sparkle didn't conceal an angry flash. She was rather tall, about 5'9", but she didn't hunch over to diminish it or use it to intimidate. Embracing her height and fabulous figure was something that Donna had no problem with. Nor, Bobby thought, would he.

This was an image, an urge that came from deep within him. He didn't identify it with lust, he wasn't surprised by it, he wasn't ashamed or embarrassed by it, though he was moderately disturbed that he wasn't. Normally, if he had found himself interested in a woman whose nephew was dying a few corridors away, he would have thought himself a scoundrel and an insensitive, brutish lout. When disappointed in himself he often relied on British denunciations. An education that included college and ditch digging had bored him with descriptive insults such as "dirt bag" and "slime ball". He used British because it was the only other language he knew. He did know some swear words and phrases in Spanish and Japanese, but he wasn't as sure of them and couldn't carry on a dialogue with himself using them.

Donna wore a purple tank top and white shorts that were more than half way to her knee. Bobby thought she was the kind of person that was comfortable in her own clothes. He noticed her earrings of Zuni silver with turquoise inlay, turquoise necklace and very little make up. She was pretty in a spicy, seasoned way. In her youth, with no wrinkles and less gravity, she must have been irresistible. Bobby was still attracted to younger women and occasionally they were attracted to him, but he found himself actually much more drawn to women his age these days. Somewhere in a grocery store one day, he saw a mother and her adult daughter walking down the aisle toward him and after they passed he could only see the mother in his mind's eye. At first he attributed this to the fact that his eyesight was beginning to fail and that he needed glasses. After the next few similar episodes he switched to the theory that the problem wasn't in his mind's eye, but his mind. However, when he began getting more erections around older women than younger women at cocktail parties he realized that it was also a physical reaction. Gradually, he accepted this change of life and was quite pleased. He understood that the possibilities had just multiplied.

Nonetheless, he didn't like thinking of himself as a scoundrel and was happy to sense the feeling evaporating. He and Donna had exchanged greetings of interest and now it was time to let that lie. They were only being honest with one another. If there was any lying to be done later it would appear that it would be the lying together in bed. An auspicious beginning in an inauspicious setting.

"Still, if you want to be alone, I understand."

Donna took a sip from her paper cup of wine. "I think I'll try some company. I've been alone for a while. Well, actually, that's not completely true. I drove over from Denver this morning, but last night I was depressed and met an old boyfriend."

"How old?"

"Probably about your age."

"Oh, a younger man, huh?" They both smiled and relaxed.

"Okay, about *our* age. We went together, kind of, for a couple of years a couple of years ago."

"Which was it?"

"Which was what?"

"Or what was which? Was it kind of a couple of years together and ago or kind of a couple together?"

"All of the above. I traveled a lot and he didn't, so he was always there when I came back home. Sometimes it was like I'd never been away and other times I hardly knew him. It was weird. I'd like to say it was for the sex, but last night reminded me that wasn't true." She paused and then shook her head. "I can't believe I'm saying this."

35

"Perhaps, you're on an emotional roller coaster and you can't be responsible for anything you say. I'm willing to go with that."

"On a roller coaster your stomach is coming up into your chest. I feel like my brain is leaving my body." Bobby looked at her with one of the kindest faces she had ever seen. "Anyway, Jeff called early and I went home and stopped all the way over the pass to get my mind straight. Obviously, it didn't take."

"Yes, Jeff did call me."

"Excuse me?"

"You may have forgotten, but my last name is Early. And you said Jeff called early." Donna looked away and Bobby could feel the thread unraveling. He was pretty good with words games, but he was not at his best when he played them.

"Oh, I get it."

"Sorry about that. I shouldn't have expected you to remember my last name, Ms. Deerfield."

"I didn't. Miss the deer in the field, that is. I did remember your last name, Bobby, but, you're right. I didn't put it together. I'll be better next time"

The thread stopped unraveling and Bobby was grateful. He didn't want it to *un*ravel before it had a chance to actually ravel. And with her play on words, it could definitely ravel.

"However, I would like to know why you call yourself Bobby. Why not Bob, or Robert, which is certainly more fashionable? Unless, it's just a stupid question?"

"No such thing, so they say, as a stupid question. Only stupid answers. Though, I tend to think that that's a stupid saying."

Donna tilted her head a little and raised her eyebrows some to indicate that that may have been a stupid comment, but Bobby was ready to plow on.

"My name is Robert, though my family always called me Bobby. That was shortened to Bob, of course, when I became mature. Which was about three years ago. Maybe." He waited and settled for a small smile. "Actually, most people kept calling me Bobby even when I introduced myself to them as Bob. I'm not sure why. At one point I had a girlfriend who didn't like the name Bob. Actually, there was quite a bit about me she didn't like, so I'm not sure why she was my girlfriend. Oh, yes, I am. The sex was good."

Donna almost spit out the sip of wine she had just taken. She had an abandoned laugh that was easy to find. So was the wine. It was dribbling down her chin. She laughed at that, too, taking one of the small folded napkins to wipe it off.

Laughing with her, he said, "So, my girlfriend called me Rob. Some friends, thinking they were making fun of her, started calling me RobBob. I thought they were making more fun of me, though. Her brother, who was pursuing a self-directed program in the Eastern religions, took to calling me Baba RobBob. I kind of liked that, though I thought it was rather presumptuous. That was before he became a commodities broker. Now he just calls me Robert, when he calls me. I don't have any commodities, so he doesn't call often."

"It seems to me that you might have some commodities, Bobby. Humor is a precious one."

"Well, I may also have some silver commodities, but it remains to be seen if there are any remains to be seen."

"That sounds intriguing and mysterious. Are you intriguing and mysterious, Bobby Early?"

"I would hope you find me intriguing, but mysterious, no. I know quite a bit about myself."

"Well, I do find you intriguing." She paused to form a demure and alluring countenance, "I'll let you know if mystery is called for or needed."

"That in itself sounds mysterious." Bobby leaned back in his chair, noted the rapidly clearing horizons and spotted the double rainbow forming. He pointed it out to Donna.

"Will there be two pots of gold, or can I wish upon a rainbow for Tad?"

"There's nothing wrong with wishing, Donna, and I'm only looking for one pot of silver at the bottom of my rainbow. Don't want to be greedy.'

"Again with the silver," Donna said.

"And we will save that for later. That way we are guaranteed something to talk about."

"You mean, beside Tad."

"That's probably more important."

Donna grew silent, the rainbow began to fade, the wine and the Jell-O were finished and it was time to go. She needed to return to Tad's room, or at least the waiting area. He needed to meet with Jeff in a couple of hours and there were a few matters he wanted to address before then.

They walked together back to the waiting area outside Tad's room, Bobby with his hands in the front pockets of his shorts, Donna with her arms across her chest. Tracy the hot rock lady and most of the others were gone.

Donna and Bobby went into Tad's room. The nurse attendant offered the small closed lip smile nurses have been giving since the first days of bad news began. She then lowered her eyes and excused herself from the room. If there was nothing to be done there wasn't any need for her to do it here.

Donna stood over Tad and held his hand in hers. He didn't look tall now and she didn't feel strong now. "Just hang on until your mom comes, sweet Tad."

Bobby moved beside her, put an arm around her shoulders and stared at Tad. He had lost quite a bit of weight the last few days, his eyes were closed and his breathing slow. The nurse had combed his hair and beard and straightened the sheet that mostly covered him.

"I'll leave you now, Donna," he whispered, tightening his arm on her shoulder and kissing her on her hair on the side of her head.

She nodded and didn't look at him as he left and closed the door behind him. He went to the restroom where he washed his face and tried to clear his red eyes. Then he breathed a couple of heavy sighs and passed through the wet meditation garden on the way back to his truck. The afternoon sun had come out again, the warmth of an August summer day had returned and Bobby headed down to the roundabout not knowing exactly where he was going. He mentioned that to God only for the purpose of continued communication, not expecting an answer.

V

What was it that he needed to do before meeting Jeff Bazzano at The Cebello Roja to discuss Tad's memorial? All too often Bobby managed to find nothing to do while avoiding something to do. There were bills waiting for him in his post office box, laundry to begin, weeding of his neglected flower beds, Herman Hesse's The Glass Bead Game to finish reading again, dishes in the sink to wash, windows to clean, oil to change in his truck and a phone call to return to his sister in San Francisco. He decided to avoid doing any of these minor interests or chores and, instead, do the irresponsible thing and visit John Hamlin.

He parked his truck on the narrow row of gravel next to his house and walked the four blocks into downtown. The streets and sidewalks were crowded with tourists wandering after the rain and locals standing off to the side engaged in conversation. Bobby knew many of them, some only by sight, but twenty years as a restaurant owner had conditioned him to remember names and relationships. There were a few that pretended not to see him and he returned the courtesy. Always someone, though, would stop him for a brief word that would turn into five minutes. Initially, he would think it was a waste of time, then a misuse of time, and finally he would try to make it worthwhile by becoming an active participant in the dialogue. Often that would motivate the other person to mosey along. When it didn't, Bobby would proceed to mention the search for his silver cache and the Legend of Caleb Century. Most of his friends had heard this story, were convinced he had completely made it up, would then laugh and bid a fond adieu. It had become a tradition of sorts, much like last call at the bar. Time to go.

While Bobby stopped to grab a copy of one of the local papers with the headline, "City Council to Charge Pooping Dogs?", Barbara Bennington called his name from a table on an outdoor patio. She was currently in her sixth year on the Council. The patio was shared between Groundswell, a coffee shop, and Wheelwell, a bike shop. They were jointly owned by a couple of former cocaine dealers that had become quite wealthy from real estate acquisitions after they had divested their business interests and broadened their portfolio.

"Hi, Barbara." He held up the newspaper displaying the headline and asked, "Do I even want to read this?"

"That crap's a bunch of shit, Bobby," she replied as he stood next to the iron fencing that separated the sidewalk from her table. "You've met my husband, Hef Bennington, haven't you?"

"It's been a long time, Hef, but yes we have met. I believe it was outside Council chambers the evening the city declared my house was being placed on the Historic Register. How have you been?"

Hef was a lawyer with a firm that specialized in protecting certain developers from experiencing delays from unnecessary encumbrances presented by those pesky people known as neighbors. He had been aligned with John Hamlin opposing Bobby Early's house being placed on the registry. Hamlin knew that if he were to ever own Early's property he would have to meet the most egregious requirements in its development. The City of Aspen would insist that the original structure's exterior appearance survive and this could dictate the accompanying architecture in extreme ways and means. Some buyers just wouldn't accept having to incorporate what to them would be an old shack into their new mansion. The shack resembled an old Victorian and didn't match well with massive wooden beams, steel girders, spreading sheets of gray glass and imposing rock work. Or, the seven bedrooms, ten bathrooms, great room, media room, restaurant kitchen and indoor swimming pool that are interchangeable within exclusive subdivisions throughout the country.

Hamlin had since had drawings commissioned that featured the shack as a quaint gardener's tool shed, an entry gate house or a children's playhouse. At only 800 square feet, Hamlin figured he would have to seek approvals to at least double its size for any of these other purposes. These approvals were always hard fought and inevitably cost Hamlin dollars from his profit. He also didn't appreciate the publicity, though, of course, Becky counseled him differently.

"No hard feelings about that, right?" Hef smiled smoothly beneath his thin, cultured moustache and he brushed a hand across his pressed silk lavender shirt.

"Not at all, Hef. I just wish I could remember why I ever wanted that historical designation anyway. It makes it a lot harder to sell that piece of crap." Bobby smiled broadly beneath his heavy, multi-colored moustache, which made his ruddy cheeks rise and his blues eyes twinkle in their squint.

"And speaking of crap, what does this headline mean, Barbara? I know I'll get more of the story from you than reading this slapped-together article that will have half the facts upside down."

"Oh, it's something stupid that the Mayor said last night. Imagine that."

"I'm trying." Bobby liked the Mayor. He was an athlete, a microbrewer, enjoyed Thanksgiving dinner on a Wednesday and was known to usually be a month behind on his rent. "What was it this time, Barbara?"

"Oh, you know all this hoopla about charging people for plastic bags at the grocery store. Well, some idiot who was at the meeting – why regular citizens even come to these things I don't know – suggested if the City is going to charge people then we will have to charge dogs – or their owners, of course-"

"Of course," agreed Bobby. Hef Bennington smirked.

"-for the plastic poop bags all over town," continued Barbara. "Now, how are we going to do that?" She was suddenly verging on apoplexy.

"By the pound?" asked Bobby. "Or, you could put the offending dog in the pound, the owner in jail and wait for the evening news."

"Exactly! It'll be Claudine Longet and Teddy Bundy all over again!" Bundy was a serial killer who leapt from the second story of the County Courthouse and eluded capture for three days before he was caught driving an old convertible leisurely back down Independence Pass into town. Longet was a serial lover who shot her ski instructor boyfriend. Both cases increased the difficulty of obtaining a restaurant reservation and decreased the occupancy ratio of hotel beds available in Aspen for a pleasant and profitable period.

"Maybe I could rent out my house," mused Bobby.

"What?" shouted Barbara.

"Why not just sell it?" said Hef.

"Can't. Historic."

"You're a piece of shit, Early.'

"Thanks, Hef. And I don't even need to buy myself a plastic bag. At least, not yet."

"My advice to Hamlin has always been to just wait you out. You don't have the resources or the will to last. You're just like all these so-called old timers. Livin' in the past, romancin' the good ole' days. Aspen's always been about money. You guys were just havin' fun, didn't care about the *value* that was here."

"Hef, the *value* was that people cared about each other and felt they were in this together. Not because they were concerned about how much money they could make off each other. Now, it just so happens I'm on my way to see your buddy, John Hamlin. You've spilled his strategy and neither one of you has a clue as to what mine is."

Bobby encouraged Barbara to keep up her good work protecting the town from the media spotlight and strolled off toward House and Home. He really had no idea of his strategy, either, but at least *he* knew that, while Hamlin and Hef didn't. Bobby looked back over his shoulder and saw Hef on his cell phone. If I was walking in the door of House and Home right now, I bet Hamlin would be on the phone, he thought, and quickened his pace.

What bothered Bobby about Hef Bennington's sentiments was that there was a truth to them. There usually is in what hurts.

He and so many others like him had coasted through the seventies, eighties and nineties to wake up one morning and see "their" town turned upside down. During those three decades and, indeed, the preceding ones, the working class had controlled the town. They set the tone for the fun and flavor of it, they pushed and celebrated the booming ski and snowboard lifestyles, they kept the local shops, restaurants and bars in business during the lean times, they protected the wetlands, the wild lands and open space lands, they held benefits and fundraisers for friends in need and strangers who asked, they created and supported a culture of friendliness and welcoming that warmed visitors and encouraged transplants and, most of all, they didn't mind if some of them made money and others didn't.

Throughout the first decade of the twenty-first century economic situations accelerated so quickly that many of these people were left behind. It was happening all across America and Aspen, long immune to the severe booms and busts of so many areas, succumbed. Among the scores of letters to the editors of the town's newspapers bemoaning this fate one stood out in sharp contrast. It read: "Quit your whining. This isn't your town anymore. We bought it." It was signed by a second-home owner who summered and wintered in Aspen, didn't take her own garbage to the curb or shop in the grocery store. She was bitter.

Bobby, like so many others, looked around and realized she was right. People with no vested interest other than real estate now controlled the atmosphere, the retail stores and the very character of Aspen.

The people who had made Aspen what it was and then been forced to move Downvalley because they couldn't afford Aspen anymore only came back to Aspen for work and, maybe, to ski. If Aspen was its own country, the Downvalley folk would be expatriates. They were older and had been raising children in their new Downvalley homes and had lost the desperate urge to fight for their former town. They were doing everything they could to hold their jobs and marriages together while realizing that the landscape had changed. Many resented the uber rich for stealing their town, thinking them callow and shallow. In fact, quite a few of these extremely wealthy people contributed generously to the traditional charities that fed the arts and cultural fabric of Aspen. And equally true was the fact that a few had brought their win at all costs attitude with them. They had, apparently, no limit and played Texas No Holds Barred. They gave the rest of the rich a bad name, but it was hard for those who felt that they had been pushed out to feel sorry for them.

45

Bobby had fallen in love with Aspen primarily because Aspen had fallen in love with him. Some people moved to town and it was almost as though they were not allowed to leave. He had come from the San Francisco Bay Area and his first job was as a ditch digger for the City. It was described as a gardening position, but he quickly discovered why the mountains are called rocky. A pick axe might get a digger ten inches down and thirty feet long in a day.

He picked and shoveled alongside an Irish wanderer named Ian whose company induced him to stay until the first snow fell. By that time it was too late, Aspen's spell had been cast. Bobby often thought of Ian, recalled their night-long conversations over pitchers of beer in a basement pub and mentally thanked him for those hours whiled away before the timing of his life had been fully set for Colorado.

His first summer came to an end and he was packing up to move back to Sonoma County when he was talked into driving a free shuttle bus around the city for the winter. He had never spent a winter in the snow before and had never skied. That winter turned into two years and, as he was packing up to move back to Sonoma County, he was talked into tending bar at a popular locals' spot named Sweet Judi's.

He had never tended bar before or even thought about it. It was quite possible that he hadn't considered that it was actually a job. At Sweet Judi's it looked like a day spent talking and drinking with friends, for which those friends happily paid Judi and the bartender. It seemed glamorous. He soon discovered that there was a shady side to the bottom of an empty glass. It wasn't long before he was drunk after work, hung over coming into work and drinking too much at work. Judi showed her sour side one morning when he came in particularly depleted. She warned him that by jumping into the deep end of the pool he was giving up the option of doing anything other than swimming for his life. He understood her, cut back and discovered he was able to actually make a living from this job if he didn't spend the day's wages every night. Eventually, he saved enough to move into The Cebolla Roja for twenty years.

He saw the town change. When he went out on vacations he saw the country and world change. He understood that all places, like people, change. He didn't need to be happy or unhappy with it, but he needed to adjust. He knew enough former and current residents who were resentful or complacent. Bobby figured he had found his cause in his house in his hometown.

***

The doors to House and Home were open to the brick mall. These bricks had been imported from St. Louis at the same time the City's buses had been purchased from Disneyland and Knott's Berry Farm. The City was flush with money and they both were lauded as good ideas at the time. Soon, however, bricks began breaking and research disclosed there were no more available matching bricks. The malls then truly burst into life. With every significant reduction in the number of matching bricks, trees, flowers, benches and sculptures replaced their space. The malls became an organic, evolving and often chaotic release and sanctuary. Street performers stretched between the cute, the talented, the original and the ugly. Mimes didn't qualify for any of these categories so they were banned to the parks. There had been an ugly incident with a susceptible child when a mime wouldn't let her out of the box.

The buses from southern California were equipped with air brakes. Apparently, no one really knew what this meant when the City ordered two million dollars worth of these incredibly colorful and rickety vehicles. The water in the air in the brakes would get cold, freeze, and the brakes would lock up. Going downhill on an icy road and sliding through a stop sign is not an effective way to encourage public transportation. By the end of the winter they had been replaced by retired military buses. The motion by a member of City Council to paint peace signs on them was narrowly defeated. This was shortly after Watergate and the Council consisted of an uncomfortable mixture of rather recently arrived liberals with the old guard of European transplants and World War II veterans. The old-timers welcomed both groups, liberals and transplants, with empty wallets that were filled by selling their ramshackle houses and struggling potato farms. The Europeans were mainly here to take advantage of the burgeoning skiing industry and were content to not be involved with politics. Some of them, in fact, intentionally kept a low profile. But most of the newly arrived Americans were carried on the wheels and wings of wanderlust, enjoying a passion for almost everything. Many had been actively engaged in the protests of the sixties and early seventies. Now disillusioned with national politics, they found in Aspen both a pristine hide-a-way and a world renowned resort. They could indulge in either persona or both to whatever degree they chose. Here, they felt they could make a difference and soon realized that they outnumbered the natives. Like any good conquerors, they imposed their way of thinking on the defeated through rules, regulations and laws rather than slavery and murder. Of course, the generational families that had survived since the 1880's and 90's, as well as those who had found Aspen on their own after the war, were not especially pleased by these left-over hippies, radicals and hedonists installing a new regime. There were some fierce election battles, long-haired men were refused service in a few restaurants and occasionally a store employee snarled at those dressed in what were called counter-culture clothes. All in all, Bobby thought, the wheel had merely turned and now his kind were the ones feeling run over.

He entered House and Home and recognized the woman at the receptionists' desk.

"Hi, Casey. Melissa on break?"

Casey smiled weakly and shook her head. "I'm the new Melissa, Bobby."

"Oh, she finally wised up and got fired, eh?"

"Yup." She lowered her voice and Bobby moved closer. "Though they'll say she quit. That way they won't have to pay her unemployment. Plus, technically they're right. She told off Becky and even had her hold the door for her as she left!"

"Well, my congratulations and sympathies to you."

"If it's all the same to you, I'll only accept the sympathy. Are you here for an appointment, Bobby? I haven't had a chance to figure out Melissa's system yet, if she had one."

"No, I don't have an appointment, but John will probably see me if he isn't out evicting one of his tenants."

"Now, that's not entirely fair, is it, Bobby?"

No, it wasn't, he thought. He was referring to an incident last winter when an eighty-six year old woman needed to be removed from one of Hamlin's apartment complexes. She had fallen while getting out of the shower and broken her hip. The complex had no handicap accommodations because it was built before such features were required by building codes. It had been grandfathered in by the building department with an agreement that Hamlin would retrofit the building by a certain date that had now passed. It was the sort of issue that neither John nor the City had the interest or motivation on which to follow through. Until something happened. John hadn't been to the complex since he bought it twelve years earlier and now something had happened.

Casey had drawn up the contract and explained to the tenant, Elizabeth Monet, that she may need to move if she developed a physical incapacity. Casey had dealt with Elizabeth privately, without John's knowledge. She had only recently been promoted from record keeping to the contract department when Elizabeth had moved in and hoped to keep the incident secret. Casey had been extremely disappointed that she hadn't been transferred to the agent staff when the Gang of Four drama unfolded. She had her license, but the firm had hired replacements from outside. It was very difficult to join the team of eighteen agents and she had looked at the sordid matter as her opportunity. Nonetheless, she had been moved a step up with contracts and didn't want to be seen as running to John with a problem.

She arranged to have an access bar installed in the combination shower and bathtub, but didn't realize that Elizabeth would be in a wheelchair when she was released from the hospital.

Elizabeth didn't wish to bother Casey with this information. For the first several weeks upon her return she managed in and out of the tub area with the help of friends who came over to visit. A few of these friends felt their visits had been unfortunately extended and had grown more intimate than they wished.

As the winter abated, Elizabeth took to wheeling her chair out of her room and through the entryway doors to spend a sunny hour or two. Several of her neighbors noticed she was restricted to the concrete porch near the doors and unable to move beyond. Two steps going down to the concrete pathway that led to the sidewalk kept her a prisoner next to the building. They fashioned a make-shift ramp and helped push her down and then back up. One day, however, a sudden snow squall came through while she was on the sidewalk and in her eagerness to return inside she attempted the ramp herself. She managed about half way before she slipped back and turned over.

It was at this moment that a photographer for the Aspen Chronicle walked by on the sidewalk. He snapped four or five quick pictures before responding to the situation, helping Elizabeth up and into the hallway. Naturally, there needed to be a story with the front page photo, even though Elizabeth was reluctant to provide it.

The next day, with a copy of the Chronicle on his desk, the Chief of the Building Department Handicap Access Staff met with John Hamlin. It was mutually agreed between the two of them that John would submit the plans for the apartment complex's retrofit within one week. A new, permanent ramp would be the first priority and, amazingly, that would also be completed within a week. It was agreed when John brought back the plans on schedule, that the city had been equally negligent and he would be required to confine the retrofit to the ramp and the street level floor of the complex. This comprised only eight rooms. During that week, John visited Elizabeth and she signed an agreement to not introduce a lawsuit in exchange for being moved to the senior center on the outside of town. John promised to pay her moving expenses and one year's worth of rent. Elizabeth considered this quite gracious and John thought it expedient. She died within two months of the move.

Casey had been concerned that Hamlin would fire her after discovering she had kept Elizabeth's accident from him, but he was actually quite pleased with her initiative. It helped to have people working for him who didn't come running for advice and decisions every time a problem arose. He had kept this in mind until the meltdown with Melissa.

"You're probably right, Casey, though it's not easy to believe John was completely altruistic by arranging for that old woman's room at the senior center," said Bobby.

"How about the fact that he's continued to pay for the room for the next occupant?"

Bobby hadn't been aware of this and it momentarily put his mind in an out of balanced state about Hamlin to which he wasn't accustomed. He recalled the times he had seen House and Home listed among the generous sponsors for such local enterprises and endeavors as the Deaf Artist Camp and Blind Skiers. Both organizations recruited hearing and sight-challenged young people from all over the country to visit Aspen and its environs to enjoy its amenities. Deaf children received sign-language instruction in the arts of sculpture, painting and music. They spent a week at a forest retreat that featured a piano with a sign hung over it reading, "Remember Beethoven!" Blind kids were brought to the mountains during the winter months to learn how to ski and snowboard from accomplished instructors and then presented with a life-time pass from the ski company. House and Home also supported various local charities and helped provide turkeys for the annual Christmas dinner at the St. Mary's Catholic Church. It was often said that God worked in mysterious ways, and Bobby thought the maxim was proved by the duplicitous efforts of John Hamlin

Bobby felt a twinge of guilt that was immediately relaxed and released when he remembered the times that Hamlin had bought and torn down condominiums that housed scores of people to build mansions for the few. He also recalled his own personal experiences with John. He settled on appreciating that Hamlin was more than one-sided, but that all the other sides were in the shade.

"That's the kind of thing that should be in the paper, not a picture of a flipped wheelchair on a plywood plank during a blizzard."

"I'll see if he's in." Casey suspected that there was more to Bobby than just trouble, even though whenever his name was mentioned John frowned. Still, she knew there was a deal that was in the works, or should be, and that it would not be in her own best interests to rile Bobby before he and John met. "And I'm sorry if I seem to be argumentative."

"You're defending your boss. If you don't, who else will? Certainly not me," finished Bobby with a friendly smile.

Casey felt almost trusting, a condition fraught with unease due to its lack of being complete. She turned to the phone, picked up the receiver, pressed a button, then spoke. She removed the receiver from the side of her head, paused, and looked at it halfway to replacing it back on its station. "He said to give him five minutes and that he would be happy to see you."

Casey offered him coffee and water, which he declined, and asked if he would like a seat. She gestured to a soft leather chair that was too low, too wide and too handsome for Bobby to feel comfortable. It was the kind of chair that swallowed someone and gave them a sense of smallness. When another person came over to introduce themselves they seemed superior, as the one seated struggled to rise.

Instead, Bobby meandered over to a large wall display featuring a proposed project available through House and Home. The artist rendering was fuzzy and sketchy. It was a given that nothing in this drawing would look remotely similar to the actual finished product. It was from a perspective and angle that wasn't present at or near the site. Yet, there was an elusive attractiveness to it that

53

made it interesting. Just trying to figure out how these many buildings and this many trees could coexist together in this small of a space invited the viewer to study it until becoming slightly dizzy. As he stepped back away from it to gather himself, Bobby noticed Becky entering John's office from around a corner. The blinds were closed, but as she opened the door he saw that there was a third person in the office.

He then approached the much smaller yet more elegant model of Aspen Elk Estates which was on display across the room. This was home. This is what had grown up around him. He observed that his house, his cute little yard and his cute little truck, were missing from the arrangement. The model represented his abode by a green open space that had patches of brown in it. Wishful thinking, he thought. He looked closer at the model and saw that the houses weren't represented in proportion with the area of land. This model was replete with vegetation and wide swaths of open space between the houses. He knew this wasn't quite to scale because as he walked or drove through his new neighborhood he saw that the houses were within fifteen feet of each other. This was a close distance for homes that sold for seven and eight million dollars. Of course, with the recession, they were now going for as low as five or six million. He was aware that they weren't worth that amount of money. At least, not in almost any other part of the world. A few other select spots commanded outrageous amounts of money for little value in return, but they were, thankfully, rare. As he tried again to figure out what had happened to his 800 square foot house amid the 8,000 square foot mansions, Casey came alongside of him.

"He's ready for you now, Bobby."

"It looked to me like it is more than just John, Casey. More like the Gang of Three. Will John have his tape recorder running?"

Casey let loose an internal shudder at the reference to the Gang of Four and gave a curious start at the mention of a recording device. Surely, she thought, he couldn't know about that. It had only been by accident, more or less, that she had discovered the machine. One night during the winter she had been working after hours when John had called the office. He had asked her to go into his office, look in the center drawer of his desk, find a matchbook and read to him the phone number written inside. There was no name associated with the number and John had hung up immediately after hearing the number. The blinds on the door to the office and along the wide window facing the floor of the main area were drawn. She opened another drawer and another, not really looking for anything, but hoping to find something. Just something that she could know about John that he didn't know she knew. Why, she didn't know. Next to a stack of envelopes addressed to clients was the recorder. This wasn't the something to know that she didn't know she wanted to know. She closed the drawer and suddenly was frightened. Suppose there were surveillance cameras in the office? Instinctively, she looked to the ceiling corners and then realized that such a move would prove that she was a sneak. But, wasn't looking in the other drawers enough proof? She hurried out of John's office, closed the business for the night and worried all the way home if she had remembered to turn the lights out in his office. For a brief moment, she panicked about leaving her fingerprints on his desk. By the time she arrived home and had a couple glasses of wine, she was restored to a brand of sanity with which she was familiar. John had asked her to go into the office, therefore, her fingerprints *should* be on his desk. She thought she had

55

heard a noise coming from one of the drawers and was afraid it was a mouse eating some important papers. She looked at the ceiling corners because she thought she heard a fly buzzing above her. It all made sense.

She had been nervous at work for a few days afterward. John hadn't thanked her for retrieving the phone number for him. She conjectured that he didn't want to remind her about the conversation or the evening and finally concluded that if nothing was said there was no problem.

And because there was no problem, there was no reason to show Bobby a curious start. She mentioned that she had woken this morning with a crick in her neck. He offered that he was a pain in the neck to some people, but that he was trying to change his ways. She didn't believe him and watched him walk through the aisle of desks toward John Hamlin's door.

VI

The blinds had been raised and the door opened just as Bobby was approaching it. Becky was dressed in a forest green sleeveless top with a complimentary shade of meadow green slacks. This particular combination wouldn't be easy to find and most women would be adverse to the attempt, but she pulled it off. She gave Bobby a warm hug that didn't linger. He appreciated that. John came around from behind his desk, greeting him with a hearty handshake and a wide smile. He wore beige slacks and a gold polo shirt bearing the House and Home logo. It was a subtle depiction of a house within a house, but Bobby always thought it looked like one house was eating the other.

"Bobby, so good to see you. I was afraid that you wouldn't be able to meet today after I hadn't heard from you since I left the note at your house."

"Thanks, John. And I followed what you said."

John gave him a questioning glance, but quickly motioned toward the third person that had been in the room. "Bobby, I'd like you to meet Joe Don Burke, your soon-to-be new neighbor."

Joe Don wore fly fishing shorts with a sharp crease down the center of each leg. The flaps above the pockets folded down smoothly and there wasn't a stain, a wrinkle, a blemish or a loose thread anywhere. Bobby thought that the closest to water these shorts had ever been was a washing machine. Joe Don's shirt was of a pin-stripe short sleeve style that threatened to burst at the buttons. His belly hung over his belt and completely concealed what might have been a waist. He sported a toothy grin and extended his hand, giving Bobby a robust handshake.

"Good to meet you, Bobby. It's good to see an older man with a youthful name."

"Well, Don Joe, my mama gave it to me and I kinda like it."

This was exactly what John Hamlin had wanted to avoid. All the worst case scenarios flashed before him.

"See, its Joe Don. A lot of people make that mistake." Joe Don's grin shrunk into a pursed smile and his eyes narrowed to squint that resembled more of a slat. "At first."

Bobby looked keenly at Joe Don and slowly broke out into a laugh. He was joined heartily by Joe Don.

"See," he waved underhandedly to John and Becky, "I told you we'd get along just fine."

John suggested everyone take a seat. There were two wooden rockers with cushions that Bobby urged Becky and Joe Don to relax in, while he chose a straight back chair with short arms. He always tried to make himself ill at ease in situations that had the potential to become antagonistic.

"See, Bobby, we just closed the deal on my lot. It's a pretty little postage stamp, but the missus and me are lookin' to have a bit more room to stretch, if you know what I mean."

It crossed Bobby's mind to ask if this meant Joe Don was into yoga, but he had already made one smart-alec remark and he didn't really want to alienate this fellow completely. At least, right off the bat. "Where are you from, Joe Don?"

"Well, see, we're from Texas. We've been comin' up here for years, mostly in the summers, and stayin' in condos. But Mrs. Burke has decided that it's time to have a place of our own where she can invite a few more people over."

"It's a lovely lot you've chosen. I'm sure you and your wife and your friends will enjoy it."

"See, that's kinda the thing, Bobby. Now, I know John and Becky here have made you a fair offer on your house and they tell me you've turned 'em down."

John bristled inside. It irritated him when clients referred to him and Becky working on deals and making them together. He had founded the firm, taken all the risks and built it into a raging success. Becky had married into it. She was an attractive asset in many ways, but figured out the bottom line in bed better than she did on a financial worksheet. Becky didn't quite see it that way and was more than ready to accept inclusion and recognition for any deals the firm made. She naturally gravitated toward spotlights and considered John's achievements her own. This was the one area of their business lives together that might manifest itself in an uncharacteristically unattractive light at home. In such a case, John found himself out of the bedroom and in the jewelry store. He leaned back in his chair, choosing not to look at Becky or Bobby. He looked over the head of Joe Don.

"See, now I know it's a market value offer for your house, 'cause I know what I paid for just my lot. I'm willin' to throw a little sugar on that cake out of my own pocket. I'll do the deal with Becky and John here and we can skip any declarations and taxes between you and me." Joe Don chuckled and leaned forward toward Bobby. "See, there is such a thing as free money." Bobby thought for just a second that Joe Don's weight and gravity were going to combine to tilt him onto the floor, but this was obviously a move Joe Don had perfected. He teetered in a delicate balance. He could go either way, much like his ethics, Bobby surmised.

The mention of Becky's name before his in this offer from Joe Don was almost too much for John Hamlin. Bobby could sense the jealousy and low level rage churning in John. He turned to look at him and then at Becky and then at John again. Becky had adopted her professional party pose. Her smile was frozen, full of gleaming white teeth, and her eyes were lit up by the lack of depth. Her stare was indecipherable to all but those closest to her. For them, the visage meant that Becky was floating somewhere inside. She was in tune with her private mantra that allowed her to grasp just enough of a conversation or event to offer incredibly effective and appropriate feedback. She became a transcendental socialite figure.

What took Bobby by surprise, even shock, was that John had duplicated the look. His gaze was impenetrable and his icy smile so phony it reeked warmth. As a couple, they had achieved the rare air of a superior political duo. They appeared as if they had been spray painted into the room from a slick fashion magazine. Bobby was impressed.

"Nonetheless," he began, and stopped to think if he was talking to the beautiful and handsome statues with hearts of stone, or to Joe Don. "Nonetheless," he repeated, "I have no intention of selling my house. I'm sure that the Hamlins have told you this."

"See, of course they have! And I like the way you are playin' it. See, I can tell that you and I have the same renegade ways and means about us. We do things differently than others. Bobby, I came up the tough climb. I had nothin' and when I got somethin' I wanted more. And now that I have more I want the most. I might not get it, but damn well I'm tryin'! I'm oil and gas Texas and I bleed money." Joe Don had southern drawled himself into having the upraised wide hands of a preacher man. His eyes pierced through the fluorescent lighting as if they were

60

slicing the truth between the two men and making it so real it could be held in those hands. "Can we talk, Bobby Early?"

"Does that mean it's my turn?"

"I'm listenin'."

Bobby could practically see his reflection in Joe Don's eyes. Joe Don would be putting Bobby's appearance through filters. The not truly garish Hawaiian shirt and the casual shorts, the short socks inside the running shoes, the tan, the long hair on the sides and back, the moustache in need of a trim, the lack of jewelry, even a watch, no hat. All these clearly visible indicators would be colliding with the words Bobby uttered, the mannerisms he used and the hidden meaning behind them in Joe Don's brain.

"I appreciate your interest in my land as much as I enjoy this first meeting that we are having. Which is to say on and off. I find you entertaining and every bit as real as this desk." Bobby slapped it for effect before he added, "And every bit as real as those fly fishing shorts you're wearing. You make a mistake with me Joe Don Burke when you think and say that I'm playing. If you said it without thinking, then you should reassess. See, this is my home. And up and around my home have grown these big houses with little flower gardens and fancy cars and beautiful women and rich men. Everything around my home has changed except it and me."

Bobby stood up quickly, turned around and looked in the mirror on the wall that had been behind him "Well, that's not true. Actually, that's not true at all." He walked over and stood behind Becky who had ceased her easy rocking in the chair. "No, just like everything else, we've changed. Both it and I have gotten older. Its foundation has sunk a little and my roots have too."

"But, see," said Joe Don, "You can't be happy here any more. It has all changed. Take the money and find another spot. There's plenty of 'em out there. Take it from me."

"But you want to take mine from me. John has miscalculated in thinking buying up all the other property and surrounding me would chase me off. It's only brought out a stubborn streak I was too obstinate to acknowledge." Bobby had said this while standing to the side of John's desk. He hadn't wanted to make Becky break her mold by becoming nervous with him behind her. There was a lovely blue vase on the desk that held a beautiful bunch of aromatic lilies. He bent over to inhale and presented a probing, waiting open face to John.

However, Becky interjected before John had the opportunity to formulate his response. "That's funny. Everybody else has known all about it."

"See, I'd heard that. I just wanted to clear the air out and let you know where I stood. I figured if I brought this up right away, you'd have time to get upset, cool down and then we could talk a deal. I apologize for my remark about 'playin'.'" Joe Don had settled back into his rocker and clasped his hands together above his belly, using it as a shelf. "And, you're right as an armadillo livin' off-road. These shorts haven't seen a river, a fly or a fish. Don't *you* make the mistake, though, of miscalculating *me*."

"It's going to be hard not too, Joe Don. I can see you are a man of many levels and, I'm sure, many wardrobes." Both men smiled at this. "I suspect you'll have a lot of surprises for me."

Hamlin shuffled in his chair. His smile had returned and he was intent on capitalizing on the civility that now seemed at his disposal. "Bobby, I'm sorry if you have felt I've tried to force you to sell your lot."

Bobby noticed that John always referred to his house as his "lot". At least Joe Don had given it the recognition of an abode. They each wanted to own it, but

Joe Don's sugar cake would be sweeter than Hamlin's plat map.

John suspected this may be one of those times in which Becky's partnership may actually prove advantageous. "Becky and I thought that it was an inevitable move for you and beneficial, as well. You're right, of course. Everything has changed in Aspen. You can make a handsome profit."

"And then move Downvalley. Out of sight, out of mind. Another person that used to be."

"Hell, no. I'd give you a real good deal on a condo here in town. I know it means a lot to you to stay around all your friends and the places you used to work."

Bobby took this as a minor jab about his general lack of employment. Still, he preferred this side of John over the smarmy, fawning, slicked up and double-downed usual front he had to face.

"Interestingly, I can do that right now. And, anyway, John, you know I can't leave until I find it."

"Find what?" blurted Joe Don.

"Oh no, not this again," sighed Becky. Her careful, studied demeanor collapsed and she hung her head. Her hair almost fell by the sides of her face, but it had been too immaculately coiffed.

"What?" repeated Joe Don.

John leaned over his desk, rubbed his forehead and closed his eyes tightly. He audibly breathed in through his teeth and then out again. "The silver."

"What silver?"

Bobby's sly smile bordered on a smirk, but it was muted by the twinkle in his eyes. He walked back around Becky's rocker, sat down easily in his chair and leaned back. "Why, didn't they tell you? There's silver underneath my house."

Joe Don coughed with disdain. If he had been a century earlier he would have harrumphed. "So? There's probably some silver underneath every house in this entire town. Aspen began with silver. See, the hills were pocked with mines and smelters. There were loose donkeys, looser women and drunken miners. They probably dropped as much as they embezzled. For God's sake, though, at today's prices you probably couldn't find enough silver in anybody's yard to pay for the damn metal detector."

Bobby was impressed that Joe Don had an idea at all about Aspen's past. He was probably right about a metal detector being a poor investment. However, that wasn't the tool of choice that Bobby had in mind.

"So, what's the point, Bobby?"

"There's a story that goes along with my house, Joe Don. It was originally a little Victorian on the edge of town. It was built around 1891 and a fellow named Caleb Century lived in it. There's a whole 'nother story about him that we can save for some other time." My God, I'm starting to talk like Joe Don, thought Bobby. "He died at the turn of the century, 1900, and that's how he was named. People just knew him as Caleb until he died.

"Anyway, the house sat abandoned for a while before a family of farmers moved in. They fixed it up some and then left during the Great Depression. Late in the forty's it was moved to where it sits today.'

"This is fascinatin' in a fly fishin' sort of way. Though, I might say whoever moved it knew a pretty piece of land when he saw it."

"Actually, it was a woman. Beverly Friedl was an architect who wanted to preserve structures from the past. She's the one who researched Caleb Century and the farmer family. She saved sixteen cabins from being razed."

"I gotta ask ya', Bobby, can I just buy the book instead? Or, at least, can you just get to the reason why there's silver under the cabin?"

Becky and John had sat in silence while he had given Joe Don the abbreviated version of the short version. "This is where it gets really good," offered John.

"Okay. Not only the reason why there's silver under the house, but why I'm not selling. Caleb Century had been a miner and he buried silver in some wetlands below the Tall Pine Mine where he worked. His own claim had long since been deemed to have been played out, but he would occasionally haul stuff from it when he was through with a shift at Tall Pine. He did it at night, he did it in blizzards and he did it in secret. This is all detailed in the journal he kept."

Joe Don was smiling again now. "So you're gonna tell me that the wetlands are where your house is and that you found this journal underneath a floorboard. Is that right?"

"Half of it is. You're right about my house sitting right on top of where Caleb buried the silver. However, I found the journal in a crawl space beneath The Cebolla Roja." Bobby smiled back again at Joe Don, then turning toward John and Becky opened his eyes into a wild, maniacal stare. He was delighted as they were jolted back into their chairs. "Now, Joe Don, you have to be amazed at the coincidence of all this. What are the odds that it would be Caleb's very own house that would be placed over his very own hidden treasure? What incredible timing that took. And for me to be the one to find his journal? Because I owned The Cebolla Roja and was trying to track down the source of a sewer gas smell? And I live in his house? On top of his cache of silver? It's amazing isn't it? You can see why I can't sell now, can't you?"

Joe Don had begun to swivel his rocker side to side and look back and forth between Becky and John. They returned slightly raised eyebrows. "Well, I can see that there would be some issues to deal with here, that's for sure. And, by golly, we have some time. See, I'm not planning on breaking ground until next spring. We'll have opportunities to get together again and talk about this."

"I don't think you heard me."

"Sure I did. You mentioned coincidence and timing and I look at our meeting here today as the perfect example. This has been what many people would call a chance happenstance, but for you and me it could be fate."

"I think I've made myself clear."

"One thing I don't understand is why you don't just knock down the house and dig up the silver."

"I'm saving it for a very snowy day and, as you can see, that's not today." Bobby rose out of his chair, thankful for the short arms on it that helped keep him alert. "I'll add this, though, Joe Don. It's been interesting meeting you and I do expect we'll be talking again sometime. Be careful when you start digging you don't come too near my fence. I built it myself and I'm not a builder by trade, so the posts aren't as deep as they mighta shoulda been."

Joe Don wasn't sure whether this was a parting shot from Bobby, but he had a couple more questions for him before he let him slip away. "How do you know the exact spot where Caleb buried the silver? And if it was marsh land then, what happened to it?"

"I believe the Hamlins can help you out with those answers, even if they might not be happy to do so. Good luck, Joe Don." Bobby reached out his hand and gave Joe Don a firm shake.

"Thanks for taking time out of your day for me," he said to John and Becky as he opened the door and left

Hamlin's office, the office of House and Home and entered back into the world of the mall.

"Well?" asked Joe Don.

John shifted in his chair again and shook his head and tried to laugh a little. Becky stepped out of the rocker. "I'm sure everything will work out, Joe Don. He gets a little excited sometimes when he talks about this silver thing of his. I'll leave you and John to finish discussing it, though. I've got to get back to work. It's always good to see you." She went over to Joe Don and gave him an arm hug, pretending to kiss his cheek. She gave the same farewell to John and left the office.

Both men remained standing, hands in their pockets and simply looking at each other. Finally, Joe Don placed his hands on the desk and leaned over enough so that his belly had a resting spot. "Let's start with this: Is he crazy or just acting crazy?"

"I don't know if anybody knows the answer to that, including him."

"So, you think he's crazy."

"He's a bit on the eccentric side of things sometimes. I believe he believes what he's saying."

"So, you think he's crazy."

"On this, I guess he is."

"I don't think he's crazy. I think he's gonna play this for all he thinks it's worth. But I don't want to have to play with him, John. He's your man. You told me you'd swing it so I'd have that property to add onto. I'm having Mrs. Burke's architects draw it up just like that. I've managed to reconcile her to the fact the damn shack is gonna have to stay. She can decide if it's a gardenin' shed or a grandchildren's playhouse or a goddamn museum with Bobby Early's head mounted on the wall! But you get me that land before I start digging. You understand that?"

"Now, wait, Joe Don. I told you I would get it for you and I will. But I never promised by the time you start building. I'll do everything I can to make that happen, but you need to think about what you're going to do if it doesn't." John was strong when it came to threats and bullying. He had killed deals before when someone pushed too hard. He didn't have the guts to be tough at home, but this was business. "I'll let you out of this contract right now. No fees, nothing. We can tear it up and walk away and find another house for you." He let what he said settle and waited for Joe Don's response.

"Let's sit back down." Joe Don suddenly looked tired and he rubbed his forehead. "Hell, one way or 'nother we'll get it. I've never enjoyed a deal that didn't come with some horseshit on it somewhere." He slowly crossed his legs, which seemed to require a special effort involving his hands and his belly. "Back to what he said before he left, though. Crazy or not, I don't really care why he thinks his property is where the silver is buried. But he does, so I want to know, too. It might come in handy along the way."

John was relieved that the deal stayed struck. He would have torn up the contract, but it would have cost him and he never liked to lose money. "He claims this character Caleb marched it off in paces from a couple of landmarks in town. They must have been buildings built before 1900. There's a few of them. The Pitkin County Courthouse is one. Oddly enough, so is The Cebolla Roja. The Wheeler Opera House. Now, how he pretends to know the length of those paces, that's part of the mystery story he walks around with. Every time I ask him something trying to expose it as a fantasy, he either doesn't answer or makes something up that's patently ridiculous."

"So, it's like he has a map in this journal. Have you ever seen the journal?"

"No," John practically scoffed. "Though, apparently, he's told everybody he knows about it. It's common knowledge, but I don't know if he's ever shown anyone. I don't hang out in his circle of friends."

"Okay, then, what about this wetlands reference? I haven't seen any evidence of that. You're not selling swampland, are you?"

"In this business, as you know, we do title searches on property. What he told you about the house being moved is true. After that, it was passed through a number of owners, most of whom were involved with the ski company, until a Rufus Smithy bought it in 1965. He had a hardware store in town until 1975. At the time, no one wanted to build in this area. Red Mountain, across the river and opposite Aspen Mountain, was the popular and lucrative area. Early bought it for cheap. I have no idea whether he has paid it off or not." John watched Joe Don attempt to uncross his legs until he finally resorted to using his hands and belly again in an odd maneuver that reminded him of a sumo wrestler exercise. "Anyway, years before all this, some records indicate that the Roaring Fork River ran much nearer the property than it does now. It's possible that it was deemed wetlands then, but it certainly wouldn't have been swamp. It's had a century to dry out and you'll see from the soil samples that it's as solid a building site as you could want."

Joe Don heaved a breath of exhaustion after his leg calisthenics. "Well, who the hell moved a goddamn river?"

"Probably one of the mining companies. Maybe they wanted it closer to their operations so it would be easier and less expensive to dump their tailings into. That's not unheard of."

"I haven't heard of it. And it seems to me the folks downriver wouldn't be too thrilled."

"I imagine not. Different times."

"Simpler times, that's for sure. Times when a man could make a buck without givin' half of it back to the government to mitigate for movin' a bird's nest."

John had experienced his own frustrations with environmental groups and governmental departments. The most odious had been with this very housing development. He had quietly bought up all the houses, lots and open space he would need, except for Bobby Early's, when he first proposed it to Planning and Zoning. They required he provide an environmental impact statement on a family of squirrels, an eagle's nest and a migration corridor for elk. He suspected the squirrel issue was mainly a personal vendetta brought by one of the members of the board that he had snookered on a land deal a decade before. The member had thought he was pulling a fast one over on John only to discover that Hamlin had already set another deal in the works that doubled Hamlin's profit the very next day. The member had cried foul and sued. John won, including legal fees, and the member had carried the grudge since.

The family of cute and fuzzy squirrels were relocated across the river after it had been ascertained that only their natural predators threatened them there. The eagle's nest was a more sensitive issue. John couldn't move the nest or the tree, so he agreed to undertake construction only after the eaglets had flown and cease shortly before the nesting period began again. This only affected the construction of two of the eleven sites he planned to sell and he would make a point of selling them last. He hoped by then the eagles would move on to quieter, friendlier territory. He also agreed to make a generous donation to the Wildlife Foundation of the Roaring Fork River and Friends.

The elk corridor, however, was problematic. Some of the allure of this development had to do with the very fact that it was a well known by-way for these majestic native animals. They were featured in all the brochures and, most critically, in the name Aspen Elk Estates. John eventually solved this dilemma by purchasing an adjacent parcel of undeveloped land, dedicating it to his friends the elk and deeding it to the Wildlife Foundation. Becky served with the foundation, but only as a volunteer. It was a meaningless coincidence, the foundation maintained, and it released a statement thanking her for her involvement. Most of the buyers of Aspen Elk Estates loved the idea of elk nearby, though not necessarily in their front, back or side yards. It cost John a little money, but he would simply increase the lot price.

By this time, Bobby realized the elk he watched through his front window throughout the winter would soon be subtly shifted several hundred yards away. Adding to his disappointment, resentment and resolve was the mention that the new elk corridor would be named the John and Becky Hamlin Elk Trail.

It was far too late for Bobby to reverse the design of his neighborhood. John, Becky and Joe Don were on the joint mission of finishing the transformation. The elk had adjusted to the changing conditions, the squirrel family had either found happy hunting grounds or happy hunting grounds had found them and the eagle's nest had been empty the last two springs and summers.

"I know about the bird's nests, Joe Don. Man has to build and birds have to fly."

"But there's a lot more sky than there is good land."

Angels could build their castles in the sky, but as people liked to say: there is only so much land and God isn't making any more of it. God probably felt that if he kept producing more land people would keep reproducing and that hadn't worked out so well so far.

VII

Donna was sitting in the meditation garden watching a mountain bluebird angle short flights from one aspen tree to another. The distinctive green leaves that paddled back and forth in the breeze orientated what otherwise appeared to be a capricious maze for the bird to navigate.

She sat on a little bench protected by the circular roof that ran around the outside of the garden. Her palms were together between her knees as she followed the bluebird as much with her thoughts as her eyes. In its flight she saw Tad's soul searching for a way out, though hesitant to forsake the safety and comfort of the familiar. She knew the bird would fly, returning to a home and life she didn't know.

The leaves of the columbines still held a drop of rain here and there as if they couldn't quite shrug the water off their shoulders. Every now and then one would roll off, landing on the bed of moss below. Shafts of sunlight shot down through the trees like hope from heaven to hearth. This peaceful little garden was a kiln of emotion.

The short wooden gate opened behind her. It was Melissa. Donna continued lost in the light as Melissa softly called her name. Finally, Melissa came along side of her and touched her gently on the shoulder. As Donna turned her head, a tear fell on Melissa's hand. She sat down next to Donna and they embraced while they wept.

In between tears and catching their breath they told each other how sorry they were. Melissa had met Tad when she first came to town four years earlier. She felt as if she had grown up with him. He was one of the first people she had met and had been like an older brother to her. She had spent time with Donna and Tad whenever Donna visited. They took trail rides in Tad's old Jeep together and joked about discovering true appreciation for a sports bra.

At first, Donna had hoped Melissa would be the girl that everybody wanted Tad to find. He hadn't had a steady girlfriend since college and most of his women friends were drinking buddies and not romantic partners. Melissa was one of the few people this last year that could motivate Tad to get out in his Jeep and experience some of the beauty that so many people came to Aspen to discover. After her first couple of visits, Donna realized that the friendship was platonic. She also was thankful that it was genuine between the two of them and that she could rely on Melissa to help her get Tad out of the bars or off the couch and outside.

A cloud drifted over, blocking out the sunlight and separating the moment so that each woman could dry their eyes and smile at each other. It was the smile of friends thankful for the other person being there.

"Were you out here when it rained?"

"No, I was actually in the cafeteria with Bobby. We saw a double rainbow."

"Good. I'm glad you've had a friend to be with. I'm sorry I didn't get up earlier. I didn't know you had come back from Denver already until Jeff told me."

"That's all right. Actually, I just met Bobby this afternoon. He seems like an interesting man."

Melissa allowed herself a short laugh. "That he is, Donna. That he is."

"I'd ask you to explain yourself, but I've met enough of him to agree with you. And I think I'd like to find the rest out myself."

Melissa leaned back, straightening an arm against her and in mock shock exclaimed, "Donna!"

"I know. As if I don't have enough guilt to carry around for not seeing Tad more often, now I have to feel guilty about finding a man attractive while my nephew is dying."

"Well, you always tried to find a girl for him, Donna. Wouldn't it be a twist if he found a guy for you?"

"Look, I'm trying hard enough not to get ahead of myself. Don't you push past me," she laughed softly.

They sat quietly for a few moments. Melissa reached for Donna's hand. "Let's go inside."

They walked to the other side of the garden where a door opened up into the hospital. Tad's room was down the hall, right, down another hall to the room next to the end. Both women were surprised that there was no one outside in the waiting area. Donna opened the door to Tad's room and saw her sister Laura sitting in a chair looking at Tad.

"Laura, when did you arrive? I thought your plane didn't land for another hour."

"Donna," Laura began and then rose from the chair, hurrying to her sister and collapsing in her arms. "He's gone."

"What?"

"He died five minutes ago. Just after I got here." The sisters cried and hugged and Melissa left the room looking for a nurse, an aide, a doctor or a receptionist to yell and scream at. She found a wall to punch and a floor to fall down on.

A nurse had heard the noise and came rushing from the room next to Tad's. She helped Melissa up and explained that Laura had asked to be left alone as soon as Tad died. The nurse had been in and out of the room with Laura during the previous fifteen minutes. She had comforted her with the belief that Tad had held on until his mother had been able to arrive. She informed Laura that her sister was in the hospital somewhere and asked her if she wanted her paged.

Laura had replied that she would wait for a few minutes and thanked her. Tad was her only son, her oldest child. She had two daughters that were married with families of their own. Both daughters had always thought Tad irresponsible and there wasn't much communication between them. Laura had come to terms with Tad's independence and his lifestyle. Her ex-husband, Tad's father, had been an alcoholic and had been killed by a drunk driver shortly after the birth of the youngest daughter. The irony had been that he was sober at the time, one of the few short periods of the year that was the case. Christmas had always brought that out in him, the opposite of many alcoholic's behavior.

She wished that Tad had at least taken a refreshing break now and then, rather than always a refreshing beverage. After their first few arguments about the subject, Laura decided that she had learned something from her confrontations with Tad's father. Alcoholism wasn't something that a person could be talked out of by another person. It was a disease of the body, mind and soul. If the body could stay away from alcohol, the mind had a chance to perform its miracles of will. She didn't have much information about the soul.

She watched from afar when Tad had hit his heavy drinking stage. The phone calls were less frequent, some went unreturned. The visits home to New Orleans, where she could mother him with good food while old friends would come over to the house, were down to once a year. She had difficulty with Aspen's altitude, so she didn't undertake visits in exchange. She had relied on Donna's impressions of Tad's health and welfare. Donna had been honest with her, which she appreciated, but she also believed that Donna didn't understand the true depths of

Tad's drinking. She believed that Donna overflowed with an aunt's love for Tad, not a mother's resigned acceptance. She believed Donna was blinded somewhat by her pure friendship with Tad and unable to see that the party was soon to be over. It was only in these last few weeks that Donna had confessed to Laura the severity of Tad's illness. Portions of his body were shutting down. He had finally quit drinking, but it was bottles too late.

Now, Donna and Laura shared one of the most grievous trials a mother can endure. The death of a child. All the true laments of the Bible, the deepest and most sorrowful poems of any people anywhere, must have been written by parents losing children. Whether in battle, by disease, through accidents choreographed by malicious or benevolent design, or with the hand of any of the many seductive forms of suicide, of which alcoholism was only one, when a child dies before the parent a void is spawned around them forevermore.

Donna held Laura and would not let her go, even as Melissa and the nurse escorted them from Tad's room. God could only do so much in these times, and he did it through others.

VIII

Bobby had left House and Home to find the sun had dried the mall bricks almost completely. He saw a couple standing next to a tall aspen tree waiting for their picture to be taken. The man placed his hand on the tree where someone had thoughtfully carved their initials in a misguided attempt to attain immortality. Rain water still cupped on the leaves spilled down upon him just as the photo was taken.

Children ran after little boats made from hot dog holders, escorting them along the thin, swift moving creeks that bordered the mall. They dislodged them from the harbors created by tree roots encroaching into the creeks, helping edge a following competitor into the same trap.

Outdoor patio tables had been dried off, reset with utensils, menus and customers. Sunlight sparkled from the freshly cleaned metal and glass up and down the mall. A string quartet had pitched their folding chairs at one end of the mall and had begun an impromptu free concert. It sounded like a variation on Van Morrison's "Into the Mystic".

Bobby noticed that listeners began to stroll away from the quartet, then rush, with children calling to their parents to hurry after them. They were headed away toward the next mall, the one where The Cebolla Roja was located. It could mean one of several things, Bobby thought. Perhaps a mime has escaped his box in the adjoining park and is wandering free in the mall, a threat to children as well as clowns trying to tie balloons. There were designated mall cops that were responsible for defusing such situations. It could also be that the Fudge Man had made an unannounced appearance. He was an older man of small stature dressed as a box of fudge. A gold lame ribbon was tied around the center of the box and, as children pulled on it, tiny wrapped pieces of fudge came popping out from the Fudge Man's belt. It precipitated a mad scramble for the brightly colored pieces and usually a few children were left with no fudge, scrapped knees and tears running down their faces. The Fudge Man would point to the Fun Factory of Fudge store at the corner of the mall where parents could be seen being dragged in by their crying children.

The commotion could also be caused by another source. Bobby came around the corner of The Cebolla Roja mall and saw most of the crowd was in front of the restaurant. He looked up into the trees out front and, sure enough, there it was. A bear. Actually, a cub. Stuck in the tree, terrified by the mass of adoring humanity and protective police people. The police had erected a yellow tape fence around the area and spent most of their time moving out of the way for tourist pictures. They were waiting for the tranquilizer gun to be delivered.

Bobby slid through the crowd and then excused himself through the bottleneck of people at the entrance to The Cebolla Roja's patio. Once inside, he was greeted by the sight of only locals and staff. These people had seen cubs up the tree before and after the first several times had lost interest. It always ended the same. The police finally cleared the gawkers, the cub was shot, it fell from the tree, it was caught in as gentle fashion as possible on a specially made blanket and it was taken away. Mature bears that needed to be relocated constituted less of a problem. If they were repeat offenders, they would often be removed to another portion of the mountains. They'd establish a new territory and enjoy a garbage dumpster-free existence. Cubs, however, suffered what the Animal Control Department euphemistically called "survival issues". They were tagged and freed three times. The fourth brought to a conclusion any "survival issues".

For a brief period, Bobby had posted photos of treed cubs in front of The Cebolla Roja behind the bar. Subsequent to the discovery of the "third time's the charm, fourth time's the harm" rule that the forest service inaugurated, however, he removed the gallery.

He glanced to where the display had once been and there was a photo of Tad Johnson. Tad was wearing a Cebolla Roja t-shirt and hoisting a foaming glass of beer. Next to the photo was a flyer inviting Tad's many friends to a benefit held at the restaurant three weeks earlier. Bobby had helped organize it and it was, by all accounts, a resounding success. Among the stories relayed about Tad, the most common was of the time he rescued a drowning dog in the raging river and almost died from hypothermia. It was the dog who had almost died, not Tad, but the story had taken on a life of its own and wouldn't be denied or corrected.

The event had featured three local bands donating their talents and was highlighted by a chorus line of women dancing the can-can on the bar. They had dressed in long Hawaiian shirts and short shorts and had performed to a number written by one of the musicians entitled, "Let's Can-Can in Cancun Soon". It wasn't exactly the most sophisticated tune or enchanting lyrics any one had ever heard, but over the last few years had become one of the most requested songs at local concerts. Response to the dancers almost drowned out the music, but the band didn't mind.

The benefit had raised $4,450.99. Bobby tossed in an extra penny to round off the revenue. All the profits from the bar and food went to the fund that had been set up to help Tad with his medical and living expenses. The servers and bartenders also contributed all their tips. Jeff

79

made sure they were well compensated. Jeff and Bobby had done the accounting together the next day. Everyone knew Jeff didn't need to be watched, but he felt better if someone else was there to validate the money. Everyone also knew that Bobby didn't have much money, but through the years he had established a reputation for integrity, sometimes to his own financial detriment.

Much of it was in bills and change that took quite a while to unfold and clean. There were checks and credit card receipts to organize and prepare for deposit. Jeff and Bobby pointed at the time of night on the computer credit card receipts and laughed at the signatures. People became sloppy and generous as the night wore on. Bobby had left a little after midnight, the latest he had been out on the town since he had turned The Cebolla Roja over to Jeff a little more than a year ago. The place was still packed, so Jeff unlocked the back door to let him out. Jeff gave him a huge hug and they were both giddy with the obvious success of the night.

Bobby was in the alley where he had locked the door behind himself so many nights during the past twenty years. He looked up and was happy to be able to see a few stars even when the town burned bright. He heard a noise near the building across the alley, House and Home. The buildings were practically back to back, though it was mostly the employees of The Cebolla Roja who used the alleys. They took deliveries through the rear doors, hauled the garbage and trash out to the dumpsters and compacters, and some of them managed a smoke break on occasion.

But tonight it wasn't an employee who made noise. It was Tad Johnson standing by a stairwell, crying. He told Bobby he had snuck out the front door about a half hour earlier, overcome with emotion. He had walked around the park at the end of the mall a few times, talking with God and asking him why he had so many friends who were doing such a nice thing for him. He was embarrassed to go back into the bar. He figured if God didn't talk to him out here, he wouldn't talk to him in there either. Of course, he was wrong about that and Bobby was happy to tell him so. Bobby reminded Tad that God had seen as many bar floors as church pews. They began laughing and Bobby walked Tad back around to the front door of the bar. A couple of Tad's friends were loitering there and they enthusiastically ushered him back inside. Bobby took his time walking home that night.

***

Now, he looked at the benefit flyer behind the bar wistfully. Only three weeks ago Tad's situation hadn't seemed that grim. It looked then like he had gotten better, healthier and more optimistic. Today there was a different truth.

The bartender called his name. He leaned over the bar and shook hands. The bartender's name was Fierce because it rhymed with his last name of Pierce. It was legally Humboldt, but Fierce had become his nickname while playing football in high school. He was openly gay and was now playing his name. The trophies he had won as the MVP as the league's star quarterback were behind the bar. Jeff had asked if Fierce wanted to showcase them, and the former quarterback was proud of both his past and present so he eagerly accepted the offer. Fierce had been recruited by college football factories across the country, but his love was snowboarding and he moved to Colorado from his small town in Montana immediately after graduation. It was then he began his gay lifestyle. Word filtered back to Montana and he eventually learned that he hadn't been the only non-practicing gay or lesbian student in his school. Not all of Aspen's citizens professed a lack of interest in others' sexual orientation. Some didn't accommodate gay or lesbian lifestyles easily, but the populace was mostly of a liberal proclivity and encouraged diversity.

Bobby had welcomed Fierce when they first met and thought his self-effacing humor charming. He began as a server and became a bartender within a year. Bobby wasn't that fond of quarterback over center jokes and the like, so Fierce kept the more outrageous aspects of his current encounters quieter when Bobby was around. Bobby felt that if he encouraged Fierce to be flamboyant both the gay bashers and those who might be finding out they were gay would be intimidated. He didn't know if he was right or not, but that's what he thought and he told Fierce such. Fierce didn't necessarily agree, but mutual respect won out and a calm decorum ruled.

The cutest little waitress in the world came over and gave Bobby the biggest hug she had. Darlene was five feet in platform shoes, though she mainly wore toed sandals. She was absolutely gorgeous in an Ann Margret way, with a proportionate figure to match.

"Bobby, it's so good to see you," she squealed. Unfortunately, as physically magnetic as she was, Darlene was also possessed of a voice that sounded as if she had just sucked helium. She was almost forty, looked twenty-three and acted seventeen if it would increase her tips.

"Darlene, you look younger today than I've ever seen you."

She was use to that fib, laughed, and stuck a hand into one of his pockets in search of his balls. He jerked back, her hand followed, and he had to turn around to find the leverage to pull her arm away. She slapped him on the butt and skipped off toward the rear of the restaurant.

Bobby saw familiar faces everywhere. He was aware, though, that in the year he'd ceased being the owner of this restaurant and bar he was gradually losing his ability to recall names. In small increments, without the daily reminders, the names of acquaintances, of regular customers, slipped off to the unused portions of his memory. He knew those names were still there, and when he did the exercises of memory gymnastics, they would either creep back in or come smashing against his awareness with such force that a domino effect ensued. Something else would be pushed out of the conscious recall section and he would have to go searching for that later. He much preferred the creeping back in mode because it didn't seem to eliminate any thing else.

He didn't recall what the conscious recall section of his brain was actually called. He was sure he had read about it somewhere. He was positive that he had spent time in a conversation with someone who was proficient in neurological matters; areas, sizes, functions, attributes, abnormalities, where the funny part of the brain was, the love part, the fear of commitment part, those parts that liked people and those parts that didn't, those parts that wanted to live forever and those that were looking forward to a long sleep in another dimension. He just couldn't remember who it was.

And that's exactly what was happening this very moment. There was a man standing in front of him that had taken Darlene's spot after she had skipped to the loo or wherever. He had no idea of who this person was, but the stranger was talking to him as if they were resuming a conversation. The stranger pontificated about the advantages of banning employee housing requirements that stifled the free market and enabled dead beats to live off the backs of the wealthy. The stranger reminded him of a couple of statements that Bobby was fairly certain he might have made. They definitely sounded as if he would have said them. In fact, he suddenly remembered making them. He had written them in one of his columns for the Aspen Chronicle. He exhaled a sigh of relief. He realized there was no reason he should know this stranger, except, of course, that a writer is wise to know his audience, and he was prepared to dismiss him as politely as possible. Nonetheless, the stranger continued to argue with the column, because Bobby would not engage him. The stranger essentially argued both sides of the issue while Bobby became more and more interested. He was fascinated by the stranger's ability to fairly and eloquently present a complicated and emotional debate single-handedly. Bobby wondered what was the name and location of the part of the brain that facilitated this quality. He vaguely believed that he had demonstrated this same ability upon occasion and he was tempted to do so now. A member of the stranger's party approached just as Bobby was ready to make the decision to begin talking or forcefully excuse himself. The stranger and his friend, whom Bobby didn't recognize either, abruptly walked away. Bobby almost began to wonder what part of the brain made people do that, then shut himself off and ceased to be curious about brain parts, at least for now.

Fierce called out, "Bear's gone!" and most of the people turned toward the front door and the patio and the tree to make sure. There was no reason to not trust Fierce, but it was human nature to double-check what could actually be verified in life. There were more stories, opinions, facts and rumors that couldn't be verified than could, so it was often a validation of one's own existence when they could.

Bobby took the opportunity while everyone glanced toward the front to walk across the bar area and take the flight of steps up to Jeff's office. Through several sets of cowboy swinging doors, of course. It was once Bobby's office and that's the way he looked at it. Now, the office, the restaurant, bar, pleasures, rewards, headaches and heartbreaks were Jeff's. He knocked on the door and Jeff opened it. He motioned for Bobby to come in and have a seat.

"Tad's dead."

"I'm sorry for you, me and everybody else."

"So am I," said Jeff. "Melissa just called me from the hospital." He had cried with Donna at the hospital, but wasn't now.

They looked at each other and nodded. "I'm glad we decided to get together and talk about his memorial today. When should we do it?" asked Bobby.

"I asked Donna. She's a sweetheart, by the way, and I was happy to see you talking with her."

"It was my pleasure," and a small smile snuck into Bobby's face.

"Hmm."

"You can 'hmm' all you want. It's just nice to meet someone attractive my age who doesn't know me."

"Oh, so you can be someone else around her? Or, is it that you could be the real you that nobody knows?

"The opportunities may be limitless."

"We all pretty much like you the way you are."

"I'm not talking about like. I'm talking about the grand search for truth."

They both began laughing. Sadness for Tad, his family and friends, themselves, needed a release. It would be a welcome epilogue to the vigil they had experienced to begin planning the party. They would fulfill Tad's wishes as best they could.

"Donna wanted to wait and talk with her sister about the timing of it. Melissa told me that Tad's mother made it to the hospital just before he died."

"That's good. I guess."

"I guess." They paused for a moment and each thought the other was saying a silent prayer. For Tad, his mother, his aunt and for whomever else they didn't know.

"Anyway, we should wait until we talk with Donna or Laura before we settle on the date and time. Tad wanted everybody there, but we should at least find out what his mother thinks."

"That would be awfully mature of us."

"Do you think we can do that?"

"Death brings out the maturity in us all."

"What do you think happens when we die?"

"Oh, let's see." Bobby looked up at the ceiling and rubbed his chin. "The short answer is either nothing or there is a continuity of life. The long answer is that the people who know we are dead throw a party or attend a funeral or both. They are happy or sad or they have mixed emotions. They say nice things about us and they mean them or they don't. Then the rest of life gets going again. They remember us sometimes, even might miss us. And then when they forget us, we're gone. Unless, of course, we leave something that those who never knew us can find. Most of us don't."

"Do you think Tad did that? Leave something, I mean."

"I don't know. I didn't know him well enough. Did you?"

"I was probably his closest friend. Honestly, I don't think so, but I sure would like to be wrong."

IX

Donna and Laura spent the night at Tad's apartment. It was one of those employee housing units that the stranger in the bar had decried to Bobby. Tad had entered the City's lottery each year for the last six years hoping to be selected as a potential buyer. When a person's number was drawn they had the opportunity to demonstrate to the Housing Authority their need for subsidized shelter and their ability to meet the requirements. It was much like a military draft lottery without the possible dire consequences. However, in Tad's case, his selection had proved to be terminally ironic.

The unit Tad had qualified for was on the outskirts of town. A one bedroom, it consisted of a multipurpose room that included the kitchen and a living area. There was a bathroom and a small outdoor platform that Tad referred to as a veranda. He rarely used the bedroom, falling asleep most nights on the couch. Knowing he was quite ill, some friends had come over the week before he was placed in the hospital for the last time and cleaned up the apartment for him. He had been too weak and disinterested to make much of a mess, so when the women arrived they were pleasantly surprised at its relative condition of cleanliness and order.

The sisters left their travel bags in the apartment and walked to a nearby restaurant for dinner. Neither felt very hungry, but they weren't prepared to spend the night in Tad's apartment quite yet.

The restaurant was slow and closed at eight. They had an hour to eat. It was across the highway from the airport and they could look out the windows and see the Lear jets and other private aircraft parked. They saw three sleek aircraft land, pivot, park and met by long black limousines while they ate their salads and had a glass of wine. It was a quiet conversation that confined itself to the events of the day. They recounted how their travels had been and told each other how tired they were.

The sun had set but it was still light out as they walked back to the apartment. On their way, they stopped at the liquor store and bought a bottle of wine to share. It occurred to Donna that Tad probably didn't have a corkscrew in the apartment, so she retrieved hers from her car before they went in. Not taking chances, she kept it with her registration and proof of insurance.

After Donna poured them each a glass, they sat on the couch and began looking around at the things that Tad had left that defined his life. A golf bag stood in the corner, the clubs dirty. Well, at least he had played some golf this summer, the women thought. A large screen TV dominated an entertainment center that also had shelves holding some books and photographs. There were pictures of Tad and Donna together in the Jeep, as well as others with Laura and his sisters.

"Are the girls going to come?"

"I think so, but I have to arrange for tickets for them both. Neither one of them say they can afford it."

Donna knew that Laura probably couldn't afford it either. Donna had never been married, didn't have children and had enjoyed a successful career in the travel industry. She was comfortable financially and had been generous with the nieces and Tad since they were born. "I can help you out, Laura."

"It's enough that you are here, honey. I've been doing better lately." Laura owned a small gift shop in New Orleans, a few blocks out of the French Quarter, but close enough to pick up the more adventurous tourists.

"Well, how 'bout if we split the cost?"

88

Laura was grateful that Donna wouldn't take no for an answer and accepted the offer. "I suppose I should call them tonight and let them know."

She called her daughters and they agreed to fly to Aspen the next day. Shelly lived in Fort Lauderdale and Pam in Houston. Laura had given Shelly her credit card number and Donna had given hers to Pam. Donna felt a little more secure with Pam having her credit card information, because she really believed Pam couldn't afford the trip. She thought Shelly was bitchy and selfish and that unless someone else paid for the flight she wouldn't come. There was buried underneath Shelly's cold exterior a tender, wounded child who was mad at her dead father and now her dead brother. She would take it out on her mother if she could. The price for her not doing so was a roundtrip airline ticket.

The girls called Laura back shortly with the flight details. They would connect in Denver and take the same flight into Aspen, arriving late in the afternoon. Donna and Laura agreed to meet them and bring them to Tad's apartment. It would be cozy in a crowded sort of way.

Donna and Laura woke early, had breakfast at the same restaurant nearby and drove Downvalley to Glenwood Springs. The mortuary and crematorium was there. Donna had sometimes wondered if there was a last name of Uary and, if so, had anyone named their child Mort? She didn't share this thought with her sister.

The women stopped at the Hot Springs Pool, the worlds largest and possibly the most aromatic, to soak out the wine and some sorrows. According to tradition, Doc Holliday had bathed here while pulling teeth and playing cards. With Wyatt Earp, the Dalton Gang, the James brothers, Cole Younger and Calamity Jane, The Doc had also performed general surgery on the town's wealthiest citizen's wallets. Tradition might have been exaggerated, but that, the locals would say, is traditional.

After the soak and a few minutes drying off on the lawn in the sun, the sisters went to collect Tad's ashes. Neither one of them looked inside the canister. There was a Latino family that was viewing a casket in a small room as they walked by and Donna translated for Laura. "She was saying he was the best husband and father and that she would love him forever. She asked him to ask Jesus to watch over her family and that as much as she would miss him, she hoped to live to be an old woman so she could tell him about their grandchildren."

They got into Donna's VW and drove to Two Rivers Park where they opened the canister together. The ashes were darker than they expected. They each took a pinch and with tears in their eyes let the ashes catch a breeze into the confluence of the Roaring Fork and Colorado Rivers.

It was just after noon when they returned to the car. Laura's cell phone gave a ring tone that signaled a message had been left. Donna wouldn't drive and talk on the phone at the same time and she didn't like to drive and listen to someone else talking on the phone, either. She waited for Laura to listen to the message.

"It was Jeff Bazzano. He called to say how sorry he is and wants to know about having a memorial for Tad at The Cebolla Roja." Laura hadn't met Jeff, she had only spoken to him on the phone twice. The first time was about six months ago when Tad first became sick. The second was two weeks ago when Tad had gone back in the hospital. Jeff had been hopeful then, telling her that the doctors thought Tad would improve. She had called Tad afterwards and he sounded fine. That was before he had been given the heavy drugs to fight the sudden failure of his liver and kidneys. Only yesterday, now a lifetime away,

90

Donna had called with the updated information she had received from Jeff. "What should I say?"

"What do you want to say?"

"I want to say, I'm taking his ashes and going home. But I can't, can I? The girls fly back out on Sunday, today's Thursday. His friends could have a memorial for him next week, or whenever. Maybe I could come back for it."Donna knew that would never happen. This would be the last time Laura would ever be in Aspen. Besides her problems with the altitude, she wouldn't be able to revisit his death place. "Did he say when it might be?"

"No. He asked me to call him back." She handed the phone to Donna. "Could you do this for me?"

"Of course." She opened the phone, found the last number that had called Laura's phone and replied to it. Both sisters used the same type of basic cell phone. The last couple of decades had introduced so much new technology that each had agreed to use the same model of gadgets so they could help each other in times of malfunction or operator error.

"Jeff? This is Donna." She listened for a minute, thanked him and said, "Tad's sisters are flying in today and leaving on Sunday." She listened again and answered, "Are you sure? That doesn't seem possible." There was another pause, she said "Thank you, Jeff" and closed the phone. "If it's okay with us, really, you, then he wants to have a celebration of Tad's life Saturday night. He wants the four of us to come in for dinner tonight and discuss it with him."

Laura had heard of family and friends joining together for celebrations of life, though she had never attended one. She had seen the wild funeral processions in New Orleans, though she had never participated in one. She planned to take Tad's ashes back with her and seal them in the family tomb next to his father's. A small cemetery with above ground mausoleums in a nearby neighborhood where oak trees swept the air with Spanish moss. Where magnolias spread their big-eyed buds, keeping watch on the past lives of this strange, romantic and proud city.

"I guess that sounds alright."

Donna realized that even though Laura wasn't completely surprised by Tad's death, she was still in some shock and would rely on her to help with decisions. "We'll get the girls, go back to the apartment and everyone can get some rest before we go into town. We can talk with Jeff and see what he has in mind. If you don't want to do anything, we can simply spend the next couple of days with the girls."

"I'm going to need your help, like I always have." She looked over at Donna, adding, "You're the best sister ever."

They hugged, which was almost impossible not to do in the VW bug, and began the drive back to Aspen. As they headed south out of Glenwood Springs the valley began to open before them and they saw Mount Sopris, looming over the Roaring Fork Valley like Mt. Fuji. It ruled the already dramatic and powerful surrounding landscape. In August, the broad shouldered mountain was wrapped in a green garment while above, toward the top, gray rock held hostages of ice and snow. The gray rock was scree, loose and treacherous to hike on, but climbing to the summit was a popular summer pastime.

Skirting Sopris was the town of Carbondale and the Crystal River, aptly named due to its clear, brilliant water. South of the highway between Glenwood Springs and Aspen, Carbondale had refused to be a bedroom community to Aspen and had forged its own identity through cooperation between ranchers and self-styled hippies. It celebrated dandelions with a festival, partied for days about potatoes, and threw a long weekend arts, crafts and music fair that had been drawing people back to it for decades.

Up the Crystal River, Redstone and its castle resided. A wealthy easterner had erected a true-to-life dream castle in the late nineteenth century. He had pretty much owned the town, doing some mining and railroading as a profitable hobby. When these played out, he moved back east, the castle fell into disrepair and the town of Redstone proclaimed a population of thirty-eight. Many thought squirrels and foxes must have been included in that number.

Beyond Redstone was the quarry and town of Marble. Stone from here was used for the Tomb of the Unknown Soldier and the exterior of the Lincoln Memorial. The unique white marble is mined from a cliff, not an open pit, and is considered the purest on this blue marble of a world. It's possible to get to Aspen from here, though it's not easy. It's a century and many major peaks of the West Elk mountain range away.

Donna remembered bouncing along the primitive roads behind Marble with Tad and Melissa. The three had spent a full day last summer traveling about thirty miles in six hours. Fields of lupine, monkshood and Indian paintbrush lay out next to aspen groves and stands of spruce. She thought that some day she would need to return to those fields.

With Mount Sopris in the rear view mirror they drove past the towns of El Jebel and Basalt, mid valley between Glenwood Springs and Aspen. The deep blue sky carried a couple of pure white clouds above the vibrant green which exuded strength and depth from the mountains. Summer rains kept the valley lush and the ranches held horses, houses and dogs. It was a beautiful area of the world and Donna understood why Tad had fallen in love with it. She wished that he had spent more time experiencing it, though. Instead, he had isolated himself in Aspen. He worked and played there, rarely venturing outside the town's boundaries.

As they drove past the road that traveled to Snowmass and its destination ski resort they approached the airport. The runways had been extended and widened over the decades, but it was still a challenging strip for pilots. There had been some horrific accidents and many a plane had pulled up or had its take-off aborted at the last minute. Sudden snow squalls and tricky winds contributed to the general hazards of flying into and out of an airport situated at eight thousand feet.

However, the weather wasn't what was on the minds of the two sisters. They were not dreading the flight, more the arrival of the other two sisters, Laura's daughters. Donna parked her car in front of the terminal and waited for Laura to return with Shelly and Pam. The girls' plane had landed twenty minutes ago and by now they should have had enough time to wonder why their mom was late to meet them.

Both Donna and Laura were pleasantly surprised that the daughters were in buoyant spirits. They had never flown over the Rockies and were practically ebullient describing the vistas they had witnessed. Their flight was only half-full and they each took a window seat. The speed with which they had landed and stopped on the runway continued to be a source of excitement for them as Donna drove across the highway and to Tad's apartment.

Once inside, the daughter's enthusiasm tempered somewhat when they saw the mementos and keepsakes of Tad's life. There were several pictures of themselves that they didn't expect Tad would have saved. The high school yearbook he kept was from the same school the girls had also attended. A bowl in the cupboard that he had always used for ice cream brought memories rushing back from their childhood times. To their own dismay, a fondness and appreciation of their brother welled up in them both and they cried for the first time since learning of Tad's death. The four women embraced and together they felt a sadness ease and a healing begin.

The sisters retired to the bedroom where a king size bed accommodated them both for a nap. Donna and Laura remained in the living room to relax and reminisce. Laura fell asleep briefly on the couch and Donna stretched out on huge bean bag chair. It wasn't made of beans, it wasn't a chair, but it was, indeed, a bag. Sewn together from sections of leather or a leather-like substance, it was heavy and uncomfortable and an ugly lime Popsicle green.

She scanned the two local daily papers she had picked up from the stands while parked at the terminal and realized suddenly that she had forgotten to discuss with Laura an obituary. She casually dismissed the thought that if a family's last name was Uary and they had a son named Mort would they also have one named Obit? She quietly stepped out onto the concrete platform that held only a small hibachi and one woven nylon lawn chair. She called the papers and learned that if she emailed an obituary in by three on Friday afternoon it could be published in Saturday's editions. She would also be able to include mention of a memorial if there was to be one.

After another hour the other women woke and, hungry, they decided to drive into town. Donna called The Cebolla Roja to talk with Jeff. She spoke briefly with him and he asked her to wait for an hour so that he would have a table ready for them. It was six now, so they could park in town without paying the outrageous meter fees and walk around.

Shelly and Pam were enthralled with the circuitous route Donna drove. She took the back streets on the west end of town where old Victorian houses mixed with more modern architecture. Every block featured manicured lawns, gorgeous flower beds and stately trees. The more recently built homes were often a blend of wood and stone, most of them carefully designed so they didn't present a hideous contrast to the older and often brightly colored Victorians. Of course, now and then there would be a house that screamed ego, suggesting the resident suffered low self esteem, was compensating for an unhappy childhood or pronouncing that his penis wasn't small after all. The younger sisters were impressed with these expressions of wealth and poor taste, but they were delighted more with the Victorians and the occasional modest house left over from the pre-ski-boom days. These were few and very far between.

Donna parked the car four blocks from The Cebolla Roja so the others could have a chance to see the ground and sense the sky before they entered the brick malls. It hadn't rained today and the grass settled softly in the shade which stretched across the town. Here and there, sunlight still came streaming up the valley, highlighting tops of buildings and the peaks toward Independence Pass. Smuggler Mountain and Red Mountain, north across from Aspen, sported great houses with massive glass that reflected the brilliant sunlight. The women strolled easily and remarked on the friendliness of so many other walkers. Cars stopped respectfully for pedestrians and the people waved back. There was a sharp, rhythmic clickity-clackity and a young man sped by on a long board. Bicyclists cruised around corners, joggers and runners strode past and hikers were reaching the end of their day at the base of Aspen Mountain.

Except for the chain stores like Prada and Christian Dior, and a few others that concentrated on high end sales, many of the stores that were owned by locals were closed by six. Shelly and Pam were aghast at this, as they were to discover the malls of Aspen weren't the malls of Houston and Fort Lauderdale. These were wide open with the creeks and trees and flowers separating both sides of completely different tastes in architecture and building materials.

They approached The Cebolla Roja without warning. The three foot tall metal grate fence that held its patio mall almost went without notice. They wouldn't have been the first people to walk straight into it while looking somewhere else. There were several teenagers every week that had practically impaled themselves in a most sensitive spot while staring at the object of their sensitive area and trying to walk at the same time. It was just part of the human condition.

They walked through the first of the many cowboy swinging doors and waited for the host to approach them. She did in due course, without anyone having to wonder if they had been noticed. Donna mentioned they were meeting Jeff around seven, the host expressed recognition of the rendezvous and showed them to their table, a larger one in the back. She told the group she was very sorry about Tad and they thanked her. The bar had been crowded when they passed through and the restaurant was full. Theirs was the only table open. Red and white checkered tablecloths covered the heavy wooden table that may have been a library desk at one time. The settings were placed and candles were lit in two glass red bowls. The table sat eight, so Donna asked if this was the correct table and, when it was affirmed it was, the four women sat down at one end of it.

A server came over presently, poured glasses of water, offered them menus and informed them that Jeff was upstairs in his office and would be with them momentarily. He introduced himself as Sammy and expressed the same sentiment as the host. No sooner had he left than Jeff appeared. He and Donna hugged before he was introduced to the other three. Jeff had little problem showing affection. He also hugged Laura, Shelly and Pam as he met them, expressing his sympathies and asking them to please sit down again. Donna had been the only one to return the sympathy, the others not really knowing how much Tad's death was a loss to Jeff, as well as so many others.

As Donna began to sit in the wooden chair again, she turned to Jeff, asking, "Are you sure we should be at this table? It's too large for just the four of us."

"I was hoping to be able to join you so we could discuss some ideas for the memorial. Also, Bobby and Melissa will be coming. This is the best table for us. So you see" he added, spreading his arms in the universal gesture of 'there's nothing to be done about it', "we will be most comfortable and well taken care of here. I should explain to you, Laura, and to Shelly and Pam, that Bobby was the previous owner of The Cebolla Roja, is a very good friend of mine and visited Tad usually twice a day at the hospital. He has the experience with events that I don't and he has been kind enough to help me in the past. He has volunteered to do so again." The women nodded noncommittally, though Jeff observed a subtle start from Donna at the inclusion of Bobby's name. "Melissa is my girl friend, and as of today, an assistant floor manager here. She left her former job yesterday and was lucky to find new employment so quickly." He presented a smile to the women and as each understood his comment a smile was returned.

Sammy returned to take a drink order and Jeff asked the women if they liked margaritas. "After all, you are in a restaurant that specializes in Mexican food," Jeff encouraged. It was agreed that a liter of margaritas would not only be a good title for a song, but would be appropriate. Donna requested a glass with no salt, so Jeff asked if he could have her salt as well as his. Sammy smiled and left to send the order to the bar while a busser placed a basket of warm home made chips and salsa on the table. "Now, please feel free to order anything you would like for dinner. We are picking up the check."

Donna and Laura both protested without success. Jeff insisted that it was his restaurant, he made the rules and that if he hadn't wanted to do it he wouldn't have asked them to come in to dinner tonight. He was thanked for his graciousness and told the women that he would be happy to answer any questions they might have about the menu. "However, Sammy's expertise will be greater than mine and he can also tell you about the specials tonight."

"That's good, because after twenty years I'm a bit bored with the regular menu" Bobby piped in. He and Melissa had come up behind Jeff as he finished. "Look who I found playing with a couple of dogs out front," he added. Jeff rose from his seat, giving Melissa a kiss hello and introduced her to Laura and her daughters. Donna embraced Melissa warmly and explained to the others their friendship. After greetings and condolences were extended, Donna and Bobby hugged and she introduced him.

"Thank you for being there with my sister yesterday" Laura said to both Melissa and Bobby. "It's nice that she was able to find someone her own age to spend time with, Bobby." Her daughters erupted with embarrassed laughter at their mother's social graces.

"I feel the same" smiled Bobby. "Though, perhaps, even a little older at the moment. In fact, I should probably sit down." Laura was at one end, Shelly and Pam on one side and Jeff sat next to Donna when he arrived. He conceded his chair to Bobby and he and Melissa sat opposite one another. The other end was left vacant.

Sammy brought the margaritas, Jeff gave his glass to Melissa and the men ordered beer. Sammy explained the specials, which were a cream of broccoli soup, a salad featuring smoked salmon, an ahi filet and a twelve ounce rib eye steak. Another basket of fresh chips was brought along with more salsa as he answered questions about the menu and specials. Jeff asked for a couple of bowls of guacamole and the diners set to discussing their options.

Donna didn't eat red meat or pork, but she was delighted with the possibility of ahi. Bobby remarked how it had been a while since he had a steak, so his choice was easily made. A while to him, in this case, was a week. The daughters chose enchiladas and chile rellenos, Laura the special salad, and Jeff and Melissa decided to share a spinach salad and a teriyaki chicken sandwich.

"You have an eclectic menu, Jeff," noted Shelly.

"It's not my fault. I inherited it from Bobby."

Bobby explained how he had worked in a Mexican restaurant years ago and, while managing to learn virtually nothing of the language, had kept some of his favorite recipes from the experience. The restaurant now known as The Cebolla Roja had previously been the Red Onion. It had endured many incarnations since the mining days, the building having been erected in 1892, originally being simply called the Brick Saloon. At that time it was the only structure in the downtown area constructed of brick. All the others were made from stone or wood, the latter consumed by any of several fires that torched the town during its mining heyday.

He had taken the twenty year lease on the Red Onion when no one else would. It had developed the reputation of a jinxed location. The out-of-town owners before him had alienated the town's residents by referring to them as riff-raff and proclaiming they intended to only serve tourists. What they didn't understand, apart from how to manage a business, was that tourists don't go to where the locals won't go. Bobby decided to enhance the All-American menu by adding his choicest Mexican fare and changing the name to the Spanish nomenclature. It was a year before he had reestablished the building's prior reputation as a place where residents and tourists alike were welcome. Hence, it became known and celebrated as one of the friendliest and most authentic of all of Aspen's surviving original locations. There was one carry over, however, that Bobby couldn't quite shake from the last owners: the ability to manage the bottom line. He was not a natural business man. He reasoned that if he and his employees did well enough that was good enough. He operated at a modest profit, he paid a fair wage and contributed to the customer's overall happy state of mind and body. Any spiritual advance was the responsibility of the patron, but there were often conversations that seemed to lead in that direction.

The group had enjoyed their dinner, Donna feasting on the ahi and sampling the daughters' chile rellenos. Another round of margaritas had been duly delivered and imbibed, tales of Tad's childhood and his life in Aspen relayed and all were pleasantly satiated from the cuisine and conversation.

Jeff found it time to broach the subject of a memorial gathering. "I don't know your religious or practical beliefs regarding this, but Tad and I had spoken of this possibility. A memorial sounds somber, perhaps, but I think Tad's hope was that it would be more of a celebration. An opportunity for his friends and family to remember him with the same sort of happy and generous spirit he personified."

"I just don't know what this entails, or what it might cost," said Laura.

"Well, you and Shelly and Pam are leaving Sunday. Tomorrow is too soon, so is Saturday, but there is no other choice. It would have to be Saturday night. We'll get the word out to as many people as we can. We'll provide appetizers and probably arrange for some music." The women, including Melissa, their emotions raw from sorrow and intensified from the margaritas, held hands as Jeff continued. "There is no cost, Laura. We've all lost a person special and important to us. This is the very least he would have done for me.'

"You are so kind. I just don't know if we can accept."

"I would like to tell you that you have no choice, but, of course, you do. Is there some reason for your reluctance that you can share with me? Anything religious?"

Laura shook her head. "No, I'm afraid there was never much of a religious life in our house."

"I can only tell you that Tad always referred to his childhood as an environment where he learned kindness and love. That sounds to me as if he grew up in a place where many churches would like to find themselves."

Bobby gave a thumbs up to Jeff and interjected, "And he was tall enough some people might have confused him with a steeple."

The women gave a laugh of relief from the tension and grave subject.

"Please, Laura, this is something that we would really like to do. It would be an honor," Bobby said seriously. At this moment, once again, both Jeff and Bobby were grateful that one had owned and one now owned The Cebolla Roja.

"You are making this a much different experience that I thought it was going to be. What can we do to help?"

"Why don't Bobby and I come out to Tad's place in the morning and we'll figure it out?" said Jeff. I think it's been a long day for the four of you. Let's get you home."

"That sounds like a very good idea," responded Donna.

"One more thing, though," interrupted Bobby, "I'm driving you ladies home."

"Oh, I'm fine to drive, Bobby"

"It's getting rather dark out now and you've had a few margaritas. All of you. I've had one beer and that was before dinner. I know the way."

"But I have a VW bug."

"It'll be cozy."

"I'll follow and give you a ride home, Bobby," said Jeff.

"I'd appreciate that. I'm not sure I should be left much longer in the company of so many pretty women."

Donna squeezed his arm. They had participated fully in the conversation during dinner, yet had somehow been able to continue the flirtatious nature of their initial encounter. This hadn't passed unnoticed by the others. A couple of times when Donna and Bobby extended their gaze at each other, the daughters elbowed one another and raised their eyebrows. Donna had mentioned meeting Bobby at the hospital to Laura, but she had neglected to provide certain details. At first Laura wondered if she should be upset about it, if it was in poor taste, but then remembered she wasn't really concerned about what anyone else might think of her sister. She loved Donna and if not now, when? Melissa and Jeff were aware of the old folk's budding infatuation and thought it cute.

Jeff received thanks again for the dinner, the hospitality and the plans for the memorial. He gave Bobby and the women a fifteen minute head start, knowing they had to walk to Donna's car.

It had cooled down considerably since they had entered the restaurant and the women were ready to walk briskly. Bobby kept cautioning them at intersections to wait for the cars to pass, but they informed him that pedestrians had the right-of-way in Aspen. By the time he had taken them the ten minute drive to Tad's apartment, mentioning how he had changed his mind about the round-about, they had grown silent and had almost fallen asleep. He walked them into the apartment, hugged each of them and returned outside to wait for Jeff to arrive. As Jeff's car pulled up, Bobby saw Donna on the platform. She blew him a kiss.

X

Bobby arrived back home about nine in the morning. He was exhausted and needed a shower. A trail run up Aspen Mountain had turned into an endurance contest with his past. Bobby of the here and now lost. He gave himself credit for the attempt and promised he would ice his knees after the shower.

A cool-off walk around his side and back yard was a routine with dual purpose. It allowed him to finish sweating and offered the opportunity to inspect his grounds. Gardening was a pleasant pastime which yielded no vegetables or fruits, but plenty of meditative moments.

"Hey, Bobby! Did you take a swim in the river? That musta been colder than a west Texas wind in the middle of January." Joe Don would have to be standing on something to be peering over the fence between Bobby's back yard and his lot. Bobby used the fence to hop on a boulder-size rock, looking eye to eye with Joe Don, who was perched on a riding mower. "I went out and rented this grasshog first thing this morning. Figured I'd see what this part of the lot next to your fence looked like."

Bobby nodded and said, "You could have just asked me. How badly are you stuck?"

Joe Don climbed off the mower and stepped into muck. "Deep enough I can't get it out myself. Care to help?"

"Let me go get some boots on."

"That'll be a pretty picture with those swimming trunks."

"They're running shorts. And, if I can't be funny, I'll try to look funny."

"Damn if you're not both, Bobby."

He came back in a few minutes in blue jeans, boots and the same wet t-shirt. Walking around the mower, he sunk almost to the bottom of his calves and told Joe Don it didn't look good. They gave a pull together on the back and then the front of the mower with no success. "I can try to bring my truck around and pull you out with some rope."

"I can't understand where this water has come from," protested Joe Don.

"Well, it's not from my sprinkler system, I can guarantee you that."

"What do you mean by "it's not from my sprinkler system"? Maybe it is."

"No, I've dug up the entire line that runs across the back of my yard and there's no leak. I was concerned at the beginning of the summer because I noticed some sinkage. That's part of the problem, I suspect, with my fence getting slightly wobbly." He pushed on a portion of the fence and it swayed a few inches back and forth. "Once you start building your house, I would consider the possibility of splitting the cost of a new fence with you."

Joe Don squinted a glare at him. "You gotta be kidding me. I wouldn't even call this a fence to begin with. It's more a bunch of boards strung together accidentally."

"Of course, I'd want you to find the source of this marshy area you have here and fix the problem first," continued Bobby. It was early in the day, but he could feel Joe Don's temperature beginning to climb.

"Where the heck is this water coming from then?"

"I told you about Caleb's description in his journal that this was wetlands. Caveat emptor."

A voice called from the street at the front of the lot. "You mind if I come through?" Bobby reminded Joe Don that it was his property and the Texan waved the man over. He was gray bearded and wore a fisherman's hat. A plaid shirt was tucked into his blue jeans and he walked carefully in open-toed sandals. "Good morning, gentleman. It would appear you could use a hand here." Bobby recognized the elderly fellow. They had briefly met when he had moved into his house, the most modest of the homes in Aspen Elk Estates. It was directly across from Joe Don's lot, on the other side of the narrow road and it backed up to the river. It had been built so there remained decent -sized side yards.

They occasionally had passed on the street when he had been out for a run and the doctor was out walking his dog, a sometimes barking Shih Tzu. At the start of a run, or at the end, Bobby was not in a proper mood of mind to engage in conversation. He felt guilty for not remembering his neighbor's name and reintroduced himself.

The doctor and the Texan shook hands in a friendly greeting. "We appreciate your offer, we surely do, Doc," Joe Don volunteered. He then smiled to himself and added, "No offense, now, but this is a pretty damn heavy piece of machinery and I wouldn't want you to hurt yourself."

"Yes, it must be quite heavy to have sunk as deeply as it appears. Perhaps, you should have quit trying to mow this grass after the first couple of times you just barely managed to rev her up and out."

A startled Joe Don spurted, "What do you mean?"

"I certainly did not intend to be a voyeur, Mr. Burke. I was sitting on my front porch with my occasionally barking Shih Tzu" answered the doctor, with a nod to Bobby, "And what with the noise and all I could hardly help myself from observing your determination to bring uniformity to the back of your lot." He paused for a moment, staring at the power mower, before he said, "However, I was not asking to be drafted for physical labor, no, not at my age. I was merely prepared to suggest I pull my truck up over here and we attach a winch to the mower." The Doc smiled. "I promise I won't hurt myself."

Joe Don was reluctant to accept the offer due to his embarrassment, but Bobby touted the benefits of a winch compared to rope and the rescue was speedily accomplished. The Doc proposed that they wash off the mower with a hose from his house, but Joe Don declined. Instead, he drove it up the ramp of the yellow, caged small flatbed that was attached to his SUV, thanked them for their help and drove away. Bobby noted that Joe Don wasn't always full of bluster and good ole' boy camaraderie. He told the Doc that it had been rewarding and enjoyable meeting him again and he looked forward to seeing him soon. Dr. Corning returned the sentiment, eased back into his truck and drove across the empty lot to his house across the way after first spinning his tires.

***

Bobby finished his shower, iced his knees and prepared to call Jeff when the phone rang. He saw it was his sister by the caller identification and answered.

"Hi, Susan. Sorry I didn't call you back."

Susan was Bobby's only sibling, twice divorced, three years younger and the mother of four children. She had spent all of her adult life living in San Francisco as a painter. She painted houses, street murals, canvas, pottery, glass, metal, and anything else she could. She had painted since she was a child and had painted Bobby several times.

"Bobby, you know how I worry when I don't hear from you." She had sworn to never call him Bob, which was not a difficult commitment for her to keep. She made longshoreman jealous when she swore and he would always be her big brother Bobby.

Bobby knew the way out of this particular guilt trip and he had the added ammunition that a friend had just died. He chose to not use it, however, hesitant to hear her expressions of sympathy. Theirs was a relationship with the inherent predictability from knowing each other as long as either could remember. Bobby was proud of her for her devotion to her artistic sensibilities and the manner in which she had raised her children. Always able to make a living with one kind of painting or another, she taught her offspring to believe in their own talents and follow through on their dreams. Unfortunately, she didn't think this should apply to Bobby.

Susan never understood his apparent lack of interest in financial security. Because he had never been married and had no children was no reason to not worry about money. Now that he was essentially out of work, she worried for him.

She rarely admitted to herself, and certainly never to him, that this perceived character flaw of his had enabled her to control their parents' assets after they had passed five years ago. Bobby had known that Susan had skimmed off the top, middle and bottom, but Bobby refused to mention it. He was like two people in her mind.

She had made the supreme gesture to Bobby by painting above his kitchen window a picture of clouds with silver linings that he could ruminate on while doing dishes. She had done this the previous summer when she visited for Bobby's closing of the restaurant.

For them both, their relationship revolved around the great spreading spokes of karma. Susan wanted to work it out and Bobby thought it already was. He thought she tried to paint them into a corner and she felt they needed to explore all the colors of their obvious cosmic connection.

"So, any romances going on?" Susan continued. If this wasn't the same question that she asked every time they spoke, Bobby would be more inclined to agree with her assessment of their common bond, but it was usually the lead in to more small talk. He felt the urge to answer "yes," but replied with "no". Two flirting episodes and a blown kiss didn't constitute a romance and he knew that even the mention of Donna Deerfield would extend their phone call beyond the mandatory ten minutes they had agreed on years before. The conversation, instead, remained on the usual subjects of her kids, the weather and baseball.

Susan was a giant San Francisco Giants fan and Bobby had switched his allegiance to the Colorado Rockies. She refused to accept the fact that he transferred his loyalty no matter how many times he explained that it was a matter of geography, daily box scores, constant media inundation and seeing the teams play each other at Coors Field. There had been one series several years after the Rockies inauguration into the major leagues when he realized that his unchanging devotion to the Giants had been splintered like a broken bat. The Rockies had rallied in the bottom of the ninth with a bloop single to center to win the game. The bat had cracked and was in pieces at the plate. The Giants had been eliminated from the division race and Bobby was not only not sad, he was happy. It took him a while to process this in his inner baseball self and when he finally told Susan some of hell broke loose.

"Fuck the Coors Field Christians and their right-wing Republican asshole fans! They cheat with their lazy fly ball pop-up mile high fake shit-happy home runs and they couldn't pitch their way out of a fart-filled paper bag!" Susan was creative with her profanity-painted hate language for the Rockies and she refrained from relying on phrases she had made up and used before. This usually brought a chuckle from Bobby and signified the end of the phone call. He corrected her that not all the fans were right-wing Republicans and that not all the players were Christians, but that even if they were, too bad for the Giants. The Rockies had just swept them again at Coors Field.

"To hell with them and to hell with you and I love you," Susan said as she hung up.

Bobby removed the ice packs from his knees, rose from his chair and stared at the silver linings as he washed his coffee pot and, then, called Jeff.

XI

By the time Bobby arrived at Tad's apartment Jeff and Melissa had been there for almost an hour. He provided a brief rendition of the power mower incident and mentioned that he had received a call from his sister. Everyone seemed to accept his explanation for his tardiness. Jeff relayed what they had discussed and accomplished without him. Melissa had taken the photograph of Tad from behind the bar and made a flyer from it. The date, time and place of the memorial bordered the picture. There was some initial caution expressed by Laura and the daughters about Tad hoisting a beer glass, but in the end they all agreed that it was a good picture of a smiling Tad Johnson.

Donna and Laura had composed an obituary that included information about the memorial and were preparing to email it to the papers. Bobby read it and appreciated the simplicity and genuine love that it represented.

By committee, because he was late to this gathering, he had been nominated to arrange for some flowers. Donna offered to help him with this project. The others approved of the two of them visiting a florist and then rendezvousing for a hike in the afternoon.

The canister of Tad's ashes rested on the countertop in the kitchen. Jeff had asked Laura and the daughters what they planned to do with them. It had been decided that Laura would take them with her, but if Jeff wanted to keep some she would accommodate him. Jeff expressed his thought to spread a small amount here and there in places special to Tad, the golf course included, and to keep a little next to a picture of Tad that he had at his house. Laura offered Tad's golf clubs to Jeff and asked him if he could donate Tad's clothing to a charitable organization. Tall people in need of a wardrobe were about to get very lucky.

Melissa and Jeff were going back into town to print off flyers and seek volunteers to post them all over town. They would also arrange to have it published in the papers. The clothes would be divided between Catholic Charities and the Volunteer Fire Department's Thrift Store. Upon inquiring, thrifty often translated as free. Jeff still wanted to find some live music for the celebration of life part of the memorial and he needed to pass the word to his staff that this wasn't going to be a normal, busy Saturday night. It could be really packed like a New Year's Eve, but there wouldn't be the turn- over of tables to make it an expected big tip night. It was fair to inform his servers that the dinner shifts would be short, allowing them an opportunity to trade it or give it away. He would be closing the restaurant at six and the memorial would begin at eight. That provided enough time for people to finish their meals and clear the building. The kitchen could shut down its normal operation and prepare the appetizers. Bartenders would restock, a band set up, tables and chairs removed to the back alley so people would have more room to mingle, flowers placed, photo montages hung and anything else that needed to be done. He would have to check with Bobby to see what he might have forgotten.

Shelly and Pam wanted to have an opportunity to go through Tad's effects with their mother to see what they might wish to keep. They would place the photos, pictures, books, compact discs and other sundry items on the bed and floor and go through them carefully until they left to meet Donna and Bobby. He had promised to find some boxes they could place things in for later shipping.

***

Donna met Bobby at his truck after explaining to the women where they would meet for their hike. He opened the door for her, she thanked him and they pulled out slowly from the parking lot. It was a gorgeous looking day they both agreed. The sky was a brilliant blue, there were no clouds, the valley and mountains were verdant and the traffic was light for near noontime. They concurred on all these important matters that each knew were trivial at this moment compared to their meeting and Tad's death. It was odd timing to them both. There was an awkwardness about their conversation. This was not a third date, it was a third encounter. Expectations were different. They were involved in a sunglasses conversation, not an eye to eye.

Donna thanked him for his help regarding the prep work for the memorial. He thanked her for her thanks. He told her that if there was anything else he could do to help he would be happy to do so. She thanked him. They each looked out their own windows at the sides of the road. Bobby nearly turned on the radio.

They pulled into the parking lot near the florist, which was close to the post office. He remembered that he had been avoiding his mail and wondered if this would be an inconvenient time to pick it up.

As soon as he parked the truck, Donna removed her sunglasses and turned to him. "Do you have a girlfriend?"

Bobby took off his sunglasses. "No, I don't even have a wife." He looked at her eye to eye and asked, "Do you have a boyfriend?"

"No, I don't. I don't have a husband, either," she said with a laugh. "Or an ex-husband."

"Neither do I." As she began to say she hoped not, Bobby amended it to say he didn't have an ex-wife, but that he did have ex-girlfriends.

"I would hope so. So do I."

Bobby just stared. She didn't leave him hanging very long before she confessed that these were girlfriends she'd had as friends who, for whatever reason, were no longer.

"I was going to say that I hope you don't think I'm too bold in asking if you have a girlfriend, but that wouldn't be true. I really don't know very much about you and the only way I'm going to find out is to ask."

"It's a fair and even start, isn't it? I know hardly anything about you either. How about if we go find out what we know about flowers?"

"I know flowers."

That she did. Donna identified virtually every flower in the shop. She commented on different arrangements and even when Bobby thought a bouquet looked perfect she was able to make a suggestion that improved it. It was like being in a flower garden with a botanist that had forgotten the scientific names and only knew the beauty of each petal. He wanted to go into a forest and bring her back a basket of branches, leaves and needles. She could weave them among the flowers, fronds and baby's breath, creating her own floral symphony.

When Donna told the florist why they were looking for arrangements, he had responded that he already had some prepared and was planning on a delivery tomorrow. They were courtesy of The Cebolla Roja. He had been taking an order from someone else when they had walked in and he had received other calls, as well. She was very touched by this and Bobby noticed her eyes welling again. He realized that the circumstances of their meeting involved emotions that were close to the surface, but he hoped that she wasn't naturally prone to crying. Some is fine, he thought, and in this situation expected.

He vowed that he would have to see her after all this was over to discover if he thought she cried too much.

He marked in his mind that he had begun to make up reasons for wanting to see her again, even though he knew he didn't need to fabricate or justify his desire. He cautioned himself that this wasn't a good sign for being objective. It had been so long since his subjective side ruled it was unfamiliar territory now. If she was going to be emotional about flowers and kind acts he was going to allow himself to be emotional about her. His heart was acting along with his loins.

He chose an arrangement to have delivered with the others while Donna was orchestrating her assemblage. He made a mental note to return here after she had left for Denver and send her one of her suggestions she had shown him. He had told his sister "no" about a romance, but he admitted to himself he was showing signs.

She accompanied him to the post office where he emptied his box, explaining that when he first came to town there was very little home delivery. Almost everyone came to the post office to pick up their mail and see friends that had become strangers. People would say to each other, "Don't be a stranger," so one means of accomplishing that was to pick up your mail frequently. Now that the post office was in a much larger building that had squeezed parking and traffic lanes so that the only practical approach was as a pedestrian, people didn't come here as much. There were many more delivery trucks, however, and mail boxes lined the streets. The main concern for some people who received home delivery was the chance encounter. There were those who timed their trip to the mail box after they had seen their neighbors retrieve theirs to politely evade causal contact and conversation.

Bobby greeted a few other box holders along the aisle and introduced them to Donna. To those who knew Tad he mentioned her relationship to him. They all extended their condolences and mentioned that they had

116

seen the flyers taped to the window out front. They hoped to be at the memorial tomorrow night.

Donna and Bobby had come in the side door, so they exited the front. Bobby gingerly peeled one of the flyers off and re-taped it to the side glass door.

It seemed to Donna that Bobby carried a rather large armful of mail. She offered to help him and he declined, telling her it was mostly bills. She wasn't sure she should laugh, but she did. As he opened the truck door for her again, he suggested they have lunch.

"That sounds lovely," she said and asked where they would go.

"My place."

"Okay." This clicked from her mind to her mouth in such an instant she wasn't aware of it until she looked at him.

"Well, that was easy" he said. Once again, he began to stumble over his words before he cleared a path of pronunciation. "What I mean, is that it was easier bringing it up than I thought it would be. I just want to drop off my mail and I'd like for you see my house. Then we can go to lunch."

"That's what I thought you meant." She smiled in such a way to make sure that Bobby didn't have a clue as to what she was thinking.

"Good. I mean…"

"You mean 'good'".

"That's right." He looked over at her while he was pulling out of the parking lot onto the road going up the hill back into downtown. "Now that we have that all cleared up, what would you like for lunch?"

"There is a place that specializes in salads that Tad took me to one time."

"That place is closed. It was called Sal's Salads. It's now a deli called Mel's Meats. Obviously the same owner,

117

but a slightly different approach to the customer's appetite." He looked at the buildings as they drove through the center of town "Ah, I've got it. We'll try the new Lost Bar and Grill. I haven't been there yet and they have an outdoor patio."

"I'd love to sit outside."

Bobby drove the next couple of blocks before turning right and meandering through some trophy homes. He made another turn so he could point out Joe Don's lot then circled around to his house.

Donna was shocked. "Why, it's absolutely charming," she exclaimed. "Oops. I don't mean to imply that I didn't think it would be, but from your description of it as a shack, well, I guess I am a bit surprised."

"It's a shack to my neighbors, but it's home sweet home to me." He pulled onto the bed of gravel that served as his driveway, parked and came around the truck to open her door. He left the mail on the seat as they walked around to the back of the house. She commented on the flowers, giving them all names, and marveled at the Japanese lacy leaf maple growing to the side and beneath a blue spruce. Admiring a hammock stretched between the spruce and the fence, she prepared to climb in. He suggested she didn't, demonstrating the shakiness of this particular portion of the fence. She now wondered what she was to find inside.

They returned to the truck for his mail and walked to the front door. Standing on the porch that featured two cane chairs, several pots brimming with flowers and hanging baskets of ferns, he said, "Now, remember, Donna, this is the home of a bachelor. I don't have people over often. This is how I normally live." He opened the door, she entered and he followed.

"Wow."

On her left was the kitchen with the silver clouds above the window looking west. Part of the same room held an old wooden table with four mismatched wooden chairs. There were no dishes in the sink, the table was clean and supported only shakers of salt and pepper and a newspaper.

"Would you like some water or something?" he asked while he placed the mail on the newspaper.

"Water would be wonderful," she said.

He opened a cabinet, grabbed two glasses and filled them from the refrigerator dispenser.

"Did you think I was going to have to go to the icebox and chop off a chunk? Then head to the well with my ladle?"

She laughed. "Maybe. Can I say that I'm relieved that you don't?"

"You can say whatever you want. Every time you speak I become more enamored."

She actually blushed. "Now who's the bold one?"

He returned her blush with his own. They were both confused and excited by these feelings that made them feel like teenagers weighted down and lifted up by an adolescent crush.

"It was my turn," Bobby said. "To keep the fair and even start I needed to catch up."

She turned away from the kitchen with the glass of water in her hand and took the few steps necessary to enter what would be called a living room. An old and comfortable looking couch was at the edge of these two rooms. It faced a small TV resting on what appeared to be a nightstand. A recliner chair was next to the TV, facing the couch. On one wall was a mammoth bookcase holding several hundred books, a mix of hardback and paper. Most were vertical, but some were stacked horizontal on top of them. In a corner was a working phonograph, bordered on each side by several rows of albums. In another corner was

119

a fireplace. She didn't see a compact disc player or CD's anywhere.

"You don't have CD's? How many albums do you have here?"

"Six hundred, more or less. It depends how you count double albums. And, yes I do have a CD player. It's in the bedroom." He extended his hand to her and she clasped it. He pointed out the bathroom in the hallway to her and then led her into his bedroom.

They stood a few feet inside the doorway. There was a double bed with a plain blue comforter on it, two nightstands with lamps, a dresser of unique design and a small desk with a high backed leather chair in front of it. There were paintings and photographs on the walls and on both sides of the single window that opened up to the back yard.

"The CD player is on the desk. It's small and I don't use it very often. Plus, I don't have many CD's. Mostly classical." He had let go of her hand as they entered the bedroom, but he took it again. "Well, what do you think?"

She wasn't exactly sure what she thought and this time she didn't mind letting him be aware of that. So she just looked at him.

"Do you like it? Do you like the house?"

"Yes, yes, I do."

"Great. Now, let's go to lunch."

Donna was relieved and disappointed at the same time. She was relieved because he wasn't making the most serious of moves on her and disappointed because he wasn't making a move at all. He brought her back out into the hallway, still holding hands, and she asked to use the bathroom.

"Of course. I believe you know where it is." They laughed at this. "I suppose this is the big test."

"What do you mean?"

"I don't intend to be sexist, but a man's bathroom sometimes isn't the most hygienic place in the house."

"I'll give you a report," she said over her shoulder as she closed the door behind her. Now, of course, she couldn't help examining the room. It could be cleaner, she supposed, but like every other room it was neat and appeared to be well taken care of. She had been surprised that his bed had been made. It wasn't as precise and professional as she made her own, but at least it wasn't a mass of lumps.

She came out of the bathroom and found him on the front porch. "I really like your house, Bobby Early. It's not nearly as rustic as I was thinking it might be. It's very warm and it seems like you seem. I have one question, though. Where's the silver?"

"We could be standing above it right now, though I tend to think it's below the bedroom."

"So, that could be a *roomful* of treasures" she said with a wink.

She put her arm through his and they began walking to the truck. As he opened the door for her, she turned, they looked at each other from inches away and they kissed.

"I wanted to get that part over with," she said. "The anticipation was making me tense."

"I thought it went well."

She smiled and said, "Me too."

Bobby closed the door to the truck and took her hand. "Let's walk, instead."

***

Within a few minutes they emerged from the forest of conifers and aspens that separated his house from town and surrounded Aspen Elk Estates. Several houses and condominium units appeared as they shifted from the dirt beside the road to sidewalks where he was pointing out

121

where the stores once were that catered to the residents. Their high end replacements were mostly empty, but these needed only to make the sometime sale to stay in business. They were told the wait for a patio table at the Lost Bar and Grill would be fifteen minutes, so they spent the time sitting in a small park watching dogs chase Frisbees and kids chase dogs. They discovered that they both liked dogs and cats but neither of them owned one.

"I was owned by a dog one time, though," said Donna. "A Shih Tzu named Pedro. He owned me for thirteen years. I lost him a few years ago and I just can't bring myself to get another dog."

"I think about getting one from the rescue shelter sometimes, but my situation is kind of up in the air right now and I'm selfish enough to not want to complicate it." He realized that she might understand this in a way in which he didn't really intend. He added, "Of course, one never knows what complications might better one's life."

Their table was being set as they returned to the patio. The menu was simple and they were quick to order. Unfortunately, the service was slow and the food marginally edible. They agreed the name of the restaurant probably was apropos and wouldn't be found the next time they came looking for it.

By the time they returned to his house it was time for him to drive her to meet Laura, Shelly and Pam at the base of Smuggler Mountain. Clouds were building in the west, but there was no wind and it didn't feel like rain. He pulled his truck next to her VW parked in the trail lot. The women were waiting and anxious to begin the hike. He reminded them that they were at altitude and if they sensed any lightheadedness they should return to the car. He made sure they had plenty of water and sunscreen and asked them to call him if they encountered any trouble. As they were parting Donna gave him a kiss on the cheek. The other women snickered some, Donna shook her head up and down and said "No". This confused people on a regular basis. Donna thought it was funny and the women forsook the opportunity to ask her to explain herself. They proceeded up the trail.

He was comfortable with them hiking up Smuggler. It was more a dirt road than a trail and popular with the locals. Visitors to the area preferred to hike trails that traversed streams and forests and were marked scenic. Smuggler offered grand vistas of Aspen Mountain and the range behind it, but it was open and really a rather quick, though steep, mile and a half push to the top where hikers would perch from an observation deck. Its base was the site of the mine that bore the mountain's name and once gave birth to a nugget weighing more than two thousand pounds. Almost entirely pure silver, it was marred by an unfortunate flaw. It was found the year after the price of silver had been drastically devalued by congress through the repeal of the Sherman Silver Purchase Act in 1893. Since 1879 silver had lost half of its value anyway, and as Aspen produced one-sixth of the nation's silver a further reduction doomed the mines and Aspen. Caleb Century had worked in this mine briefly and wrote in his journal that the bosses were bastards.

The women encountered mountain bikers, runners, spandex-teasing, super-fit, bejeweled ladies of the afternoon, dogs on leash, dogs off leash and the occasional elderly couple that they could actually pass. They conversed with anyone without iPod earphones that would return their southern "Howdys". Donna concealed a miniscule trace of the accent, but she could hear it creeping out the more she spoke with her relatives. She recalled how effective it had been with certain northern gentlemen when she was younger. She thought now that it had been a silly game in a silly time, but that for the most part it had been harmless and fun. There had been occasions, however, when the gentleman no longer remained such. A southern accent communicated a lack of intelligence to these arrogant and aggressive creatures. There was once when she needed to employ mace. The experience had yielded unto her a more sophisticated and less naïve view of the world. Not necessarily of men, though. She had remained remarkably open and honest with the species, though she had dropped any exaggeration of the accent.

The sun was intense as they reached the vicinity of the observation deck. Any shade available had already been spoken for and sat under. They eyed the approaching clouds as a harbinger of relief, not the storm that would manifest itself within minutes.

***

Bobby returned to his house to see Joe Don and John Hamlin in his back yard. It had only been in the last year that he had begun locking his door. He had arrived home one day to sense more than see that someone had been inside searching for something. There was the extremely faint aroma of expensive perfume, so dim it indicated that the wearer wasn't aware of it. Items throughout the house had been moved or opened and replaced in almost exactly the original position. Bobby had an irritating habit to anyone that had lived with him for any length of time of keeping certain pieces on shelves, desks and nightstands in precisely the same spot day after day. After dusting or cleaning, these special tokens of profound events in his life must be placed back to their happy spot. Normal bric a brac to the visitor, but cherished mementos to Bobby. Lamps, vases and ordinary objects whose chief purpose was utilitarian or decorative could be rearranged and Bobby might not notice for days, months or years.

He never found out who it was or what they had been looking for, but he had a key made for his front and only door. He couldn't bring himself to ever lock a window, though.

The trespassers adopted an air of rightful occupation. They stayed their ground and attempted to broadcast to Bobby that they were very serious and their conversation critically important.

He exited from his truck laughing. "Good afternoon, my young friends. May I be of help to you?"

John Hamlin detested this attitude Bobby adopted at times. It was condescending and insulting. He preferred Bobby predictably cantankerous. Joe Don was more concerned with being caught on Bobby's property without approval.

"I didn't properly thank you for your help this morning," offered Joe Don.

"I see. You're entirely welcome. Simply trying to maintain the good neighborly policies that I'm sure are stressed in the Aspen Elk Estates' Homeowners Association manual. Even though, of course, I am not a member." He paused to give John a steady gaze, waiting for the realtor's real reason for their presence.

"Actually, Bobby, we also came out to take a look at the possible source of the water that seems to be pooling behind the fence here. Frankly, it's unexplainable unless it's coming from your property."

"I would take exception to that, John. Though, I agree it needs to be explained and remedied. I can't have my fence continue to sag and wave in the wind like it seems surely to do once this storm rolls in." The clouds were gathering ominously and puffs of breeze were building in strength and duration. The rain was still Downvalley, however, and there was always the possibility that the storm's path would shift north or south.

"I'm aware it would be expensive and possibly damaging to some of the landscape work you have done, but I suggest you get a backhoe in here, move some of these boulders, and dig down to find the source of the problem," said John.

"Oh, you do? Well, you know I place great value on your suggestions, John. Particularly the ones that begin, 'If you know what's good for you.' I suspect you would like to end this latest suggestion with those words, but our company inhibits your candor."

Joe Don did not have an appreciation of being referred to himself in the third person unless it was himself speaking. "Joe Don is in agreement with John on this. See, when I was last out on the back part of my lot, maybe two weeks ago, there wasn't any water. You can call it wetlands or marsh or whatever else you want, Bobby, but it all comes about because of water. That water is comin' from somewhere and I'm bettin' it's here along the fence."

"Of course, you are, Joe Don. If I was in your boots, I'd say the same thing." Bobby glanced down to see that the Texan's boots still showed the mud on them from earlier and continued, "Nonetheless, I'll wait until you start digging before I do."

Bobby knew this wouldn't be until at least the spring. It would take him that long to acquire approvals from all the planning and building sub departments. It wouldn't take quite an act of congress to force him to remove his landscaping, but it would certainly involve a court order. His personality and affections were displayed in the rock, wood and plants he had placed throughout the years. He had moved rocks and timbers, moved them back, transplanted, cultivated, weeded, measured and, indeed, watered. He had studied his yard and his landscaping from every angle during every season in search of harmony and serenity. He wasn't likely to remove any of it without a sheriff's officer standing over him.

"See, Joe Don, what we have here is not a failure to communicate. You remember that Paul Newman movie, 'Cool Hand Luke'?" When Joe Don nodded, he continued, "What we have here is a stand off. Or, actually, more of a sink-off. John's trying to convince you that I'm the problem, which isn't too difficult considering that you think that already. However, I'm thinking that mother earth will make the decision. Land rises and subsides all the time. There are instances when we can predict it and many more in which we can't. I'm afraid you have something going on under your lot and I'm worried for you." He then looked back at John and cautioned, "Or, else, I'm worried for John when you sue him for selling you faulty property." He had no idea if there was such a thing as faulty property, but he was fairly sure Joe Don and John would translate the idea into deceptive practices and illegal representation mumbo jumbo that could be used in a court of law.

"Damn it, Bobby, you're really starting to tick me off!" John turned to Joe Don. "Joe Don and I are of one mind on this. We see the slope of the land, we see the way you water these plants back here and we see the rain that we've been getting almost every damn day this summer."

"I don't mean to interrupt and it's not really me that is. 'Cause, speaking of the rain, here it comes and I have no overwhelming desire to invite you inside for cover. You'd better hustle to your cars," Bobby yelled as he trotted to his porch and the wave of rain crashed on the shingled roof above him. Lightening bolted in several parts of the sky and thunder came booming quickly after. He watched the Texan and the realtor sprint and slip their way to their cars. Joe Don followed John out the long driveway through Aspen Elk Estates and Bobby began thinking about Donna Deerfield again.

The women might have made it up to the top and back down by now, but it was just as likely they were still

127

on the dirt road. If so, the dust of the day would absorb the first heavy sheets of rain and turn the soil into a slip-slide. He wondered if he should even think about driving back to the trailhead. They were adults and quite likely had probably been rained on before. He remembered his cell phone was still in his truck. He stepped inside for a hooded light jacket, reminding himself that one of these days he was going to buy an umbrella, and raced out and back. He saw there was a message.

It was Donna telling him they had started back down before the rain began and they were trying to make it to her car before.... Interference or thunder or just normal sketchy service ended the message. He now had her number and tried calling her back. He was only able to leave a message. It had developed into a world of messages. People left each other messages everywhere. The most troublesome were the ones that informed someone that there was a message for them and to call back. Of course, text messaging had replaced voice messages for many, particularly the young. As in all things hip and streamlined, though, older folks had received that message and were tip-tapping their way to abbreviated vocabularies. Bobby considered the possibility that hieroglyphics were next. We could be moving to a pictographic script where texters would send entire stories, conversations and rumors in just a few symbols. This could be retrograde advancement or accelerated regression. It could be the two steps back part of the one step forward formula. He didn't know, but he did intuit. Consequently, he presumed the damsels were in distress and he should ride to the rescue.

As he pulled into the parking lot, he saw the four women muddy, limping and laughing. The rain had passed as quickly as it had arrived, but everything and everybody was soaked. He walked over to them and could see that most of the limping was caused by the mud on their shoes.

Shelly, though, was in some pain, so he had her put an arm around his shoulder. He stood her next to the VW and went to his truck for blankets he kept behind his seat. Donna helped him lay them out on her seats and the backs so that they'd be somewhat protected from the wetness and the mud. Laura and Pam squeezed into the back of the bug and Donna helped Shelly into the front passenger seat. She came over to where Bobby stood by his truck.

"Thanks for coming back to our aid, Mr. White Knight," said Donna.

There were fire engine sirens in the town below and Bobby reflected that The Cebolla Roja was probably out of power. "It was my pleasure, princess. You womenfolk should get back and take some hot showers."

"I really had a very enjoyable time with you earlier. It was terrific seeing your home. I'd like to see it again, sometime."

"Maybe after all this is over."

"I'm glad you said that. We had such a good time on this hike, and it's been so long since I've seen my nieces, I really want to spend tonight with them and see them as much as possible while we're all here."

"I think you should."

She moved closer to him. He looked over her shoulder and saw the women in the VW looking back at him. He smiled at them and at Donna.

She put her hands in the front pockets of his coat and gently pulled him closer. "But I want you to understand that if they weren't here things would be different."

"I think they would."

They pecked, she turned, and both the car and the truck moved out of the parking lot, down the road and took opposite directions once they got back into town.

XII

After showers and a short rest the women decided to take a drive up to Snowmass Village. It was the middle of the afternoon and the sun was back out. Donna was the only person among them that had been to Snowmass, and that only once. She had been with Tad for a Thursday evening free concert on the slope of Fanny Hill. The Neville Brothers played, they knew all the tunes and it was like a trip back to New Orleans without the mosquitoes and humidity.

Snowmass Village was a planned resort that had been built specifically for skiing. It was a little over eight miles west of Aspen by road and not much less than that by a bird. That is, if the bird had no other plans and took a direct course. It was an expansive ski and snowboard mountain, catering to all levels of proficiency. The commercial area that contained the shops, restaurants and lodging had been constructed slope side. It was like a Tibetan village in terracing, but in place of prayer wheels there were bars.

A similar concept of planning and structuring a town solely for the purpose of skiing had been employed a few years earlier. Vail had been built alongside Interstate 70 with a Bavarian beer mug in hand while looking at pictures of the Swiss Alps. It had a certain new world old world charm, but for some it brought visions of a Walt Disney movie set plunked down in the American old west of trappers and hunters. Immediately, Vail and Aspen were rivals. Snowmass Village was a harmless in-between type of growth that was hidden off the main road. One had to make a special effort to get there and had no one else to thank or blame.

On this August Friday afternoon it was beautiful but difficult to reach. Across from a golf course was a rodeo and next to the rodeo was a large parking lot. Visitors were encouraged to leave their vehicles here and ride a free shuttle up to the shops and restaurants in the village. Parking was at a premium and the general layout of roads and facilities may very well have been designed by a Vail architect while sampling a Bavarian beverage.

Donna took the good advice and the women spent the now late afternoon strolling past pricey shops and pretzel stands. They were enticed by the aroma of a pizza oven being opened and closed and chose a patio table close to the ski run. People were riding the chair lift up and down the mountain for hikes, picnics or simply the panoramic views. Donna had a fear of heights that precluded her from such adventure and the other women realized they had reached their maximum altitude for this trip. They were over nine thousand feet and they felt like they had started smoking. Breathing was a thousand feet more difficult than in Aspen, just enough to temper their bravado.

After they finished their Italian American cheese pies, they voted to catch a shuttle to the rodeo lot and drive back to the apartment. The rodeo festivities were usually midweek and they were all rather pleased they didn't have to make excuses not to watch cowboy and clown antics. They didn't dislike horses, cows, bulls, cowboys or clowns. Put them all together, however, and it wasn't their bottle or two of chardonnay for this particular evening.

***

The cool evening soothed Bobby as he drifted in the hammock wondering what the cause *really* was of the soggy ground along his fence and beyond. Birds were clamoring around his feeders, the finches content to hold a spot until another more aggressive bird chased them away. The coming of darkness would hide them all wherever they go to sleep. The sun had touched the top of the mountains to the west spreading an orange and blue light through the mist of clouds across the far horizon. He could faintly hear the river lapping at its shore and splashing onto its boulders. It grew quieter as darkness descended and he pulled a soft blanket over his body to keep warm. Patches of sky opened up above him and were filled in with stars becoming gradually brighter. He loved this time alone in his backyard.

A few years ago, before the older houses had been bought and razed, it had been noisier. There were still a few families then and the cacophony of children screaming, yelling, laughing and crying had been, most of the time, a joy. He had known all of his neighbors. They all said hello and when they left they all said goodbye. Some of them had been happy to leave. It was an opportunity to take the money and run, either Downvalley or to some other locale completely. The ones who didn't really want to move saw the writing on the wall in the office of House and Home and then on the contract offer. People put their hands out in front of themselves. One hand was weighted down by what they owed. If they sold, the other hand went way up. They would be out of debt and have a significant amount of windfall money to chase and maybe plant another dream. This was just prior to the recession and prices had escalated enormously. Other folk were buying houses one year and the next selling them for a fifty percent profit. It was madness, Bobby knew that. There had been a point that turned out to be the peak when he had seriously considered selling. The value of his house had reached a range he hadn't imagined, his own values were reaching their breaking point, and when combined with the realization that he wouldn't be continuing much longer with The

Cebolla Roja, he was tempted to flip a coin, consult the I Ching or talk to a financial advisor. He thought the I Ching would probably give him the best direction, but he couldn't make this decision by an oracle and he doubted his spiritual purity to obtain the true hexagram. He flipped a coin with heads being sell and tails stay. He didn't like the one that came up, so he visited a financial advisor.

Benny the Bookie had always provided Bobby with the most sage and practical financial vision. The principal one was to never bet again. Bobby had gambled himself into a several thousand dollar hole many years ago and wanted to get back to even in the Super Bowl. Benny and Bobby agreed that if he won he would never bet again. If he lost, he'd pay Benny a hundred dollars a week until the next Super Bowl and never bet again. He won and never bet again. On sports, that is. Otherwise, every day, every step, every choice is a bet and the difference between winning and losing is all about the timing.

When he was first contemplating leasing The Cebolla Roja he had consulted Benny. Benny reminded him that this was just like a bet. In a bet, the bettor either took or gave the points that would make the contest evenly matched. In the long view, Benny made the odds slightly against Bobby due to the poor reputation burdening the building and his complete lack of experience of ever owning any sort of business. Bobby later thanked his financial advisor. He became aware that Benny's negative forecast had motivated him to apply all of his resources into The Cebolla Roja's success.

When consulted about Bobby's choice between selling the house for a handsome profit versus remaining while mansions bloomed around him and his dwindling bank account, Benny bet that Bobby would stay. Bobby thought Benny was hoping to deceive his old gambling pal and trick him into selling, but Benny knew that no matter

133

what he said Bobby was going to stay. He was betting that, similar to The Cebolla Roja experience, his former gambling buddy would fight a little harder than he might otherwise if someone was telling him he couldn't win. It appeared Benny was correct, though Bobby admitted to himself that weariness was setting in.

During a man's lifetime the night sky might be a constant, but his own will isn't. It ebbed and flowed. When it weakened, faith that it would be strengthened again was all that carried him until the next dawning. When the will seemed all powerful was a good time to lay in provisions. They would be needed when it was proved it wasn't.

Balancing his weariness in his battle with big business was his revitalized energy regarding personal relationships. It's surprising how a chance meeting two days ago had given his spirits and a much underused part of his body a lift. But now it was time to lift himself out of the hammock and into the house. Among his musings while the night fell was whether to stay up late or get up early for a sight seeing session with the Perseid meteor shower. It was one of the first nights it would be approaching its peak, so he might sleep through it, knowing the sky was a constant.

He entered his house, turned on a light and poured himself a glass of Jameson Irish Whiskey. He went to his album collection that he kept meaning to refer to as vinyl and selected a Peter Green solo record. Dimming the light and putting on some old fashioned headphones, he laid back on the couch listening to his favorite blues guitar. This highlighted the greatest advantage that CD's maintained over LP's according to Bobby and his not so sensitive ears. If he wanted to skip a couple of songs and hear the third he needed to get up and lift and move the needle. With a CD, the remote did all the work and passages could be played over and over or skipped entirely. To his mind it was amazing technology, but he couldn't bring himself to discard the albums. Not only would he have to expensively replace them, but the fate of the LP's concerned him. He wasn't buying any more and, as he remembered, he was in no mood to sell.

He mulled these critical matters while sipping the Jameson slowly and found himself in exactly the situation he regretted. He wanted to skip a couple of songs. He rose from the couch, went to the turntable, couldn't see the tracks properly and took off the headphones so he could turn, walk over and turn up the light. That's when he heard the phone ring.

He saw by the caller I.D. that it was Donna Deerfield. He answered.

"Hello, Mr. Early, I hope I'm not calling too late." The smell of white wine wafted through his phone.

"Well, hi there, Ms. Deerfield. By the way, there's no date of expiration of those kinds of jokes."

"It's difficult to be late with an Early joke, huh?"

"Indeed." He saw he hadn't lifted the needle on the turntable yet, so he did that and took a sip of the whiskey. "So, what have you folks been doing tonight, if I wasn't allowed an obvious surmise?"

"See, that's one of the characteristics I like about you. You have a vocabulary."

"I only use it when I talk"

"However, I must point out that there is really nothing obvious about 'surmise'.

"I might have surmised that."

Bobby heard giggling in the background. The women were in the contagious stage of silliness and he wasn't, so it would behoove him to either play along or ask the cause of her call. "I take it you are at Tad's and can I do anything for you?" he asked, deciding to travel equidistant in both directions.

135

"I'm sorry, Bobby. Yes, we're at the apartment. I've had a bit much to drink, perhaps, but I want to ask you a question. We are going to meet at the golf course in the morning and spread some of Tad's ashes. Melissa and Jeff are meeting us and we wondered if you wanted to, as well."

"Certainly. What time?"

"Nine o'clock. We'll see you there," she said with the beginnings of a slur.

"You will if you remember."

"Remember what?" she laughed. "Good night, Mr. Early."

Bobby wished her a good night and returned to his glass and headphones. He awoke a couple of hours later with the headphones off, the needle rubbing against the album's paper label and a groggy memory of having another glass. He forgot about the meteor shower and went to bed, perchance to sleep and certainly to dream.

XIII

He woke to the sound of heavy machinery rumbling on the road in front of his house. He vaguely heard the sound fade before it reappeared behind his back yard. Peering through the window he saw a yellow backhoe slowly churning across Joe Don's lot toward his fence. Thinking this should be interesting, he climbed into some clothes, started the coffee pot and walked around the house to the fence. The driver of the backhoe waved at him and he waved in return, stepping onto the large boulder from which he'd seen Joe Don yesterday morning. The driver halted the backhoe's progress, jumped from the cab and came over to speak with him. He explained to Bobby he wasn't digging today, or anytime soon. His piece of equipment had been rented for Bobby's use whenever he so desired. He gave Bobby his company's card and told him to call when he was ready. Bobby mentioned to the driver that he had heard rich people didn't enjoy throwing away money and that he had no intention of calling. The driver replied he was hoping Bobby wouldn't call, because at a daily rental rate the driver might find out for himself if it was true rich men don't throw away money. He added he just happened to be the owner of the equipment. A work truck drove by, the backhoe driver said goodbye and got into the back of the truck as it drove away.

During his shower, after some strong black coffee, he recalled that he missed the meteor shower last night. The rush of the water in the morning would fill in for the flash of fire in the sky at night. At least for today.

He called House and Home, leaving a message for John Hamlin that Joe Don had parked a backhoe on the lot and he expected it to be removed by the end of the day, or else he couldn't be held responsible for any possible vandalism or damage from natural acts of nature such as falling meteors. He refilled his bird feeders and left to meet the others at the golf course.

He saw the VW bug, parked near it and went to find the women. They were sitting on the deck having coffee and wishing that the idea of a Bloody Mary wasn't so repulsive to their stomachs. It was already a warm morning and the golf course was filling fast. A popular spot and sport with locals and visitors alike, it had grown up nicely over the last thirty years since being expanded from nine to eighteen holes. It was City owned, a public course and residents were afforded the opportunity to purchase a season pass at a generous discount.

Jeff and Melissa walked out onto the deck from the club house and pro shop and greeted Bobby. They had met the women earlier and went inside to discuss the idea of spreading Tad's ashes with the people who ran the course and might take offense. The young man behind the check-in desk had known Tad and was planning on attending the memorial tonight. It was fine by him, but he needed to attain approval from the head pro. He came back in a few minutes with the request that the ashes not be spread on a green and be done quickly. The first foursomes would be coming up the eighteenth hole within the next fifteen minutes. These were golfers that loved to play early, usually starting by six a.m., finish early and have the rest of the day made or ruined by the way they scored and hit the ball. It was alternatingly a very rewarding and frustrating way to live. The pro had requested the ashes not be spread on the green because human ashes are not quite as fine as the imported sand for traps, which regularly inhabited the greens. He didn't want any putts knocked off line.

138

The women finished their coffee and the sevensome walked around the eighteenth green to the fringe area between two sand traps. Laura suggested that the white sand might show the ashes too much. Shelly and Pam commented that they didn't know anything about golf except that their husbands used it as an excuse to neglect weekend projects. Donna was strangely quiet so far, keeping her sunglasses on and not engaging Bobby or anyone else in conversation. Melissa and Jeff admitted that Tad had loved playing the eighteenth hole primarily because it led to the nineteenth hole, otherwise know as the bar. Bobby, who had played golf only once with Tad, in a foursome that included Jeff and Melissa, reminded them that Tad had chipped in for a double-bogey on this hole. He indicated the approximate spot and they agreed that forty yards in front of the green was the best area to say a few words and let fly a few fingers full of Tad's earthly remains.

Donna pointed out two hang gliders that were flying above the course. Bobby went over to her and pretended he needed her to show him precisely where they were. As she raised her arm in the direction, he planted himself in front of her, not looking up, but only at her sunglassed eyes. She slowly lowered her arm, then with a gesture of resignation put a finger to the top of her sunglasses and brought them down to rest on her nose. The shiner was visible, but Bobby suspected that she thought it worse than it was. She had woken in the middle of the night and walked into the bathroom door frame while searching for the light. He told her it was sexy and they lifted their eyes to see the hang gliders weaving above the course.

Jeff and the others also looked up and he noted how unusual it was to see gliders so low on this side of the highway. One was a bold blue and gaudy gold stripped fabric while the other was iridescent pink and neon green.

139

The designated landing zone was in an open field on the other side of busy Highway 82. The gliders didn't seem to be able to find an updraft, a thermal that would lift them back across the road and away from the course and nearby Red Mountain. They circled each other for another minute before they collided. The pink and green glider had closed the distance too quickly with the blue and gold. They were entangled and falling together about a hundred yards in the air above and away from the sevensome. Jeff and Melissa and Bobby began running in their direction. The gliders were spinning around each other, plummeting toward a group of forty foot tall conifers. Just above the peaks of the trees the gliders flew apart and tumbled to the ground on either side of the grove.

Jeff and Melissa raced to the blue and gold heap and Bobby the pink and green. Both flyers had managed to hit the ground running, if only for a few steps. The man below the blue and gold wings was rolling from side to side complaining about his legs. The woman wrapped in the pink and green was sitting up by the time Bobby reached her. It was a miracle that neither of them was dead. Miracles happen every day, but unless they make it to YouTube they are rarely recognized as such.

Donna was at Bobby's shoulder as he leaned over the fallen flyer. "We need to call 911," she exclaimed. As she spoke, sirens were heard coming from the direction of the hospital, across the highway and just a half mile from the open field where these gliders would rather have landed. Someone must have seen them collide and called. Golfers from all over the course were sprinting or driving their carts to the scene. All of them had left their golf balls where they lay, except for one group that putted out and took the opportunity to play through. Within minutes, three ambulances were bouncing across fairways to reach the downed flyers. Laura and Pam had followed Jeff and

140

Melissa, with Shelly limping behind. The man was in severe pain and it was the consensus of everyone standing around him who had ever had one or watched medical dramas on TV, that he suffered a broken leg. Bobby and Donna had been carrying on a conversation with the woman, who remarked that this would not have been her first choice of how to celebrate her last day of her honeymoon. She blamed her husband for the crash, the whole idea to begin with and sure hoped he didn't lose consciousness so she could tell him right here and now. This was not to be. The couple found themselves separated again in different ambulances. Bobby assured the bride that she would find a later opportunity to express her feelings. She replied, "I knew this was a mistake. And not just the hang gliding."

Donna and Bobby shared the humor of this on the walk back to the eighteenth hole, waiting for the others to catch up. The husband's stretcher kept catching on the back bumper of the ambulance. He was shouting something about it being all his wife's fault. At least they cared for each other and thought of the other person first.

The sevensome joined the foursome that was preparing to play the eighteenth on the walk back from the scene. The foursome was understanding, offering proper respect for the ceremony the sevensome was about to perform and urged them not to be in a hurry. Nonetheless, the recent events, combined with knowing that they were holding up play, rushed the participants some. They each said a few solemn words as they rubbed the ashes out of their fingers, wondering if the updraft would now materialize. Jeff closed the ritual with a comment that Tad would have enjoyed the air show of the morning immensely, knowing that the honeymooners were alive and somewhat well. "Who knows," asked Jeff, "Maybe he had a hand in that last spin that set them free." On that note, the

141

sevensome waved the group behind them up and proceeded toward the clubhouse deck.

Jeff, Melissa and Bobby all ordered water or a soda. The four women decided that a Blood Mary was now a desired beverage. They were planning on returning to the apartment and, under the guise of finishing sorting through Tad's effects, taking naps. The memorial was to begin at eight and they asked what time they should arrive. Jeff recommended by seven-forty five so they would be seated at a table reserved for them and feel comfortable when people began to enter.

Bobby was discussing with Donna the option of him driving them in her car so he could drive them back to the apartment when they wanted to leave. The others agreed that it was a welcome plan and that he would be at the apartment by seven-thirty. The women left after finishing their drinks and paying the server. Bobby, Jeff and Melissa checked the amount the women tipped and added to it. The percentage was fair and in accordance with accepted practice, but they had to live in this town and restaurant people always over tipped. It was a habit probably started by someone who wished they hadn't, but it was ingrained as a tradition by now. It was like trying to stop a golf swing when a fly flew by the nose after the player had already started back down. Bartenders and servers just had to continue with it.

Bobby, Melissa and Jeff talked over some of the details concerning the upcoming evening before they reached their vehicles. They concurred the day had started in an interesting fashion. Instead of witnessing events leading to a double funeral, they had beheld an uncanny act of timing saving two lives for what clearly seemed a mutually shared karmic debt. This day, like every other, was about life and death, but this day displayed its design clearly in the sky, on the ground and in fingertips stained with ashes. Jeff and Melissa assured Bobby all chores were assigned or spoken for and that all he needed to do was to get the women and himself to the memorial on time.

***

Inside Tad's apartment, the women stopped to contemplate this morning's entertainment. They were relieved that whatever presence it was had intervened to save the flying honeymooners. Whether it be Tad, God, someone or something in between, or the wind and nothing but the wind. Seeing how well suited they were as a pair, "until death do us part" appeared to be more a life long sentence than a promise of devotion and loyalty. Still, watching them die before their eyes while holding Tad's canister of ashes would have been too traumatic for them to continue with plans for this evening. They all enjoyed a laugh, again, thinking about the couple before they wished each other a restorative nap.

Shelly and Pam retired to the bedroom, where Pam immediately fell asleep. Shelly's sore ankle from the fall during the hike bothered her enough so she tossed and turned until she gave up the nap attempt. They were all going to finish packing up objects and keepsakes of Tad's to send back to their homes after everyone had rested, so she decided to look through some of them again. She sat on the floor flipping through a photo album and investigating books. She was surprised to see Tad had been so interested in astronomy and theoretical physics. She had assumed him to be more of a jock than he really was, apparently. In fact, he was a jock with a scientific bent. Many siblings are amazed about the subsurface lives of their counterparts and Shelly now included herself among them. She laid on her front, pressing her elbows and forearms on the floor to look more closely at the photos. She lifted her head a little to relieve her neck and saw a brown envelope tucked underneath the bed, held by two wooden slats close together.

She reached up for it and had to push the mattress to retrieve it. Pam stirred, but didn't wake. Shelly opened the envelope and began reading poetry Tad had written and kept to himself. There were sonnets, haikus and some other rhyming poems that had a scheme she didn't recognize. These were villanelles. She read through them and was startled to think these were written by her brother the jock turned astrophysicist. Why he had never showed them to her was a question she posed and quickly answered. Because they had ceased communicating and she thought he was wasting his life. Perhaps he had misused it, instead. Perhaps this poetry was his real talent and he had been afraid to show others. Or, maybe, he had shown a few to his friends and they had lacked appreciation for his words. She didn't know, probably never would, but she thought some were beautiful and some very good. She was anxious to show them to her mother, sister and aunt, but decided to read them again while the others slept.

When all the women had read the poems there were tears in their eyes and longing in their hearts. Gradually, they began to speak of how grateful they were that these poems had been left for them to remember Tad. Amidst their deeper sorrow that his talent and gift had been extinguished there was a rising joy that his spirit would live on in their hearts through these words. There were dates on the poems, they had all been written within the last three years and they were signed with his initials. After the women had touched the poems and the poems had touched them, they handled each of the items left from Tad's life with a more profound, even felicitous, sense of sharing their son, brother and nephew the poet. They weren't thinking of having lost a talent too early and too young. They were filled with a sense of wonder about how their feelings had changed so much from what they had originally anticipated when they were flying into Aspen. Instead of a memorial they would be attending a celebration of life.

***

As Bobby was driving back into town he received a call from John Hamlin. Against his better judgment and in accordance with his worst, he answered it. Hamlin wanted to know what Bobby meant about a backhoe being parked behind his fence on Joe Don's lot. The Realtor knew that Joe Don was going to be high maintenance, but he hadn't thought it was going to begin today. Hamlin had swung a deal with the contractor who was to build the Texan's humble mansion. He was to be the go-between and mediator in any disputes, disagreements, misunderstandings and outrageous demands arising from shoddy workmanship, unrealistic expectations and any other inevitable and expected developments during the construction. He was already regretting the role and the plans hadn't been submitted to the City yet. He was experiencing doubts concerning the supplemental profit he would be receiving from the builder and whether it would prove worth its while.

Hamlin told Bobby he was unaware of the backhoe until Bobby's call, had not talked with Joe Don since yesterday and was in the dark as much as he. Bobby countered that he wasn't actually in darkness at all and could explain the purpose of the backhoe to Hamlin. He did. Hamlin suggested that Joe Don was only being neighborly and Bobby kindly recommended a place where Hamlin could stick his neighbor. Both men were cognizant the conversation was not directed on a course for compromise and agreed that it might be best if they continued it on Joe Don's lot.

145

Twenty minutes later they stood in front of the backhoe. Hamlin was sharply dressed and wore woven leather loafers. Bobby was decked out in his running shorts, t-shirt and short socks inside his running shoes. Neither man wanted to go too near the muck that could be easily seen just beyond where the backhoe was parked. The cab door had been locked and a sun protector placed on the inside of the windshield since Bobby had spoken with the driver earlier.

Hamlin told Bobby that Joe Don had left Aspen last night on his private jet without mentioning anything about this big piece of yellow machinery. He had spoken with him only minutes ago and Joe Don had stated an intent to leave the backhoe there for Bobby's use or until his construction crew began digging in the spring. He understood Bobby's consternation about having to look at this harbinger of construction to come until next spring, but proclaimed Joe Don's right to park whatever he wanted on his own property. Bobby sensed this was going to prove problematic. He didn't want to begin a run angry, so he was prepared to abandon the discussion for the present. As he turned from the backhoe and the view of his fence he saw Dr. Harold Corning approaching.

The doctor was accompanied by a woman of similar elderly appearance and Bobby assumed it must be the doctor's wife. It turned out to be Dr. Harriet Corning, his older sister. She was highly agitated and her brother was attempting to calm her, to little avail. She seemed slightly confused as she looked to her brother for assurance, but she remained adamant that the big piece of yellow machinery needed to be removed at once and for all time. She enjoyed her view of the young gentleman's fence from her chair in her library and she didn't appreciate the obstacle interfering with her sight line. Something about finches along a fence.

146

"I would only inquire whether or not this backhoe is to be employed in the near future, and, if not, why we would be content to accommodate its presence?" asked Dr. Harold. "I assure you that my sister's opinions are vital to my happiness and I strongly endorse her sentiments. We, of course, understand that at some point forward we must endure construction vehicles and noise. Others suffered the same interruption of their lives while our house underwent its own evolution. However, we were informed this process was not due until spring."

Bobby grinned as Hamlin stuttered something about finding out who and what was at the bottom of this and he would get back with them presently. The sibling doctors ambled back across the lot and the road before Bobby spoke.

"You've really done it now," he scolded.

"No, I haven't!" argued John

"Sure, you have. How can you allow this, John?"

Actually, he couldn't. He reminded himself that he had granted a clause in the doctor's contract that stipulated there would be no construction activity on what turned out to be Joe Don's lot until all the planning and building permits had been secured. At the speed with which the City's departments moved, even in these sparse construction times, these documents would not be ready for enactment until the spring. He rolled it over in his mind. He could be sued by the Cornings or battle with Joe Don. Either course required compromise with Bobby Early.

Bobby didn't know what chord he had struck, but he could see by John's look of consternation that there was what might seem an insurmountable dilemma he faced. "I mean, why did you have to sell your last lot to Joe Don? Surely you could see he is going to be trouble at every turn?" It then occurred to him what John might have been thinking. "Ah," he continued, "But it wasn't your *last* lot,

147

was it, that you were thinking about? It was what you think is your *next* to last lot. You weren't thinking that Joe Don would stir up Dr. and Dr. Corning. You were thinking how you could use him to drive me to the breaking point and, kabamo, you have my lot, finally. Well, could be you've turned loose a wild mustang on a dude ranch, John. It's either going to be a helluva ride or you are going to get bucked off. You don't think I would want to miss that rodeo, do you?"

Hamlin knew he had no choice but to remove the backhoe himself. He and the builder were partners of a sort in this entire project. He sighed, "The backhoe will be gone Monday. My apologies for my client's impulsive behavior."

This isn't what he should be doing at this moment on a gorgeous Saturday morning, thought Hamlin. A man of his means, who owned a handsome little portion of Aspen, Colorado, should be enjoying himself in whatever manner he wished. And that would be teeing off in the City Invitational golf tournament in about an hour. He should already be at the clubhouse meeting the celebrities and high-profile banker he was grouped with. There should be glad-handing, elbows rubbing, back patting and fake laughter erupting at this very instant. This represented another of those business opportunities that he relished. Very few golfers played with John more than twice. He was an excellent player. Plus, he cheated. He was rarely caught, but, when he was, admitted his "mistake" readily and penalized himself a couple of shots. He still won most of the bets. It was best for him if he could establish a connection early in the round and confirm an appointment before it was over. From there, he could stay off the golf course where he might get caught cheating and stay on the realtor course where he wouldn't so likely be observed fudging figures. Surely, he thought, this is not what God had planned for him. Standing near muck with a hold–out real estate hobo look alike dressed in running shorts, wondering how to explain to an ornery Joe Don that he had sabotaged his plan.

"It's good that you've listened to reason, John. I could almost envision the headline for my next column: 'Realtor Deprives Couple of Retirement Serenity'." Bobby knew that he would never write it and he knew John prayed that he would. It was far too personal and would be playing into John's hand. If Bobby was going to lose this fight he would rather look back on it as not having enough weapons, in this case resources, than because he was being nasty and stupid.

"Don't keep pushing me, Bobby."

Bobby knelt down to retie his shoes. He didn't want to have to stretch out all over again and he was getting itchy from standing in the tall grass next to the muck and not running. "John, we just keep pushing each other. We both want to win, but losing will mean a lot more to me than to you. I'll take you at your word that this piece of yoke yellow machinery will be gone Monday, not *by* Monday. That's my first gesture of truce talk for a while, so let it settle before you respond." He raised his palms up outside his shoulders and with a clenched jaw started his run up the mountain.

XIV

The women finished packing boxes to mail to themselves, took a little walk up Buttermilk Mountain, drove into town, walked around looking at clothes they weren't going to buy and came back to the apartment late in the afternoon to rest up for the evening's activities. Buttermilk Mountain was the first ski mountain along Highway 82 on the way into Aspen. It was built for beginners and kids, though it had some steeper terrain. It was also home to the X Games, an event that the local public schools finally gave in to and closed their doors while the games were in progress. Snowboarders, snowcrossers, snowmobilers, noises, tricks, wild, enthusiastic young crowds, ESPN TV, night lights, free shuttles from out of town, busy, packed Aspen and huge publicity took over with big buses and big money every winter to almost everyone's delight. Bobby loved it. Today, though, it was quiet, green and a little too much for the hung over women with an altitude adjustment to make.

Bobby completed his run by tripping into a copse of Gambol oak. Often called scrub oak, it generally doesn't grow beyond fifteen feet tall and almost exclusively in a grove. It, like aspen, proliferates with runner roots, making it very difficult to transplant. Bobby continued to attempt growing a bonsai style grove in his front yard year after year and met with utter, complete and embarrassing lack of success. He had two green thumbs for most flora and fauna, but the oak refused to be a compliant partner. He had suffered many bouts of scratches and cuts while trying to transplant them, though, and today's unintended scramble through them proved no different.

He showered, treated his scratches, which turned out to be minor and settled into his hammock. Jeff had taken care of all the last minute details they could think of and there was really nothing for him to do except relax. He had no problem accepting God's plan for him this afternoon and fell asleep while swinging in a gentle breeze beneath the shade of a mighty blue spruce tree.

Jeff and Melissa had spent the day planning the music for the night, spreading the word through more posters and many mouths, taking delivery of a couple dozen flower arrangements and preparing to shut down the restaurant when six o'clock chimed on the grandson clock behind the bar.

John Hamlin had arrived at the golf course in plenty of time to join his foursome on the driving range and putting green. All the tee times had been pushed back an hour due to some sort of an aerial accident earlier in the day. By the time the story reached John, seven people had been injured, four on the ground, all women. The delay, however, disrupted John's timing and sense of urgency with which he had driven to the course. He was edgy and seemed to be in an irritated rush. This didn't sit well with the two movie stars and high-profile banker with whom he was playing. They avoided his company and chit chat on the course and ignored him at the party at the nineteenth hole afterwards. John knew whose fault this was and it wasn't his. It was Joe Don and Bobby's together. The thought made him pause for a moment. Damn, if they ever teamed up together, I'd be screwed. He relaxed when he thought it through and counted the ways the two of them were fortunately and naturally opposed to each other. He finished a vodka screwdriver while following several stunning middle age women through the party. The day had sucked, in John Hamlin's perfect appearance world, but the sight of these sexy women and the realization that he really held all the cards in this game with Joe Don and Bobby, turned up a smile on his face. Besides, he had a sexy, beautiful woman of perfect appearance that would be meeting him at home tonight. All would be well.

As the sun disappeared behind the Downvalley mountains and the light was shaved from brightness, Bobby began the short and easy drive to Tad's apartment. It was the quiet light that spreads when the air is calm and trees can still be seen in relief. Coolness comes off the mountain tops and up from the rivers to soothe working bones, playing bones and dead bones. Born again bones drifting in the wind to make more dust to dust and spirit to spirit around and around these mountains and valleys here before and long after bones are born and die. A drive slowly meditative, where his brain is almost silent, brings Bobby to the door where four women wait in comfortable anticipation, not knowing what to expect from a last night in Aspen and the celebration of one of the loves of their lives.

Bobby drove the VW into town with Laura in the front passenger seat and the others in the back. Everyone felt she should enjoy the prime view and the seat of some distinction. They parked a couple blocks away from Wagner Park and walked across it, observing the remnants of the day's rugby match between the Aspen Gentlemen and an out of state side that had made the trip for the scenery. The Gentlemen were aptly named, in a physically dominating, politely brutal and consistently victorious sense. Among their many contributions to the town was Ruggerfest in the middle of September. Teams descended from around the country for a tournament that featured matches and an old-style sportsmanship that specialized in song and beer appreciation. The Gentlemen, following several unfortunate incidents of fisticuffs by overly enthusiastic visiting players, generously established and enforced a ban on fighting, brawling and threatening behavior in the bars and public spaces of Aspen. This, of course, led to the ruggers hosting mainly private parties where they could properly conduct themselves. A team member found to violate the behavioral edict in a public place banned his entire team forever. Nonetheless, the entertainment value of the games, the sight of large, burly men walking the streets in short shorts and bandages, the revenues the spectacle provided the restaurants, lodges and shops, was traditionally and happily welcomed. This was the sort of colorful quality that initially attracted many to Aspen, even the new and out-of-proportion rich. These people remained on the outside edges of the swarm of activity, but enjoyed relaying the nature of the event to their out of town visitors. For, Ruggerfest usually marked the turning of the leaves on the mountains. Whole mountainsides began shifting hues overnight and once again the town and region were ablaze, even if for just a short while.

The green was still abundant in the pale light shading just above dusk as they walked onto the brick mall. Planters brimming with petunias, pansies and columbines were spaced between beds of delphiniums, lantana and lobelia. As they approached closer to The Cebolla Roja they noticed the patio was empty of people, but that there appeared to be a line of faces stretching away from them. Bobby lit up in a smile and let out a small whoop. At least fifty friends had already gathered and were waiting for another twenty minutes before the door would open. A male and female pair of bouncers, two of the most congenial people Bobby knew, allowed them through the patio and into the restaurant where they pushed through some cowboy swinging doors. A sign had been hand lettered and hung in the large front window that notified customers that the restaurant would be closed to the general public tonight and please come back tomorrow. In the center was a picture of Tad Johnson.

A sound check for the music was underway, long tables had been set up and were being filled with appetizers and salads, servers were fluffing flowers and Jeff was in earnest conversation with Antonio Ceja-Lopez, the bar manager. They both turned and came to greet the women and Bobby. Antonio and Donna were quickly exchanging pleasantries and condolences in Spanish, so Jeff led the others to a table tucked into a little nook just past the bar. Here they would be somewhat shielded from constant interruption and at the same time available to meet and greet folks as they passed by or stopped. He told the women they could give their light jackets they had brought and their purses to him and he would make sure they were secure in his upstairs office. Bobby whispered to Jeff as the women discussed this and seemed reluctant.

"I assure you that you won't need any cash or credit cards tonight, ladies, and that if you tried it would be refused." At that, the women turned over their carryings and Jeff went through some cowboy swinging doors with them.

Donna gradually made her way to the table, pausing every few steps to continue her bilingual exchange with Antonio. He finally extricated himself from the enlightening history of Donna's Mexican journeys so that he could regretfully continue to help his bartenders stock the bar.

Darlene, the cutest little waitress in the whole wide world, came by as Donna joined the table. She took a drink order, told them what a great guy Tad was and that she could speak from personal experience, knowing the long and short of it. She belted out a laugh over her reference to their height difference and left the women to wonder if she referenced anything else. The women shared glances that confided that this might not be the saddest night ever.

Bobby was chatting with the musician tuning his guitar. The guitarist sang a verse testing the microphone arrangement. His voice was a mix of Hoyt Axton and Dave van Ronk with a pinch of nasal tininess from Richard Farina. Bobby joined him in harmony attempting his closest impression of Bob Dylan. For people who appreciated Bob Dylan's voice, or not, the similarity was uncanny. Bobby liked to say he was obliged to Dylan, because, if the voice was an acquired taste, Dylan had already done all the work.

Jeff and Melissa asked Bobby to join them in the kitchen. They informed him that there were at least a hundred people in line and it was almost eight o'clock. Together, they agreed that the amiable door bouncer personnel would have to keep a tally so they didn't go over their occupancy limit of one hundred and eighty-four by very much very often.

Poster boards with pictures of Tad and friends lined the walls, complimentary appetizers graced the tables, the staff acknowledged they were prepared and the doors were opened. The crowd didn't behave like one. They drifted in, ambled about, ordered a drink, helped themselves to a plate of food and found a few old friends to talk with. Within ten minutes the building was full and the happy guardians of the gate needed to ask people to wait or come back later.

The Deerfield women who sat at Tad's Table were stunned so many people had arrived so quickly. Bobby explained that the music would start in a couple of minutes, then Jeff would make some comments after the first, short set was finished. He asked the women if they would then be comfortable in saying a few words. They all assented willingly. The guitarist approached the center microphone and the crowd cheered. Johnny Winwood was a local legend of immense talent and little ambition to make it big outside of Aspen. He played everywhere in the area all the time, reprising local hits from the past and introducing new songs recently penned. He announced the two other musicians that would be joining him tonight, Willy Garcia and Jack Robertson. The all-star super group of Aspen would also have the pleasure of showcasing Mary Joplin, Winwood added. Mary was the vocal queen of folk, rock, ballads and blues in the music world when it cyclically thrived in the town and its environs. In the first forty-five minutes of playing, the band moved from Bo Diddly through Chuck Berry, Jimi Hendrix, the Rolling Stones, the Beatles, Traffic, the Band, Bonnie Raitt and Aretha Franklin, spending as many minutes in segues as in songs. It was a robust and impressive opening set that sparked as many people dancing as the floor could contain.

More food was brought out, more drinks were poured by the three bartenders and Jeff approached the mike. He provided a fitting and accurate summary of Tad's years in Aspen and had difficulty containing his emotions when he talked of their personal friendship. He mentioned that the bartender's tips tonight would be donated to the cause of establishing a Tad Johnson Bench in the mall in front of The Cebolla Roja. He then invited Laura, Shelly, Pam and Donna to speak. Laura thanked Jeff for the celebration and all those who were in attendance tonight. She welcomed her daughters to help her complete a sentence without crying and the three of them were in such a state that Donna offered to add to the stream of tears. A spontaneous burst of applause swept the building and, as it eased, Donna told the crowd how much this evening meant to the family. She closed her brief words by thanking the people here for showing Tad's family and each other how much he had been loved and respected in his adopted town.

156

Mary Joplin followed them to the microphone, raised her hands high in a request for quiet and softly began an a cappella rendition of "Amazing Grace" that brought smiles to the women in attendance and tears to the men. Appropriately, some of the attendees were emotionally emptied and needed to go outside for air and a moment alone. This allowed others to enter and thus was begun a gentle and cooperative shuffle of partiers, mourners and satisfied participants for the next three hours.

During breaks in the music, friends were invited to say a word or two or fifty-six before they were asked to make space for the next story, reflection or appreciation. Occasionally, a eulogist had too much of the spirits to remain within the spirit and had to be helped along in the interest of fairness, but throughout the evening a benevolent and grateful mood prevailed.

Donna and Bobby had danced more than talked. In the pursuit of capturing a few minutes of quiet they asked Jeff if they could step up to his office. Through the cowboy swinging doors they went, returning in a more timely matter than anticipated by Jeff and Melissa, or the three women who had smiled after them as they departed from the table of honor.

In the upstairs office, Donna and Bobby engaged in a passionate kiss that they were barely able to keep under control. It was only because their hormones were sixty years old that they weren't rolling around on the floor.

As they caught their breath Donna said, "Well, this hasn't happened in a little while."

Bobby wanted to ask what she referred to, but chose to refrain. "Donna Deerfield, I must tell you that this is quite an attraction I have for you that I seem to be walking around with."

Donna wanted to ask him what he was referring to, but decided to just look down.

"Look, Donna" he began, "No, not there. I mean, look here." He pointed to his eyes. "You have to leave tomorrow and you need to be with your family tonight. You'll probably think I'm some kind of square, if they still exist, but I'd actually like to get to know you. Sounds as if it could be a song, doesn't it?"

Donna swayed to the tune as she tried to remember more than the title lyrics. "Yet another thing we have in common. I'd like for you to get to know me, too." She ushered a sweet laugh and added, "But only if I get to know you, also."

"It's a deal then." He reached out his right hand in an offer of a handshake. She accepted. They shook hands firmly, he presented a soft kiss and they went hand in hand to the office door. "We'll talk. We'll give each other a chance to talk and to listen and we'll see what happens."

"I think you might have just swept me off my feet," said Donna, as they left the office and pushed through some cowboy swinging doors at the bottom of the stairs.

The celebration and memorial were slowing down after eleven. There were still a few hours until closing time and Bobby knew the bar would stay busy waiting for the grandson clock to strike last call. As much as it might have been the shank of the evening to some, that had passed for Bobby and the women. They found Jeff and Melissa and the women expressed their deepest appreciation for a visit and an evening they would forever cherish. Laura presented Jeff with a small container of Tad's ashes and a spare key to his apartment. Jeff had volunteered to mail the boxes to the women and he had offered to check on the place, making sure it was empty and clean for the next renter. Donna suggested she be responsible for any paperwork or legal issues that might arise throughout the process and Laura gladly accepted. Donna was marginally more adept with the computer, plus she lived close enough she could make a trip to Aspen to deal with any developments easily. In addition, there might be other incentives for her long commute. "Speaking of Bobby," she chuckled, "I think it's time our chauffer drive us home, Jeeves."

Arm in arm, the five of them walked away from The Cebolla Roja, through the mall and across the park to the VW. They arrived at the apartment at the bewitching hour. Laura, Shelly and Pam thought this appropriate, watching Donna and Bobby holding hands and whispering their farewells. No one thought it would be long before they were together again.

XV

The airport terminal was busy with people who couldn't afford their own planes. One of the saving charms of Aspen's airport was the lack of pre-boarding time required. The Deerfield women arrived thirty minutes before take-off and they were as good as on the plane. Since September 11, 2001, regulations had increased the time allotted for passengers to bitch, complain, stew and get drunk while waiting for an opportunity to be stuffed into ever-shrinking seats. The close-knit family that is America was encouraged to cast a suspicious eye on their fellow traveler and to stay out of the way of unfriendly airline personnel. Baggage allotments had been reduced and carry-on fees increased. On-time arrival and departure schedules were written in the wind. Flexibility applied to flight schedules just as it did to the gymnastics of fitting into and remaining bound to a middle seat of a row. One of the features that airlines had improved, however, was the creativity of their apologies. It was always someone else's fault. If government regulations weren't to blame, it was nature, which, of course, meant it was God. Who was going to be upset at a pilot who complained to God about God and didn't receive a satisfactory response? Hadn't everybody experienced the same result some time? Therefore, the most appropriate persons to receive rude treatment were the desk personnel who provided the essential service of checking-in passengers.

At the moment Donna, Laura, Shelly and Pam walked into the departure portion of the terminal there was a loud argument underway between two potential passengers and the desk staff. The would be passengers forcefully explained to the clerk that they simply had to get back to New York as quickly as possible. This necessitated a flight to Denver and a connection with a layover only long enough for baggage transfer. The clerk countered that she would help them as soon as she was finished checking in ticketed passengers. This was unacceptable to the New Yorkers. They furthered their case by stating that their husbands were going to trial tomorrow on mortgage fixing charges and that it had been difficult enough as it was to pack so quickly. They needed action immediately. That request the clerk was able to accommodate. Within a minute the offended wives were in a holding room undergoing interrogation by the TSA, the Transportation Security Administration.

Laura, Shelly and Pam were now prepared to be accepted through security and sent along their way. It was a sweet farewell for Donna. She hadn't felt close to her sister or nieces for the past few years. Maybe this would be one good thing to come out of Tad's tragic death. As the women walked through the gate and to the plane she also thought of another good thing that had come into her life. She resolved she would stop to see Bobby on her way back to Denver.

Seeing the New Yorkers in the holding room as she walked by, she thought that they were the kind of people that gave rich, arrogant New Yorkers a bad name. Travel had been her pleasure and business for the last thirty years. She admired the skill with which the clerk had defused the situation. A screaming scene in Aspen involving New Yorkers wasn't unheard of, but it usually occurred during the Christmas holidays. Neither the paparazzi nor The New York Times were skulking about the terminal this sunny Sunday morning near the middle of August. The felonious banker's wives were completely out of season.

She drove back to the apartment and retrieved Tad's poems that she was going to have printed and bound for the family. Taking a few minutes to reflect, she had a good cry before she decided that she would just drive straight back to Denver and skip seeing Bobby today. By the time she had driven five miles toward Glenwood Springs and its intersection with I-70, her eyes had dried and she turned around.

She stopped in the downtown drugstore, one of the few remaining businesses that continued to thrive from the 1960's. Purchasing a couple thank you cards and a Sunday Denver Post, she drove her VW a few blocks away from the store and signed a note of thanks to Jeff and Melissa and then one to Bobby. She walked to The Cebolla Roja and left the card for Jeff and Melissa with Antonio Ceja-Lopez. The young couple had yet to show this morning and, if Antonio was correct, they might not make it in today at all. Donna chatted in Spanish with Antonio about what a wonderful tribute it had been last night until Antonio excused himself to fill an order of drinks for which a server was patiently waiting. Antonio suspected that Donna simply enjoyed speaking Spanish so much because she was so adept and accomplished. He would be correct.

Another day and the world begins again, she thought on her way through the cowboy swinging doors. Donna had to leave or expose herself to remorse and sorrow in a place that had provided such happy memories for her only last night. She drove to Bobby's house, half-hoping he wouldn't be home. There had been a spell cast the last four days and to see him today might break it. But if it was that fragile, it was best to find out now.

Bobby opened the door, surprised, and invited her in. For a brief moment he felt the rush of awkwardness he felt with her on their ride to the florist, but it vanished with the soft breeze that followed her inside. He thought that was a good sign and decided to leave the front door open. He occasionally mulled over the use of the term front door when it was the only door he had, but he had concluded that it was in the front of his house and that should be reason enough. He was trying to simplify his life in the midst of the biggest upheavals of it. First, the loss of the restaurant. Now, possibly, the loss of his house. And, third, the emergence of this lovely vision of a woman standing before him in his very own living room. He offered her the opportunity to turn down a cup of old coffee, but she didn't. She gave him the card she'd written and they took their cups to the front porch. He mentioned how he didn't have a back porch and explained why it was okay to call it a front porch anyway.

They remarked upon the glorious weather and the marvelous gathering of the night before. Bobby had returned to The Cebolla Roja after taking the women home and chatted some with Jeff and Melissa. He related to her that Jeff had closed the restaurant on a night that usually reaped a very nice profit. Bobby had brought that up at the end of the evening. Jeff had hugged Bobby with tears of joy telling him that he never imagined that such an evening would prove to make him so rich. Jeff continued to fill the space in Bobby that was meant to hold good feelings.

Donna showed him Tad's poems, telling him of her plan to make a small booklet of them. Bobby read a few of them and stopped. He remembered the conversation he'd had with Jeff about legacies and if Tad had left anything that might survive the memories of those who knew him. Perhaps, here was the reason someone might remember Tad who had never met him or heard about him. Bobby asked her if he could have a copy for himself and that he was sure Jeff would like one, as well. She thought there could be no more appropriate thank you gift from the Deerfield family.

They talked about Donna's impending drive home over Independence Pass and why it was best that they wait before jumping each other's bones. Remarking upon how mature and clinical they sounded, they almost abandoned this restraint. But Donna needed to be at work tomorrow morning and they each shared a picture of waking up together to see how that played out. It was planned spontaneity with life and love's tender moments and passionate movements. A roll of the dice, a tossing of the I Ching, a prayer to God, the hands of fate, the ships of destiny, all the world's a stage and who is waiting in the wings? It was all about the timing and they agreed that they would accept that and not put themselves on a deadline to see what happened. Without knowing it, they had been living with Tad's timer. Now they would let it be, to see who or what took the timer from here.

They stood beside her car, discussing whether he would be able to visit her in Denver soon. He thought he might be able to work it into his busy schedule of writing a column a week, tending bar now and then and infrequently working at the book store, but he would have to get back to her on that. She took him seriously at first and they realized they, indeed, had plenty to talk about. She promised to call him when she arrived home. They kissed and she drove away.

At the top of the pass, she took her small container of ashes and walked as far as she could from her car. Taking a pinch, she thanked Tad for being in her life and let part of his remains scatter quickly in the icy air. She went back to her car, removed a joint from her glove compartment, took a hit and then drove off down the eastern side of the pass. The marijuana helped her escape the series of what seemed non-stop events of the last four days. It also helped her appreciate them. She cruised comfortably back through Leadville, down to I-70 near

Minturn and Vail, over Vail Pass and eventually into the sprawling city of Denver and its companions on the plains.

When she arrived home she checked her answering machine on the land line she kept. It was a generational hold over that many people her age couldn't forsake. She figured out one time it was extra money spent every month that, if she discontinued the land line, her savings over the year would pay her mortgage for a month. Suppose, though, someone was looking for her in the phone book and she wasn't there? And she would have to inform all of her friends and acquaintances that she no longer could be reached at this number. What if she missed telling someone and it was the one person who needed her at that particular moment the most? It was easier to keep the phone. It was also harder to keep it when she played back the message that told her she needed to fly to Chicago tomorrow morning for the week.

When she called Bobby to tell him she had arrived safely and was leaving tomorrow, he expressed regret because he had managed to shift his schedule all around so he could come to Denver tomorrow.

She chuckled and said, "Well, that wouldn't have given us much time to miss each other."

"It turns out I didn't need much time. I missed you before you came into my life and I just didn't know it."

"I can see this talking and getting to know each other more is going to be a very enjoyable adventure," she replied. "I like the way you started out."

"So do I. I wasn't sure I had it in me, but, apparently, I might."

"I'd like to be the one to find it. We can uncover ourselves."

Bobby paused for a moment before responding, "See, it's talk like that which will only increase the horniness level and make this more difficult."

165

They talked for another hour, laughing, explaining, relating, divulging and discovering. He learned she taught seminars to representatives from corporations concerning travel arrangements for their employees and clients. She helped orient these travel departments in matters sophisticated and sublime. Unfortunately, the employees assigned to these fields were often in search more for entertainment than work, which made her task less enjoyable. She was called out of town when a particularly important client needed her expertise. Otherwise, she managed the staff that customarily accomplished these duties and rarely left Denver for business purposes anymore. Agreeing Donna would call tomorrow from Chicago, they bid adieu. Walking around the rest of the afternoon and evening on different sides of America's watershed divide, they both felt a fresh spring bubbling up in their lives. It wasn't a torrent or a lazy river. It came from down deep and refreshed the spirit. It was welcome and the source, though known, thirsted to be explored.

They talked Monday evening. Donna was staying in downtown Chicago and had just heard "Dead End Street" by Lou Rawls on a 1960's rock and roll radio station. Rawls offers a spirited description of the wind, the almighty hawk that sails through the windy city in the winter. Donna commented that she would run naked in the streets if this would cause a cold, harsh wind to blow through Chicago in the middle of August. Of course, this only excited Bobby. He was quickly concluding that images such as these which Donna occasionally introduced into the conversation were not entirely accidental.

She asked him to call her Tuesday night and he did. They discussed her day spent instructing cruise directors on the most effective methods to greet and disembark passengers. Bobby's suggestion that they "take it up with the Captain," it turned out, was not the proper response. An hour seemed to be the rapidly established norm for these informative chats, so at the end of that period Donna said she would call him tomorrow about the same time. Curious as to whether this was to become routine, Bobby asked. She replied, "Of course not. We won't always be able to talk at six or seven in the evening. I know you have a life and other commitments. And so do I, but I do think we should talk every day at *sometime*."

Bobby didn't think that *everyday* was necessary, but Donna was adamant that if they were truly desirous of knowing one another, this was the best way. They needed continuing communication about the important, the trivial, the serious and the funny thoughts, experiences and ideas they each entertained. These were the key to knowledge and knowledge was power. And power allowed them to make the right decisions about what kind of person the other was and if this relationship was even worth pursuing. They were at an age and time in their lives where if they wanted to have sex with someone, even each other, that was fine, but if they wanted to have more than that they would need to discover whether it was with this person or not.

Bobby wasn't opposed to this. In fact, he was enjoying it. He simply didn't think that it was as crucial as she did that they actually spend an hour talking when they might just say hi and bye sometimes. He was wrong.

They spoke Tuesday and Wednesday and when Thursday arrived they discussed the news that Donna was going to need to stay in Chicago, that Toddlin' Town, for another week. There had been a major shake-up within the corporation for which she was conducting her seminars and she may need to start all over with a new crew of trainees. There was every reason to believe that multi-national corporations were no smarter or wiser than multi-national people, but many regular folk kept hoping that there would be a difference in numbers. With each bank collapse, bailout and executive scandal, their hope vanished like the hedge funds and profits on paper.

The next morning Bobby searched the headlines for the story about Donna's client. It had been moved down in the list of importance due to an even larger and more well-known international corporation experiencing some equally profound revelations at the top.

Bobby was hardly a financial success, but he ruminated on the matters in a professional manner. He reasoned that it was really the large corporations that ran the world, so to speak. They were crumbling like cracked dominoes of fragile currency and, yet, the electorate was demanding that business men and women be drafted as their political leaders. As if situations were not harsh and hopeless enough, there was a movement to discard idealism entirely. To replace politicians who had sold out their commitment to public service by installing businessmen, who disdained the concept, seemed a deal between devils. He figured God would tell him it was a man made problem and it was up to man to fix it. Someone else would tell him it all begins with loving your neighbor. Well, the problem there was that the neighbor he was ready to love was stuck in Chicago.

Of course, he had another, different, kind of neighbor down in Texas who was still complaining to John Hamlin about the removal of his backhoe. Bobby relayed the story to Donna and she found it interesting enough that she asked Bobby about the silver.

XVI

After Bobby acquiesced and shared more of the details with Donna about the silver cache beneath his house, their conversations took a turn. He had been concerned that she would consider him mentally questionable, possibly delusional, obviously obsessive and living in a different reality, without accepting the positive qualities of these character traits. What actually transpired was a pleasant surprise and a validation of the initial whoosh that consumed his fibers of sensitivity the day he met her. She wanted to know more about Caleb Century, how Bobby marked off the paces from which particular 1892 landmarks, what his plan to retrieve the silver consisted of and when that might happen. He told her he would disclose the answers to these questions, but only in person. And that they would be revealed in segments as their relationship matured. She suggested that by "mature" he meant sexually intimate, but he denied this. "I have no intention of acting maturely when we are having sex," he said.

In fact, he divulged all the information she requested over the course of the next week's conversations. She absorbed it and confided that if he believed it, she would. Naturally, Bobby was aware that it was no skin off her nose, sweat off her brow, shirt off her back, if she believed it and it didn't come true. He wasn't resentful about that, however, and was grateful for the moral support. He was excited that someone else in his life was excited about what he was excited about in his life. And he was ecstatic that it was who it was.

During the two weeks that Donna had been working in Chicago and they had been conversing daily on their cell phones, they had tip-toed into the ether of emails. Donna had also sent cards to his post office box, so he now went there on a daily basis and found himself disappointed if there wasn't mail from her. He examined the developments and faced the fact that he was falling in love with her. "Now, how could this be?" he asked himself. He had only seen her for four days and, of those days, some encounters were brief. They had been communicating long distance for about two weeks. He understood how his feelings would grow more deeply as his appreciation for her strengthened. "Am I falling in love with the idea of love again?" he asked himself. When not asking Donna questions, he was in the mood to ask questions of himself.

He brought up the idea of falling in love with love to Donna after she returned to Denver. She was familiar with the concept and found it completely plausible for a true romantic to experience. However, she wasn't convinced that Bobby was such a soul and, in fact, was rather sure that he was actually falling in love with *her*, not some idea. And she told him so.

That weekend they broached their first argument, which they both secretly wanted to have happen before they saw each other again. Things had been going along so smoothly and delightfully, they were cautious about the expectations of near flawless imperfection they each probably held about the other. Donna was concerned that turning sixty had pushed her beyond the physically attractive edge and Bobby was becoming worried that not being financially secure would eventually scare Donna away. So, logically, they argued about their plans for Labor Day Weekend. She didn't want to make the drive to Aspen because she would be swallowed up in traffic going both directions. Friday or Saturday traveling to the mountains would be a nightmare due to all the adventurers on their last summer weekend jaunt. Sunday or Monday would be a traffic jam of tired and cranky commuters coming back into Denver. Bobby thought it was a crazy idea to spend the long weekend in Denver when the Aspen Snowmass Jazz Festival was featuring Allen Toussaint, the Doobie Brothers, Crosby, Stills, Nash and Young. Allison Krause and Big Mama Thornton. He admitted that, perhaps, Big Mama Thornton might not be there because she was deceased, but she would certainly be present in spirit. It was never too late to buy two general admission tickets and mingle with the little people.

They had a week to settle their differences, so they dropped the argument, which they called a gentle and amusing disagreement, and returned to the playful banter they had previously employed. In the end, both of them admitted they had been attempting to fabricate an argument so expectations were lowered. Consequently, they agreed the choice between Aspen and Denver on a warm early September weekend came down to sanity versus insanity, foolhardiness versus right thinking. It was rare Bobby was on the sane and right side of things.

Donna drove up Saturday morning and arrived while Bobby was still out on his run. He had left her a note if this should prove the case. As he suggested, she helped herself to some juice and then used the bathroom. How thoughtful, she reflected, that he knew she would require the facilities. He also had written that she could bring her traveling bag into the bedroom, but that he would be happy to do it for her when he returned. She smiled at the gentlemanly gesture and considered whether to play the coquette with him. Her flirting when they first met had been deeper and more poignant, so she resisted the temptation to indulge herself and brought in her own bag.

171

She walked back outside and around the fence to the area Bobby had spoken of when telling her about the power riding mower and the yellow backhoe. Much of the grass had grown over the tire tracks and the muck had dried. She walked backward away from the fence to view Bobby's roof and house lines through the backyard trees. From the fence she receded until she bumped into Dr. Corning.

"Excuse me, young lady. May I help you?"

Donna turned and was startled speechless. "I'm sorry," she said. "Is this your property? I was lead to believe it belonged to a Texan named Joe Don Burke." She peered into the sunglasses of Dr. Corning and asked, "Surely, you aren't his wife?"

"My, goodness, absolutely not!" answered Dr. Harriet Corning. "I can't stand the man and I've only met him once." She jerked back and added, "Oops. Perhaps I shouldn't have said that. Are you a relation or friend of his? I know you aren't his wife or you wouldn't have asked me if I was." She laughed conspiratorially. "I haven't lost that many of my marbles, you know."

By the time Bobby returned from his run, hot and sweaty and hoping to impress Donna with his manly fitness, there was no Donna to be found. The VW was in front of the house, her bag in the bedroom and her near empty juice glass on the counter. He correctly concluded that all was well and she had probably gone for a stroll. After his shower, when she hadn't returned, he became a little concerned. He dressed and went out as a search party of one. He wasn't much of a tracker, so he walked with the road that went back a bit before forking. He chose the direction that looped between the Corning's house and Joe Don's lot. Dr. Corning greeted him as he walked past. "Aren't you looking for your girlfriend?"

172

Bobby came to a halt, much as, or so it seemed, did time. She couldn't be his girlfriend yet, he thought. But, wasn't that where he thought it was headed? And how old do people have to be before they can't be girlfriends or boyfriends? He had the distinct impression that neither Donna nor he had attained that horizon, but was that because once inside a relationship of sorts there was no seeing clearly? He assumed this was the situation because he was clearly befuddled. And he was certainly asking himself a plethora of questions these days. Pretty soon, he thought, he was going to have to ask himself why.

"My girlfriend?" he asked.

"Well, Bobby, she's a girl and she claims to be your friend. I can't ascertain the latter for certain, but she qualifies as a girl from every angle I've subtly spied from near and afar. If she's not your girlfriend, perhaps you wouldn't object to inquiring whether she might be receptive of a suitor." Dr. Corning chuckled and waved Bobby toward him. "Would you accept a friendly invitation to join us for a glass of iced tea? The women are on the back porch, shading themselves, I'm sure."

Bobby followed Dr. Harold Corning through the house and onto the back porch. At every step, Bobby had wanted to stop and take in the surroundings. There were walls of books and paintings, *objets d'art* occupying every table top and window sill ledge, and fantastic furniture that defied Bobby's concepts of age and style. It looked like what he imagined a forgotten basement in the Smithsonian Institute would look like. There was the impression of a Victorian collection tilted in an M C. Escher drawing that caused him a certain dizziness as he almost stumbled through the house.

As they emerged onto the back porch, which looked out toward the river, he turned to the male Dr. Corning, asking him, "Do you actually *live* here?" As the question escaped his mouth he realized it might be taken as a rude and invasive question, more an assertation on the quality and concept of the furnishings than he meant it.

Dr. Harold Corning presented a piecing gaze into Bobby' eyes and his artistic soul. Then he laughed and stated it was only due to his beloved sister's influence and bizarre collections that the house didn't appear as a hunting lodge might. He did accept responsibility for the arrangements of much of the furniture and many of the paintings and that, no doubt, contributed to a general atmosphere of disorderly confusion.

"I think it is one of the most attractive and arresting series of rooms I have ever experienced," interrupted Donna before Bobby could advance the conversation. She rose from a wicker rocker, glided gracefully around a low glass table and approached him. "Hello, darling," she smiled as she kissed him. He had been transported from long distance relationship guy to boyfriend to darling in a matter of moments.

"Well, hello, sweetheart," he said as he kissed her back.

They drank iced tea and chatted with the Drs. Corning until they were worried about being offered watercress sandwiches. It had been an enlightening and entertaining visit. Among the revelations was that Donna had been so initially shocked to see the female Dr. Corning because she had taken a class from the doctor in college. Dr. Harriet Corning was an esteemed professor of psychology and had influenced many brilliant and simple minds at the University of Colorado, Boulder. Dr. Harold Corning had contaminated and enriched, so he opined, many similar intellects at Colorado State University, Fort Collins, as a professor of theoretical mathematics. These were Front Range cities, north of Denver, that Bobby knew vaguely and Donna well. Both doctors, with their respective spouses, had visited Aspen throughout the decades for cultural and athletic endeavors. The spouses had succumbed to disease and old age and the siblings decided that they may as well finish together how they began, living in the same house together.

The iced tea party also divulged common political alliances. All four of the conversationalists had campaigned for Cheryl Finnister to unseat Senator (R) Stanley P. Shockanawe in the previous election. It was a rare occurrence when any of these four voters were in the winning corral, but Senator (D) Finnister had succeeded in closing Shockanawe's reign of environmental terror. It was fortuitous, of course, that Shockanawe's base of support felt betrayed by revelations of marital indiscretion, drug use and a video wherein the senator mocked children quoting Bible verses. Finnister didn't win, so much as Shockanawe was repudiated by his own kind of people for not being their kind of people, after all.

Bobby and Donna had cautiously tread the sacred ground of subjects, politics and religion, midway through their long distance phone call period, as they fondly referred to it. It was with a palatable sigh of relief that each delivered and received the welcome news that they shared left-over liberal leanings. It began when Donna related a story of the ugly breakup she endured with a former boyfriend. He had resorted to labeling her one of the nastiest words in the language. Bobby would not even give voice to the term, as he agreed that such language was inexcusable. "I'm pretty sure I know what you are thinking, Bobby," Donna said, "But he called me a Republican!"

Introducing their religious views proved to be a less dramatic moment. Donna casually mentioned she had attended Catholic school as a child, Bobby expressed his sympathy and they quickly found common ground in One God and the Brotherhood of Man. As the conversation

175

evolved, they exposed differences in the particulars, but both shared convictions that belief, faith and spiritual progress were cornerstones of their lives.

Bobby had added, "I knew some cornerstoners back in San Francisco who got religion when they got high and they were never gonna die and they were born to be wild." This reference to Steppenwolf's hit tune transferred the discussion to works of literature, Hesse, and his mention he had finished rereading The Glass Bead Game. Donna was fairly certain she had read that particular work, but admitted, like many others from this generation, she had read Hesse when she had been smoking pot in a timely manner. This was termed "marijuana maintenance" in contemporary circles. The practice of ingestion through smoke or edibles on a physician or self-prescribed basis to keep unwanted awareness at bay. It might be the awareness of physical pain, mental anguish or spiritual confusion, but it provided relief and forgetfulness.

***

As Donna and Bobby walked hand in hand back to his house, she thanked him for asking how her drive had been this morning and confessed she had taken it without the customary pull-out for a puff. He no longer engaged in the ritual and he refrained from trying to make a judgment on it. Like with most anything, he thought moderation was a wise path, as long as moderation wasn't taken to an extreme.

As they approached the front porch, they reviewed the time spent with the Drs. Corning and laughed at the candid nature of the Drs. language couched in formality. Donna relayed to Bobby that she had learned Dr. Harriet Corning had taken a crowbar to the side of the yellow backhoe before it had been removed and that she, Dr. Corning, sincerely hoped Bobby hadn't been falsely accused. In fact, John Hamlin had been strangely silent for the last two weeks and Bobby had invested some hope into the idea that John had accepted Bobby's proposal for a truce.

They entered the house and Bobby remembered he had forgotten to ask about Donna's luggage. This jogged a memory of the time he had written a country song title, "I Drink to Remember Why I Drink to Forget". The chorus, he envisioned, would be something along the lines of "That's right, that's what it was!" He had never aspired to be a country songwriter, because he didn't think he would appreciate all the personal experiences necessary to write truthful country songs. And, if a songwriter was going to write a country song from formula, hoping to strike gold, he may as well live and work in a tune mill in Nashville. He'd rather stay near the abandoned lumber mills of the Rockies where the silver, he believed, wasn't buried too deep and was as true as a song from the heart.

Donna told him her bag was in the bedroom. He gazed through the hallway and recognized the simple bag resting on a small refinished cedar chest, below the window. She was wearing blue shorts above the knee, a t-shirt that read 'imagine" and sandals. Bobby knew that the t-shirt's message probably referenced John Lennon's song, but he couldn't quite stop himself from extending the possibilities of what he might imagine. They both looked like they were ready for sex, thinking about sex and resigned to waiting for sex. The anticipation was to continue, senses were to heighten and satisfaction with the first time was quite possibly going to be fulfilled in the mere finishing of the act. If it was physically and emotionally rewarding, all the tension in the waiting would be further released.

There was a certain shyness to them both that was endearing to each other. They had the cock-eyed grins of kids knowing nobody would be watching the candy store or the cookie jar the next time they came around. But, with the kids, there was always a look over the shoulder, just in case someone *was* looking. In *their* future, they would be the ones looking at each other, for each other, all over each other, on top of each other, around each other and within each other. It was an exciting vision they seemed to be sharing separately together as they smiled and stared at one another.

Donna broke the gaze first, asking if she should change into warmer clothes. The concerts were outdoors across from the rodeo on the way to Snowmass Village. They were fortunate there was no rain forecast throughout the weekend, but a September evening in the Rockies can turn chilly quickly. The concerts they were mainly interested in were in the afternoon, but, once caught up in the music, they could be coerced to stay for the duration. They packed a change of clothes into a canvas bag that Bobby normally used for groceries.

Gradually, they became more at ease and more playful. It had been three weeks since they had seen each other and their eyes were becoming accustomed to the sight again. The span of conversations spun in emails and phone calls allowed some things to go unsaid, such as, what a gorgeous day it was.

"I know this sounds trite, Bobby," said Donna, "but what a gorgeous day it is."

"It's amazing how what is trite is so often true. Pretty much like this very statement. However, this isn't trite, not at all." He went to her and, in the kissing, a truth moved back and forth between them, exhibiting that the terms "darling' and "sweetheart" may not have been ahead of their time.

"You know, Donna, I'm quite smitten with you."

"You know, Bobby, I'm smitten with you, too."

"Shall we go for some lunch, darling?" he asked.

178

"Sounds delightful, sweetheart," she answered.

They walked easily into town and happened upon a shady table on the otherwise sunny Cebolla Roja patio. Bobby inquired as to whether Jeff and Melissa were on the premises and was told they were expected. Bobby knew the young couple was going to the concerts and hoped they could all travel together.

It was a busy Labor Day weekend and they had been fortunate to find a table. After they were seated, the next customers had been put on a wait list that grew quickly.

The service was fast, the food was good, and they were ready to leave for the bus depot sooner than they had planned. Free bus shuttles transported patrons to the festival throughout the day and night. They kept some drunk drivers off the road, many cars parked at home and provided a welcome and visible service for the weary taxpayer.

As they hadn't seen Jeff and Melissa arrive yet, Donna wanted to walk inside the restaurant to revisit fond and sorrowful memories before they left. Bobby waited outside. Jeff and Melissa soon approached through the crowded mall and they greeted one another with air guitar mannerisms. As this pantomime performance was underway, Donna walked out through the patio and joined them. She had a thumb toward her mouth and was obviously playing the air saxophone, but Bobby could only think of himself. He realized at that moment he would actually be somewhat relieved when this relationship graduated from such constant sexual reference. He had been transformed from celibate in body and mind to being still celibate in body but a wanton luster of deep eroticism in mind. He was vaguely disappointed in himself. However, he was trying to use the transition to clarify in his philosophy how far and fast man's nature could cross the thin line between civilization and animalism.

Jeff asked Bobby if he had his tickets yet, because he heard the concerts may sell out the day. This had never happened before, so Bobby, naturally, had been unconcerned with buying tickets in advance. Donna stared at Bobby as if she had realized she may have been falling in love with a total idiot.

"I can't tell you how happy I am you didn't buy those tickets. I have two extra VIP tickets that I forgot I had until Melissa spotted them as we were leaving the house." VIP tickets allowed patrons front area access and seats if they wanted to refuse to dance, move with the music while on their feet or otherwise contribute to a festival atmosphere. Though, Bobby readily admitted, these days and nights he didn't stand or dance quite as much as he once did. He also wasn't as quick to criticize those who remained seated, either. He was more likely to assume that the sedate patron was recovering from a hernia operation or knee replacement surgery. It was that age group, his, that monopolized these tickets. The women may have been younger, though.

VIP tickets could be purchased for outrageous sums of money, or they could be given to people who owned restaurants, liquor stores, bakeries or any other outlet for purveyor's products. Sometimes the people who could afford the tickets and the people who were given the tickets actually knew each other, but often they were strangers sharing luxury. Previously, Bobby had been a recipient of these cherished ducats, but the sponsors of these events moved on to the present purchasers of their products. The sponsors apologized to Bobby about this lack of largess they formerly gleefully gave, but both they and Bobby understood the shifting accounts of financial reality. The prized wrist band one wore in exchange for surrendering their VIP ticket at the entrance also entitled them entrance into the free food and drink tents. The flaps on these tents were thoughtfully kept down so the common festival attendee wasn't exposed to the aroma of gourmet cuisine or intoxicated by wafting fumes of complimentary cocktails.

The four of them proceeded to the bus station where they stood in line with the little people with general admission tickets. Many of these faces were recognizable and some of their names were familiar. Bobby had shared his VIP tickets with a few of them over the years. He felt it had been better for his karma than his business. Generally speaking, these had been shows he wasn't really interested in seeing and someone else always wanted to witness. As they waited in line, Donna mentioned to Bobby that he had been rather lucky Jeff carried spare tickets he was willing to share. "Sometimes things work out better, happen happier, if you procrastinate," Bobby grinned.

Donna slid her arm in his and whispered, "I hope you don't plan on procrastinating later."

"That's the thing about procrastination: nobody plans it. It just happens. That's why we're bucking the trend."

"Speaking of bucking..." , Donna trailed off in laughter. Bobby gratefully realized that these obsessions were not his exclusively.

The four squeezed onto the bus together and hung on to the ceiling rails for the ride to the concert grounds. They entered in the middle of a set by Marcia Ball, which was followed by Allen Toussaint and then the Neville Brothers. There was marijuana smoke in the air above their heads and dust rising up from the ground. Stomping feet in and out of rhythm shook the ground while giant amplifiers reverberated the air.

From the vantage point of their privileged position, they were able to occasionally retreat behind the speakers

181

to carry on a conversation. They also drifted in and out of the courtesy tents, eating and drinking for free while tipping heavily. There were introductions for Donna to friends and friends of friends. There was dancing with different partners and multiple partners and the changing of the clothes in the VIP restroom trailers rather than in the port-a-johns. Bobby hoped he wasn't spoiling Donna.

During a break between the Neville Brothers and Dr. John the Night Tripper, John Hamlin snaked himself through rows of white wooden folding chairs to introduce himself to Donna. Bobby was retrieving a clear plastic cup of white wine for her and a dark beer for himself. She had heard tales from Bobby, so she was prepared to dismiss him upon the handshake. His personal magnetism rarely failed on the handshake and dialogue laced with flattery soon established affection, if not trust. She was not immune to his charms. He was a very difficult man to dislike until a person got to know him. He had noticed her dancing with Bobby and admired him for his great good fortune in sharing company with a lady of such grace and beauty. Donna curtseyed and replied that Bobby had also mentioned the loveliness of John's wife, Bobby's former girlfriend, Becky. John offered that Bobby had proven he was a superior judge of women through his previous relationship with Becky, and was truly validating it now with the radiant Donna.

Donna asked him what he wanted and John told her he would appreciate it if she would consider talking some sense into Bobby concerning the sale of his property. It was none of her business, she replied, adding she was really quite anxious to watch Bobby's plan to find the silver succeed. John was confused, unable to quickly gauge her interests. Were they with Bobby, or was she plotting somehow to abscond with the riches? Whenever he asked himself questions it was a sign of trouble. He concluded she was only interested in Bobby, because, contrary to Donna's professed belief, there was no silver with which to find success. It was difficult for John Hamlin to comprehend motives that weren't his own. Therefore, he proceeded to tell Donna he had been very disappointed in Bobby's vandalism of the backhoe. She informed Hamlin his assumption was in error and the guilty party was actually one of the elderly Drs. Corning, but she would never tell him which. Hamlin walked away in disgust, thinking his problems had only been compounded. The only thing he could think worse than having Bobby as a thorn in one side was now having Donna in the other. Nonetheless, he remained confident of his persuasive powers and optimistic about the final outcome.

Bobby had observed the encounter between John and Donna from afar. As John turned and walked away, Bobby returned and told her he was disappointed he wasn't greeted with a curtsey. She informed him the gesture allowed an opportunity to bow one's head and mumble what one pleased. It had become popular among peasant girls when courted by men above their social means and below their quality of character.

As the set up continued for Dr. John, the final performance of the day, Donna and Bobby shuffled on through the seated VIPs and into the larger crowd milling about between exhaustion and anticipation. Jeff and Melissa were staying for the closing show, but Donna and Bobby were calling an end to public intercourse.

They drifted to the bus takeaway zone and found it to be far less crowded than they would if they had waited another hour. They were through waiting. The dancing had been stimulating, the conversation suggestive and the destination known.

They arrived in town, stepped off the bus and walked smartly to Bobby's house. The sun was fading behind the Downvalley mountains while they poured glasses of wine and started up the turntable and themselves.

XVII

Sunday morning began with songbirds, coffee, showers and Thelonius Monk on the turntable. If they had been younger and not had Sunday evening to look forward to, there would have been a reprise of last night's lovemaking. The enticements and seductions had taken much longer than the actual activity itself, but all the buttons had been properly pushed and the first experience, they happily agreed, bode well for the future.

Thelonius Monk was replaced after one side by the Grateful Dead's "American Beauty" album, which was followed by Buffalo Springfield. CSN&Y were on the concert schedule today and the newly consummated couple was reminiscing about their rock and roll show adventures. Donna had partied with Janis Joplin and Bobby had almost been accidentally pushed off a cliff at the Big Sur Folk Festival by Joni Mitchell. These were rather tame with some other stories of which they were aware. However, many of the other storytellers were either dead now or unable to function in society.

It wasn't true that a person hadn't been to the 1960's if they remembered them, but it was true that everyone had been affected. Even those on the outside looking in were changed by all the altering that was taking place on the inside. Quite a few of those in the military or straight world drifted over the mutable boundaries into the music, politics, lifestyle or just fashion of the so-called counterculture. Later, many more moved back into the safety, security, responsibilities and apathy from whence they had come. Fashion changes.

185

Donna assured Bobby that she was a grown woman and could fend for herself while he went up the mountain for a short run. He confirmed that he had found out for himself she was a grown woman and told her he was merely trying to be polite. She shooed him out the door after admiring his short socks and soon left the house for a walk. She encountered the Drs. Corning and the three meandered together until Donna's patience with the pace grew thin. Before she went ahead, she asked them if they had been to Bobby's house yet. They said they hadn't, so she invited them over. When Bobby returned from his run, Donna was still attempting to construct a story of how the Drs. had invited themselves to Bobby's house. Not finding a fabrication even she might believe, she told him the truth. She had invited people to a house that wasn't hers without consulting the owner of the house. As a new girlfriend she had certain privileges, but she wasn't sure this was one of them. It was like sweat off his finely tuned runner's body, he told her. It was an attempt to change the "water off a duck's back" metaphor, but it wasn't worth explaining or repeating, so he said, "I just haven't had a woman to civilize me in a long time. I guess that means I'll have to take a shower." While he showered, he suggested that Donna drive to the store for iced tea and watercress sandwiches. She immediately assented and he had closed the bathroom door before she asked, "What?"

Bobby was dressed and talking with his guests before Donna returned. She carried a jar of sun tea and a clear plastic box of sandwiches that had the crust removed.

"I bought the tea from some kids on a corner and I had them cut the crusts off at the deli."

Bobby opened the plastic box of sandwiches, took out a half sandwich and peered at it. He declared, in mock horror, "These aren't watercress!"

The Drs. Corning, in unison, shouted, "Good!"

Donna, confused, said "No, they're not. They are chicken salad with nasturtium petals that I picked from the planter at the entrance to Aspen Elk Estates." Donna took the half sandwich from Bobby's hand, showed it to the doctors, who not so adeptly tried to withhold their amusement.

Dr. Harriet Corning took the half sandwich and removed the top layer of bread. "You know, dear, that the nasturtium is botanically related to the watercress plant, but it really is no substitute." She paused a moment while Donna absorbed Harriet's bubbling mirth. "No, for it actually is quite delicious."

Bobby confessed he conspired with the good doctors to have some fun with Donna about her vittles and beverage errand. Donna accepted it as proper payment for inviting house guests while inhabiting the role of guest herself. Iced tea, chicken salad sandwiches with garnish of nasturtium and cloth napkins were laid out on the kitchen table. Harriet went from eloquent coherency to disjointed incomprehensibility within sentences. Harold simply smiled at Donna and Bobby when this occurred, as if it was something by which they shouldn't be surprised. They sat at the table, nibbling, sipping and talking for about an hour before the Drs. asked to be excused for their afternoon nap.

Bobby and Donna walked them back along the road to their house. Donna escorted Harriet inside, while Harold addressed his sister's early onset dementia. He termed it "infant dementia". "It enters like a small, enfeebled child, but will grow to take over the house," he said. His sister was aware of the memory losses because she had a rare capacity to remember that there were blanks in her memory bank for which she couldn't account. Harold didn't believe this feature would persist, but he seemed contented facing her progression. "This happened with our mother and she passed on to the next life within days of full memory loss, so we are hoping for the same with Harriet."

"You seem certain of a next life, Dr. Corning," said Bobby.

"I do, indeed. Isn't this life we are living now the one after the one we were living before? So, it's quite apparent reincarnation means continuity of life. We are a joy to God's eye, my friend, not the burden so many would have you believe."

Donna emerged from the house and as she walked toward them on the winding walkway, Dr. Corning added, "By the way, I hope you have not suffered any foul repercussions from Harriet's crowbar assault on the backhoe. She blamed her dementia for the act, but I think she has merely become emboldened upon hearing of your resistance to Hamlin and the cowboy."

"There hasn't been a word from them."

"Usually not a good sign, Bobby. I'd enjoy speaking with you about all of this sometime, if you are so inclined."

Donna approached them as Bobby told Harold that he'd be in touch. She thought that was sweet of Bobby, thinking he was concerned about Harriet. He was, but there was also something in Harold's countenance that intrigued him. As if he might provide Bobby with an insight.

The new couple wandered back to Bobby's house. The cell phone signified a message and he retrieved it. Jeff was offering VIP tickets to the shows again today. They agreed they'd probably be happier without the free drinks and rich food. Bobby returned the call and left a message for Jeff, thanking him for the offer. If they went, they'd buy their own tickets and be little people.

Donna was in the mood to adopt Harriet and forego the afternoon shows, but Bobby reminded her there would be plenty of people at a rock concert she could easily befriend who would be in need.

They danced the hours away beneath a marijuana cloud that burned the eyes more than the brain and then hopped the bus back into town. Donna offered to buy dinner for them at a moderate Italian restaurant, in appreciation for Bobby sponsoring the day's entertainment. Judging that it would be an approximately equal expense, they shook hands on the arrangement. They continued to discover they were becoming good friends, even as the romance deepened.

That night they made love and let the night be their soundtrack. The river could be discerned through the quiet air and elk or deer heard clopping across the road and through the woods. They slept until sunrise and made love again. The river was drowned out by road noises, the birds were singing and they were a bit loud themselves.

Donna left in the afternoon, when it seemed if she didn't, she might never. Bobby promised to try to come to Denver the following weekend, if she didn't want to make the drive back to Aspen. A fondness was growing for the town and the people she had met, but she also attributed this to her falling in love with Bobby. He was returning the favor. Love was in their words, their touch, their thoughts and their plans. They had found, they each thought, a person that would last in their life. Moving in together or getting married wasn't an option, nor was it a matter for discussion at this point. Deliriously happy together, with so much in common, they were immersed in the moment and, of course, the next few weekends. They agreed to look that far. No longer a flirtation, absent from fantasy, they were committed to discover if this was the person they didn't really need, but certainly wanted.

Lurking in the depths of longing, there exists a hope to share another's life. There had never been the expectation, but always the possibility. On good days, the probability. Content by themselves, they didn't discount that they might be even happier and better people with someone else. Especially, if that someone else wasn't around every day.

There were many rivers to cross and hurdles to jump before they would find out if living together would be more satisfying than living apart. One of these would be how Bobby dealt with Denver and Donna on her home court. It was gratifying to him that so many people knew him and acknowledged him while they were at the concerts throughout the weekend. Of course, there were others that dismissed him and ignored him, but these were mainly the usual bitter politicians and people of privilege that he skewered in his columns. He reflected that he might have to abstain from any forthcoming self-righteous attacks on the rich after his weekend wearing a VIP wristband.

He was fairly well known, reasonably well liked and quite comfortable escorting his girlfriend around the grounds. Never had his friends and acquaintances seen him so obviously enamored with a woman and they were delighted. However, visiting Denver, where he would know no one except Donna, well, that would be similar to her situation in Aspen. He hoped he had enough courage and self-reliance to venture into foreign fields. And so it came to him that "fields" was the answer. In singular form, however, as in Coors Field.

He checked the Colorado Rockies schedule and ascertained the National League baseball team would be playing at home the weekend after the next. That meant Donna and Bobby would endure a separation of two weeks rather than one, but they had just survived a three week exile and actually prospered. Bobby was optimistic.

Donna was agreeable to the suggestion, but insisted the phone calls occur twice daily and that he check his email inbox more regularly. Baseball games were among the most boring enterprises she had ever attended, but she would try to be fair and be equally disinterested in both teams. Bobby explained this wasn't the best attitude with which to approach the national pastime, but she accurately pointed out to him that the new national pastime was no longer baseball. It was the cell phone.

Bobby kept himself occupied the next almost two weeks talking on the phone with her and replying to her emails. In between, he studied the ebb and flow of the water along and behind his back fence. He also managed to write a column that did feature his infiltration of the VIP world at the Labor Day Weekend concerts. It was an expose, of sorts. He fabricated recipes and told his readers that this is how "the other one-percent" celebrates its victory over the general admission crowd. He divulged the ingredients in a vodka and orange juice screwdriver and pleaded to avoid a lifetime ban from the Grey Goose tent. Finally, he admitted that he had been a sham and this wasn't his first VIP experience. He added that he hoped it wouldn't be his last. Cryptically, he closed with mention of "Once I uncover my silver…."

The day following the publication of the column Bobby received a call from Becky Hamlin. She asked if she could come by for a visit. She had a new proposal. If there was anything Bobby was wary of, he replied, it was a former girlfriend and present enemy offering to propose. Becky pretended to laugh and suggested an hour would be enough time for her to finish her current business. Bobby, though skeptical, told her to come on over for a visit.

Almost to the minute, Becky arrived, dressed in a short, fly-away skirt and plunging neckline blouse. Bobby remembered her body sufficiently well to not need any obvious pointers, but applauded her thoughtfulness. She dismissed her wardrobe as something she wore to the grocery store and dry cleaners.

"Not the last few months we were together," noted Bobby.

"Would it have mattered?" she queried.

"No, but still, you would have looked better."

"You know, Bobby, I never look back upon our break up as a mistake, but that's not to say I don't miss you."

"What's to miss, Becky? We never talked, we had virtually nothing in common, we annoyed each other with our daily habits and our personalities clashed."

"Well, the sex was good."

"That's true."

Becky moved from her chair on the front porch. She didn't come closer, but it seemed as if she did. It was the way in which her body had shifted its emphasis. "Do you ever miss it?"

"Becky! You didn't come to offer me sex for my signature on a contract, did you? Where do I sign?" He knew she had no intention of any ruse so obvious and this is what concerned him.

"You don't have to sign at first. Maybe later, though, when I have more incentives to offer than just the secret roll in the hay."

Bobby had wondered if she had always wanted to be a farmer's daughter, for she had reverted to her usual sexual fantasy spot. Personally, Bobby could only imagine extreme itchiness and inappropriate pricks from the hay, so to speak.

"Becky, I think you're toying with me. You have way too much to lose. Granted, perhaps, not your self respect, but if Johnny found out, yikes!" Bobby rose from his chair and stepped closer to her. "No, you're offering me something, but it isn't sex, is it? You'd get me to the point and then tell me what it really is you have to bargain with. Why don't you skip the charade and give me your best offer." Bobby put up a palm to halt her response. "No, wait. Give me your first offer, because I know you want to do this in stages. It wouldn't be a real estate deal without negotiations."

Becky smiled sweetly at him. "You know, I wish you had stayed in real estate. It would have been fun competing with you." She sat back down in her chair and leaned forward so Bobby could stare at her cleavage more easily. "I'm serious about the sex, but I do have a financial interest in you, as well. I'd rather have the contract with my name on it than John's. Lately, I think he's trying to push me to the background and I need a deal to grab his attention."

"Has he been ignoring you in bed, too? Is that why you want to play a double header?"

"What does that mean, exactly?" she said with a sneer.

Bobby laughed and said, "Sorry, I had baseball on my mind."

She hadn't completely dropped her practiced sneer, but countered, "And, no, of course not, John has not been ignoring me. If anything, I can't keep him off of me."

"It says a lot that you would want to."

"I didn't say that either."

"Look, Becky, even if this wasn't just plain wrong, it's never going to happen." Bobby walked away from the cleavage and the fly away skirt and leaned against the far post on the front porch. "Did John tell you I have a girlfriend and that I'm in love?"

Becky started at the second revelation. She actually had been aware Bobby had a lady visitor to his house, but she was shocked to hear him confess that he was in love. After months of trying to pull those words out of him for her own ears to hear and, now, here he was offering them as normal conversation about someone else. "I'm very happy for you, Bobby. Does she know how fickle you can be?"

"Becky, we are all different with different people, aren't we? You never sold your soul to me like you have to John for his money, and I want to thank you for that."

The afternoon air had grown stale with a bitter aftertaste as Bobby watched Becky flip him off as she drove away. He felt embarrassed by some of his comments and his pervasively negative attitude. Whether Becky meant what she said about having sex with him, he knew that it would never come to that. She might cheat on John, but not with Bobby Early. She did present the possibility of sweetening the offer from John and that meant the stakes had been raised. He wondered how high they would bid to surpass the other, and if Joe Don would top them both just so he wouldn't have to pay them a commission. The Texan surely wasn't pleased with the removal of the backhoe. Bobby knew there would be repercussions eventually.

The phone inside rang and Bobby saw it was Donna. He answered it and said, "Hello, my lady love, what are you wearing?"

"Nothing. Come on over."

Bobby laughed, Donna laughed and he told her of his visitor.

XVIII

The half marathon between Snowmass Village and Aspen was scheduled to run the weekend Bobby was planning to visit Donna in Denver. He had not missed a race for seventeen years. The weekend was also Ruggerfest in Aspen and he hadn't been absent from one of those since the early 1970's. It was a true display of love, as he saw it, for him to arrive at her door Friday evening. Apparently, Donna recognized this and welcomed him naked.

The sun was beginning to set when they left her small and enchanting house for the walk into LoDo for dinner. Lower Downtown was proud of its nickname this last decade and more. Abandoned warehouses and rundown buildings had been restored, rebuilt and reoccupied. Coors Field and Major League Baseball contributed mightily to this revitalization and the businesses knew it. Restaurants were named after baseball references and refurbished lofts flew the Colorado Rockies' flag from their windows. Especially this September, when the team was piecing together one of its patented late season charges to gain a spot for the playoffs.

This was precisely the type of talk Donna didn't want to hear. At least, not tonight. She assumed she would be forced to hear it tomorrow going to the game, during the game and, if the team won, after the game. There was only a week left to the season, the Rockies were two games behind in the standings, and one would need to be a moron or without radio, TV and internet reception to not be aware of this amazing, civilization-altering event. It was bigger than Y2K, the Mayan calendar and, in Colorado baseball purist's minds, the 1927 New York Yankees.

195

After only a few sentences, Bobby wisely picked up on Donna's complete silence and decided to reserve any more commentary for tomorrow. They entered a sushi place that Donna loved and slid into a romantic booth. Colorado Rolls were the house specialty and the waiter claimed the entire state of California was suing the restaurant. They were that good.

As a display of true love, as she saw it, Donna presented a racing bib to Bobby at dinner. There was a ten kilometer race around downtown on Saturday morning and she had registered him. He had planned for a brief run tomorrow before breakfast, but this was a surprise gift that stole whatever part of his heart that had remained not hers.

He finished in the middle of the pack of ten thousand runners, about the same positioning he would have found himself after the half marathon completed by about three hundred and fifty freezing, dedicated runners. It had snowed last night in the mountains, while Denver's morning temperature was sixty degrees. As the saying went, if one didn't like the weather in Colorado, wait an hour. Or, if one lived near the Continental Divide, drive ten minutes to the other side.

They went to breakfast after the race and Donna showed off her neighborhood on a roundabout walk back to her house. Quaint houses with delicate gardens were tucked in between well kept apartment buildings and specialty stores. Neighbors seemed to know one another to some degree and Donna appeared to know them all to many degrees. She stopped and chatted with almost everyone they passed, introducing Bobby as her long-lost boyfriend from Aspen. He certainly didn't look rich, they remarked to Donna later.

They rested on her backyard patio for much of the afternoon. There was the occasional fire truck siren, diesel engine noise from passing big rigs and barking dogs, but not any more than in Aspen, thought Bobby. If there were a river, wild animals and mountains closer than twenty miles away, the two, Donna and Bobby's backyards, wouldn't be so different.

When he saw how much she identified with all her friends and how proud she was of her neighborhood, he knew it would not be easy for her to leave. No easier than it would be for him to leave Aspen. He didn't think that driving here, but he did now, and he was glad he understood what she would be sacrificing if she ever departed.

When they left for the evening game, they allowed themselves a couple of hours to roam through the Tattered Cover, one of the country's great bookstores. Bobby had offered to buy dinner, but Donna, trying to get in the spirit of things, said she would feast on ballpark fare. This would be the only time she ever said this.

A late September evening in Denver sparkled beneath the high lights surrounding the stadium. The setting sun inspired streaked clouds to spill colors laced with orange, red and pink. Facing the home team Colorado Rockies were the hated Los Angeles Dodgers. This was a rivalry created mostly by the Dodgers' dominance throughout the years. An expansion franchise from the early 1990's, the Rockies had always struggled against the west coast glamour team. However, this weekend would witness an opportunity for the Rockies to find themselves in the division lead if they could sweep the stinkin' Dodgers. They had won Friday night's game and, if they took today's and tomorrow's, Rockies mania would engulf the entire Rocky Mountain region and beyond. At least, that's how Bobby saw it.

Fans were dressed in anything from shorts and tank tops to tuxedos. The game was sold out and Rockies' memorabilia was competing with cold beer for volume sales. Silver and purple, the team's colors, were marching up and down aisles and infiltrating sections and levels of the seating areas. Bobby and Donna were ushered down toward the field. Donna kept descending the steps, waiting for the usher to stop at their row. The affable, elderly gentleman finally halted at the row behind the Rockies' dugout. He turned around and smiled at the lucky ticket holders. He told them they should keep their feet off the dugout and hoped they would enjoy the game.

They sat down in the two seats to the right of the aisle. Bobby looked at the tickets that read row two and said, "I guess row one is in the dugout"

"These are pretty amazing seats, Bobby."

"Oh, I don't know. I think there're made of hard plastic, that's all."

Donna pushed him playfully and placed her sneaker soles on the edge of the dugout. Bobby went to tell her to remove them, but the usher arrived before he could get the words out. She promised to not make him ask her again and the suddenly stern usher returned to his affable self.

Bobby had been given the tickets from a friend who still sold liquor in its many varieties, flavors and prices to The Cebolla Roja. Jeff wasn't a baseball fan and, though Bobby remained suspicious of this character flaw in his friend, he was grateful at the moment that Jeff didn't wish to avail himself of the tickets this weekend. The ducats belonged to the company his friend worked for, and just by the luck of the draw did his friend have the rights to them this weekend. Donna asked Bobby how he lived with himself for taking these expensive tickets and the VIP passes to the concerts only to lambast the privileged and the few.

"Very comfortably, thank you," he replied. "You see, I don't think it's my due, so I don't mistreat anyone around me when I am the beneficiary of kindness and generosity." He paused, pulled out a napkin from the pocket of his light jacket and pretended to wipe off the imagined scuff mark Donna's shoes had left on the dugout. "Unlike some people I know, I might add." She shoved him a little harder this time. The national anthem was sung, the players introduced and the game began.

"Strike one!" shouted the home umpire. This is going to be a long game, Donna thought. She knew baseball games here could be longer than in other cities, because the ball flew faster and farther in the mile high city of Denver. She accepted Bobby's offer of a beer and some Crackerjacks and resisted the temptation to put her feet up.

By the seventh inning stretch, Donna had eaten parts of a pizza slice, some nachos, half a bag of popcorn, an egg roll, several onion rings and had consented to trying pink cotton candy. Another large cup of beer washed these flavors from her mouth and when it came time to sing "Take Me Out to the Ballgame," she was in fine form. A couple of Rockies players lifted their heads over the dugout roof to see who it was that was singing like a cross between Bette Midler and Aretha Franklin. The game was scoreless, Donna was enthused and Bobby enthralled. If forced to choose at this very moment, the game of baseball or Donna, he would have been fit to be tied, just like the game. Fortunately, no one was asking him to choose and he had both at the same time. Life, he thought, couldn't get any better. Until, that is, when the Rockies won the game in the bottom of the ninth on a solo home run with two outs and the count three and two. Coors Field erupted. Bobby received the strongest shove of the night from an exuberant Donna. The beloved, perennial underdogs, the Colorado Rockies, had defeated the stinkin' Los Angeles Dodgers in a pitching duel. This would lead off the evening news tonight and top the morning headlines tomorrow, or so Bobby proclaimed. Donna hoped Bobby would calm down by the time they left the stadium. He did. Just enough to suggest they hit a few bars on the way home to celebrate.

It was in the last one where a minor skirmish broke out. Fan loyalty had been fueled by alcohol and the late hour to help cause tempers to ignite, even flare. Bobby had mentioned "stinkin' Dodgers" one too many times. A young man wearing a Dodgers nylon jacket had taken offense and wouldn't accept Bobby's half-hearted apology. Donna was undergoing an out-of-body experience in the ladies' room, in the sense that there were once solid items that wanted to leave her body. She attributed this to her ballpark diet and didn't witness the beginning of the confrontation. Even if Bobby had been younger, he would have been no match for the Dodger fan. Donna emerged tired, but cleansed, from the ladies' room just as the Dodger fan threw a round house punch that narrowly escaped Bobby's chin. Unfortunately, it clipped Donna's shoulder. With no choice now but to embody chivalry and not appear the complete coward, he boldly raised his palms and warned the Dodger fan that he was a trained self defense expert. The Dodger fan countered that Bobby was full of bullshit and nobody who is proficient in the arts of self defense ever says that, but in the movies. As another blow was prepared to, probably, this time, land on its intended target, the bar's bouncer bear-hugged the fan and escorted him not too kindly to the sidewalk pavement out front.

As Donna and Bobby exited out the back door and race walked the few short blocks to her house, he apologized for his overzealous behavior while inquiring about her shoulder. There was no bodily pain she had suffered that could add to her mental anguish, she explained. Then, at the front door of her house, she turned, laughed, and asked him if he really knew martial arts. He told her that his hands were registered deadly weapons. In the kitchen, he added. He adopted a pose, attempted a kick to a front porch post, slipped and fell on his butt. It seemed only fair.

* * *

The next morning, Donna suggested that if Bobby wanted to see the final game of the series that he go alone. She wasn't feeling quite up to all the certain excitement for some reason. After a proper period of accepting Bobby's remorse and further apologies, she forgave him, but still didn't want to go to the game. The smell of cotton candy continued to burn her nostrils and she couldn't brush off the beer breath. Bobby claimed that Donna was actually suffering from pennant fever, but he walked to Coors Field and found a couple of kids to whom to give the tickets. He wondered why his butt seemed sore and then remembered. For only an instant, he wished he had actually taken a martial arts class.

The handsome and lovely couple spent the afternoon strolling the 16th Street Mall and jumping out of the way of electric street cars and buses. Much fancier than Aspen's outdoor malls, they were also considerably faster, Bobby learned. They sipped coffee at tables up and down the mall while reading the Sunday newspapers. Occasionally, Bobby used the men's room and conveniently returned with the score of the baseball game. He casually mentioned that the Rockies won, nine to eight, in four and a half hours, placing them in first place with a week remaining in the season. Donna nodded and told Bobby she was happy for him. Testing their quiet time together in the midst of unbridled activity and city clamor, they otherwise communicated silently. Once again, they were pleased with what they discovered and disturbed by the looming question of, "What happens next?"

After Donna had gone to work the next morning, he allowed himself a few minutes to walk around her house and study her art, knickknacks, library and multitude of flower vases. He walked back to the 16th Street Mall, bought a mixed bouquet that resembled one she had created while they had been in the flower shop in Aspen and placed them in a vase on her kitchen table with a note. There were not enough personal, hand written notes these days and, together, Donna and he would try to improve Bobby's handwriting by practice, practice, practice.

***

When he arrived back in Aspen, Bobby visited the Building Department to discuss excavation. Knowing how tediously long the approval process for permits could take, he deemed he should begin in the fall for the spring project. It was explained to him that the requirements, in fact, might prove to be even more excruciatingly extraneous than his past personal experience indicated. This optimistic outlook came from a friend within the department. The crucial impediment was the hard earned status of historical registry.

A hearing could be scheduled for the middle of October, so Bobby entered his name on the docket and spent the next few days contacting the members of the department privately. He hoped to acquaint them with his situation and the justification for his request. The three members of the hearing board all seemed amiable to his reasoning, which concerned him. If they thought his plan sounded reasonable, they would think an objection would be equally credible.

He approached John Hamlin with his proposal, hoping to discern if John would offer opposition. John indicated that he would actually support Bobby's efforts. There was no reference to Becky's recent visit. If John knew about her front porch opera of overture, it probably was the version that featured Bobby as the beast and Becky the innocent beauty. Bobby counted on John's familiarity with Becky's mutable morality to maintain his innocence.

John told Bobby that he would get back to him before the hearing, but he never did. When the hearing began, John Hamlin and Joe Don Burke walked in together. Donna Deerfield sat with Bobby Early.

XIX

Donna had planned to leave Sunday afternoon, the day before the hearing. She and Bobby had spent the previous several days on an excursion to southern Colorado to view the last of the leaves changing in their autumn splendor. In Denver, the aspens would be turning through the rest of the month, with maples, oak, birch and other varieties of deciduous gifts from the world of trees. In the mountains, however, the vast networks of aspens had spun their golden loom across the hillsides, blanketing valleys and ravines with a variety of rich yellow abandon. Tied together by running roots, entire forests changed from green to hues of yellow, orange and red overnight. The myth that aspens only favored the color of the sun was disproved around various curves of every highway and in the multi-hued, leaf-covered pitch of the many trails they hiked.

After they had canvassed the southern secrets of the state, Bobby shared with Donna the meaning of the Monday meeting. She wanted to stay and attend the hearing with him, even though she judged it to be merely a formality. Bobby seemed to have corralled the support of the hearing officers, as well as his most powerful opponent. They both walked into City Hall with an easy and comfortable confidence that should have alerted every fiber of their being that trouble was guaranteed.

Two of the three expected members of the board were in attendance, but the third participant was a surprise. City Councilwoman Barbara Bennington had joined the others behind the short, curved wooden table at the front of the room. Bobby glanced around to see if her husband, Hef

204

Bennington, the lawyer and confidant of John Hamlin, was present. If he was, thought Bobby, he was scurrying around like a rat somewhere and couldn't be seen. Though the memories were fond of his last encounter with the Benningtons, he also recalled that the sidewalk chitchat was followed by his introduction to Joe Don.

The Texan, sitting next to John, was looking especially smug at the moment. Hamlin was disarmingly dapper in a silk suit, completely in character with the ultimate smoothness he routinely tried to transmit. Obviously, Bobby and Donna had not received the memo about attitudes and wardrobes. Nonetheless, Bobby remained confident that his project would pass with the approval of the two appointed officers, even if Barbara dissented. Majority rules in America, reflected Bobby. Then he attached the addendum: Of course, there's always the matter of money...

He also took a moment out to remind himself that America, specifically the United States Thereof, didn't have a monopoly on corruption and had not birthed political influence. The recent world monetary crisis confirmed that these sterling silver qualities were the gold standard in many nations and on all continents, with the possible exclusion of Antarctica. In was only because the news from the southernmost land mass traveled with the speed and general public interest of a climate warming iceberg that Antarctica escaped scrutiny. Bobby was a firm believer in and ardent supporter of democratic institutions with all their frailties and flaws. Sometimes money won and other times the voters made horrible decisions, but the USA's system was the map for mankind in matters of self-government. It was easier to expound to himself these ideas when it seemed assured he would win what he came for today. And, yet, remembering that his votes had come out on the losing side of more elections than they had triumphed, he urged himself to be circumspect. The events began predictably. Bobby was asked to present his proposal and provide due cause.

"First, I'd like to thank the board for granting me a speedy hearing and express my hopes that Frank Herner recovers quickly from whatever malady has struck him down."

Barbara Bennington nodded perfunctorily and said, "Contrary to your assumption, Mr. Early, Frank asked me to sit in for him today. He's aware that I'm familiar with excavation proposals and advised me that the board would appreciate my expertise."

"It's clear that you would be referring to the four or five homes you have demolished and had rebuilt, Barbara, but are you an expert in the area that concerns my house?"

The chairman, Steve Turner, lightly tapped his short handled gavel and stated that Barbara Bennington was as well qualified as he and the other member of the board, Wayne Lane. He also emphasized that certain formalities would prevail throughout the hearing, and among them would the use of proper names. Bobby decided now would be a good time to start becoming concerned.

He took a few minutes to explain how he intended to jack up his house about four feet and dig under it until he found the silver that Caleb Century had written was there. The fact that other historically registered structures had been lifted by similar procedures and then reset on new and improved foundations, some with five thousand square foot basements that included bowling alleys, had established precedent, he claimed.

Steve Turner and Wayne Lane were familiar with Bobby's conviction that silver was beneath his house, though neither granted it any credence. Barbara Bennington had heard John and Becky Hamlin, in addition to her husband, speak of this fantasy that seemed to all of them the sole reason for Bobby refusing to sell his abode to House and Home. They didn't understand that his house was his home and that he would continue to want to live there even without recovering the silver. They also didn't know, no one did, that there would come a time, without the silver, Bobby would *have* to sell his home. Donna hadn't asked, and Bobby hadn't told her, but he figured he had another year left before he would be forced to capitulate to the economic forces of winners and losers. He figured, he reminded himself, because he hadn't calculated. Not wanting to see the numbers in red and black in black and white, he refrained from measuring them against his needs.

The fact that all three members of the board believed, without even a sliver of doubt, that Bobby was misled at best, and a fool at worst, did not necessarily cause Bobby to consider that his proposal would be denied. It was no skin off their nose, no money from their bank account, no public humiliation for them and no filling the empty, unprofitable hole back in for them. He could not see how they could possibly care less what he did, as long as he followed the usual rules to failure and paid all the bureaucratic fees. Bobby had closed his simple and unadorned presentation with an expression of appreciation for the traditional "unbiased and perennially fair reputation of this fantastic and glorious board." Donna said underneath her breath, as Bobby leaned back in his chair, "I think you had them until your summation, comrade."

The board then invited opinion and objection from anyone in attendance. John Hamlin offered a rebuttal to Bobby's depiction of raising a house up on jacks of any sort as a common occurrence. "This approval normally takes months and, in some cases, years."

"Objection, your honors," interrupted Bobby. "Mr. Hamlin is citing cases where complete remodels and additions, indeed, even modern day mansions, have sought board and department approval."

"Mr. Early, this is not a court of law and, if it was, you would be well advised to procure an attorney or face contempt of court charges," replied Steve Turner, pounding his gavel.

Donna pressed Bobby's forearm and hoped that he wasn't thinking that he knew martial arts again. Bobby instinctively jerked his arm at her touch, but returned to reason instantaneously. "Quite correct, Chairman Turner. My apologies."

The board members looked at each other and effectively raised their eyebrows as if there was a common assent brewing. Steve Turner continued, "Do you have anything further to add, Mr Hamlin?"

"I only wish to emphasize that the board rarely approves such a project as Mr. Early is proposing in an expedient manner. I suggest the board consider taking an appropriate amount of time for due diligence."

The members each seemed to be choreographed into mimicking one another with expressions that included a furrowed brow, narrowed nostrils, tight-lipped frown and beaded chin. It was so effective that Bobby put his head in his hands.

"Nonetheless, I would like to introduce a client of mine that may very well be unduly affected by any excavation on Mr. Early's lot," added Hamlin, motioning to Joe Don Burke and introducing him to the board.

Joe Don proceeded to enlighten the board to the encroachment of water and its attendant effects upon his land. "See, I'm concerned that I'll have to deal with this muck and mud next spring when I begin construction of my house next to Mr. Early's lot."

It had been hard enough for Bobby not to react to Hamlin's use of the word "lot" for house, but Joe Don's was just too much for him. "Mr. Turner, surely the board will not continue to allow slander and innuendo to proliferate within these hallowed walls," he interjected.

"Mr. Early, another outburst like that and we will adjourn this hearing," countered Steve Turner.

Donna had become alarmed at the sudden turn of fortune since they had entered the room. She was also becoming concerned with Bobby's lack of composure and asked if she might address the board. She introduced herself as a close friend and advisor to Bobby and requested a brief recess.

The chairman responded that unless there were any further comments Mr. Burke and Mr. Hamlin wanted or needed to offer, then a recess would serve also the purpose of providing an opportunity to render a decision. Joe Don replied that he would darn well like to add one more thing. Hamlin sunk in this chair.

"See, I had arranged for Mr. Early to use, without charge, a backhoe to dig along his fence to discover the problem, probably a busted sprinkler line or water pipe. But, no, instead, he whacked this piece of machinery with a lead pipe or somethin'…"

"That was Dr. Corning," interrupted Donna before she covered her mouth with her hand.

"What," exclaimed and questioned Joe Don.

"Oops," muttered Bobby.

Chairman Turner slammed his gavel continuously while an argument erupted between the opposing parties, before finally bringing them to a level of order and quiet. "The board will now deliberate in private and we will reconvene in thirty minutes." He finished and laid the gavel on its side.

Bobby apologized to Donna and Donna apologized to him. "I may have gotten a little carried away here," said Bobby.

"I didn't help any, but, yes, I think you did. What happened?"

"I thought it was such a sure thing that when it started going the other way, I just lost it. Not my best moment."

John came in front of their table, hands in his pockets and a smirk on his face. "Am I safe to stand here so close to you, Bobby?"

"I can see clearly now, the rage is gone," sing-songed Bobby.

Joe Don came along side John and looked equally sure of himself. "We gotta a deal for you, Bobby. Wanna hear it?"

"Pull up a couple of chairs, boys," answered Bobby. Donna slipped her arm inside his and squeezed. As Joe Don and John went to their table to retrieve chairs Bobby turned to her and whispered, "We may as well hear what they have to say." Donna's heart skipped to hear Bobby say "we," because she knew that he had always felt alone in his belief and in the struggle. "I'm through with the dramatics, by the way," he continued. "I think I simply overreacted to having someone by my side that I thought I needed to impress. Can you understand?"

"I think I overreacted a bit just being by your overreacting side." She removed her arm from inside his and laid her hand out, palm side up. "Pals?" she asked.

He reached his hand to her and grasped it surely, but gently. "Forever," he said.

Joe Don and John returned with their chairs and set them at the opposite side of the table. "Bobby, this is something Joe Don and I have discussed and we are in agreement. We have an offer to make you and it'll mean you can dig for your silver with no further problems."

"Go ahead," replied Bobby.

"We will drop our opposition to your plans to raise your house and mine below your floorboard. In exchange, if," John paused momentarily, "Notice I say "if," you don't find the silver then it's time to strike a deal and sign a contract."

"What if I don't accept?"

"Then we continue to throw every City Hall review committee at you and delay your dig until you exhaust whatever dwindling resources you have left."

Donna's head swiveled to Bobby, but he was impassive. Finally, he said, "What makes you think I'm going to be denied my permit today?"

Joe Don hooted and smacked the table with his fist. "Goldarn, if you don't remind me of a Texas Ranger ridin' into a box canyon of outlaws!" Joe Don guffawed and added, "Only thing is, that Ranger never rode out."

Donna started to say something, but Bobby stopped her. John leaned back in his chair and said, "I'd preferred Joe Don to not have put it that way, but he does have a point. Do you really think you have any chance to win an approval today, or any day?"

Bobby looked back and forth between the two men that were causing him to lose a sense of spiritual equilibrium and replied, "Do you think you can influence their decision?"

John smiled thinly and nodded. "We can try."

"It's a deal, then," said Bobby.

"Wait a minute," threw in Joe Don. "We need to sign somethin', have this in writin'."

Bobby stretched his arms out in front of him and rested them on the table. His eyes squinted and he held John is his stare. "Is that right, John?" It was a Clint Eastwood moment.

"No, I guess not, Bobby. You are a lot of things, but you're not a liar. Truth is, I'll be sorry to see you go."

211

"No you won't," smiled Bobby

John laughed and said, "You're right, *I'm* a liar, though."

"Yes, you can be, John. Shake?" John and Bobby shook hands. Bobby turned to Joe Don and extended his hand. Joe Don looked confused. "Joe Don, my word is good and the silver is there, so you may as well shake because I won't be going anywhere at anytime."

"If you don't find this imaginary silver then you *are* gone, though, right?"

"If it's not there then neither am I. You have my hand on it, as well as my word."

Joe Don reached for Bobby's hand slowly and with obvious trepidation. He hated to be swindled and he suspected everyone. Bobby shook his hand and thought to himself, good, this will keep him up at night.

John and Joe Don excused themselves from the table, returned their chairs and left the room through the same door the board members had exited. A few minutes later the five of them came back in the room and the deal was done. The board announced that they were issuing a permit to Bobby to jack up his house and excavate below it. They smiled at Bobby as they shook hands with him and offered congratulations. After the board members left the room for a final time, Donna turned to Joe Don and John and said, "Mighty deep pockets you have there."

"Don't be so presumptuous, Donna," said John. "I'm sure this will have to be paid for someday, but as a businessman I have many different options."

"Oh, the facts are that this costs you nothing, John," Bobby interrupted. "I'm such small potatoes that granting me the permit is like giving a ghost a hall pass. Nobody will notice. The board doesn't owe you anything and you don't owe them anything. I'm the one who owes. That is, unless I find the silver. And then the party isn't over, it's

212

only beginning. I'll have every one of your clients digging up their yards looking for boulders and bars of a fine, shiny metal."

Donna laughed and she and Bobby left through the front door. Bobby handed the clerk his stamped approval petition and was advised to come back to pick up his permit any time before he began his project. He offered her the peace sign and told her he would see her in the spring.

They went to The Cebolla Roja to celebrate with a hot and spicy Mexican lunch, a couple of margaritas and a plan to return to the house for a siesta. Instead, they made love and then went for a hike. Donna was leaving tomorrow morning and they weren't sure when they would be together again. She continued to impress upon Bobby that they were together even when they were apart. Though he agreed in principal and knew it to be true in a spiritual and lovey-dovey sense, he had to point out that wasn't really a fact. Some of the last leaves of the aspen trees around Bobby's house were falling on the roof when they resumed the conversation of living together for a few weeks. They wanted and needed to see if the burden and bounty of time hurt or helped them.

XX

When Donna left in the morning, she drove over Independence Pass and wished she hadn't. A brief, but serious, snow storm followed her up the pass and over it. Halfway down the eastern side she out ran it, but the storm had almost created a whiteout and she felt lucky to have escaped it. Traditionally, the pass was closed to all automobile traffic from Halloween until Memorial Day Weekend. Gates were closed on each side of Highway 82 well below the pass. To Aspen's east, the road was open and plowed for about six miles. Skiers, snowboarders, snowshoers and snowmobilers could still gain access around and beyond the gate, but at their own risk and with no patrols. Only the Search and Rescue teams were available to aid those in distress and, sometimes, those teams discovered too late that people were in a life and death situation. Then it was a recovery mission. As in most matters, those with the best preparation and planning were the ones who survived when the blizzard hit, equipment malfunctioned, bones broke or avalanches slid.

And, so it was, that Bobby Early decided he should prepare and plan by investigating this idea he had for raising his house up on jacks and digging below it to find a silver cache. It seemed like a reasonable enough request that he could make of a company that moved houses around for profit. But he didn't know and he didn't have a clue. Now that he had gone to the trouble to obtain the permit, perhaps he should find out a little more precisely what was involved.

First, he visited a friend of his in the construction business that might be able to direct him to a reliable and

214

cheap company to do the work. His friend informed him that Fierce Pierce, the bartender at The Cebolla Roja, could probably help him. Bobby stopped by the bar the day before Halloween to see how this could be possible.

Fierce was behind the bar, it was two o'clock in the afternoon and there were three patrons in the entire building. Two were at a table in the back and the other was leaning forward on his bar stool, in a stupor, hunched over a draft beer. Fierce was pleased to see a familiar face and one that could speak, so he joined Bobby at a half moon shaped table near the large front window.

The lone server, Sammy, was relaxing in a small booth, reading a local newspaper that was full of big ads and little news. There was another off-season election scheduled for next week. At the top of the ballot was the forty-first running of the Entrance to Aspen vote. There were a few full page ads in favor of the expansion to four lanes with a straight shot and no curves, there were many letters supporting the opposite, and no one mentioned a three lane option except for Bobby Early in his weekly column. Anyone not having read a newspaper for a year to the exact date would have concluded nothing had changed and they would have been correct. The headlines and arguments were precisely the same. Whichever side won the vote this year would face a citizen's initiative the following June. The initiative would win and a person could save themselves some time by not reading next year's newspaper on this exact date. Unless, of course, they wished to own the collectors' edition that discussed the forty-*second* running of the Entrance to Aspen debate.

Bobby accepted Fierce's compliment on Bobby's column and offered his own opinion that the City should have two entrances, one four lane and the other, two. Bobby assumed this was because Fierce openly supported alternate lifestyles, but Fierce replied, "No, it's because I want to see all these idiots run into each other and then figure it out. God, I've only been here a few years, Bobby! I don't know how you old-timers handle it!" Fierce hurriedly clasped his hands over his mouth, but not before Bobby saw Fierce's upper lip cover the lower lip. His eyes were saucers and Fierce held the pose until Bobby shifted on his swivel stool and patted Fierce on the knee.

"Well, young fella," began Bobby, "It's because we've been fightin' so long, we don't know how to do nothin' else." Bobby had slid his lower jaw a little to the side and raised a lip as he said this with a slight lisp. "Jus' like all the other fundamentalist absolutists in the world."

Fierce dropped his hands and patted Bobby's knee in return. If Bobby had been gay this would have been the start of a beautiful April-November relationship. Instead, it was the beginning of Bobby's rude awakening to the difficulty he faced in simultaneously excavating silver and saving a house.

Pierce told Bobby that, while in high school, he had worked in the manly fields of construction, mining and house relocation. These summer jobs had kept him in terrific shape for the ensuing football seasons in which he amassed the trophies that were now behind The Cebolla Roja bar. They hadn't convinced him that he was heterosexual, like his pastor had hoped, but they had persuaded him he didn't wish to pursue manual labor after high school. He told Bobby that a firm would have to be hired to set timbers and steel girders between the house and the jacks and the jacks and the foundation. The plumbing and electricity would all have to be disconnected and the entire insane project would keep him out of the house for months.

"This conversation isn't going as well as I'd hoped," said a resigned Bobby.

"Look, why don't you just face a couple of obvious facts? The first is that your house is so old that it isn't going to handle being lifted and put back down very gracefully. The second is that you should sell the place, propose to that girl you've been seeing and move to Costa Rica."

"What?"

"Listen, sweetie," continued Fierce, "You know that I love you like a great uncle, but you're not getting younger and you could spend your golden years on the beach."

"I prefer to think that I'm in my late bronze period, and I plan on the silver ages before my restful golden years."

"I'm sorry, Bobby. I know you have this dream, but I don't want you to break yourself trying to achieve it." Fierce explained that to hire a company of machines and men to undertake the project of raising his house, tunneling underneath it, pouring a new foundation and placing his house back down on it would cost tens of thousands of dollars. Bobby knew that by the time he'd spent that, his funds would be perilously depleted. In addition, he'd have to camp out in his back yard with the mysterious water perhaps seeping his way. He was beginning to feel he had been all wet, as it were, with his proposed plan.

Bobby Early was slightly discouraged and depressed from all this talk of futility, failure and demise, so he asked Fierce to pour him a beer. As Fierce walked behind the bar, Bobby casually mentioned, "Shoot, I should have just stuck to my original idea."

"What's that, Bobby baby?"

"Get a shovel and dig it out from my crawl space."

Fierce tipped the glass he was pouring beer into and it flowed over the bar. He nearly shouted, "You have a crawl space?"

"Sure"

217

Fierce Pierce wiped the meandering beer off the bar, filled the glass and brought it over to Bobby. "Is it dirt?"

"Why, yes it is. I couldn't use a shovel through concrete, now, could I?"

"Don't sass me, old man, or else I won't tell you that you were just handed your silver spoon."

***

After Pierce had finished his shift, he came over to Bobby's house. Donna had arrived minutes before Pierce and a half hour after the snow began. She had missed the mess on the roads that would develop throughout the night, but she wasn't particularly happy about the drive up from Glenwood Springs. Pierce was camouflaged in white from the heavy snow through which he had walked, when he knocked on the door. Bobby, realizing that he was in the best mood of the three, offered to make them hot chocolate. Instead, Donna opened the refrigerator and poured herself a glass of chardonnay, while Pierce opened cabinets looking for some of Bobby's Jameson Irish Whiskey. In a few minutes, both of them were in better spirits, Bobby noted. They frowned at the tired pun and proceeded to follow Bobby to his bedroom. Pierce made the requisite amount of sexual innuendo jokes as he watched Bobby open the closet door.

"Where is it?" asked Pierce. "Where's the access door?"

"Well, I have to move a few things," replied Bobby. He reached into the closet and his golf clubs, an open safe, a box of photographs and a dirty clothes hamper filled with old running shoes. "There you go," he said to Pierce and pointed to the outline of a trap door cut out of his closet floor.

Pierce looked askance at Bobby, rolled his eyes to Donna and bent down onto the floor. "Do you happen to

218

have a light? I mean one that might be from this century and doesn't operate on kerosene?"

"I've been meaning to put a light in here, but I can usually remember where I put my clothes. I reach in and always seem to find something close enough to what I was thinking." Bobby went to the kitchen and returned with the flashlight. Pierce had managed to pry an edge of the door loose and lift it away from the floor. He reached for the flashlight and shined the beam down into the hole. He stuck his head into the space and Donna and Bobby watched him wiggle around as he was attempting to look in all directions. It was rather comical to Donna, but Bobby was becoming anxious about Pierce's assessment. The bartender emerged from the hole, turned off the flashlight and leaned against a wall of the closet. "Oops."

"Oops?" echoed Bobby with a raised intonation.

"Alley oops oops," faintly murmured Donna, recalling a silly song from their early youth.

"Take a look, Bobby." Pierce handed him the light. Bobby pushed around Pierce and dived into the hole with the flashlight before him. He didn't go far. He pushed himself back up and braced himself against an opposite wall from Fierce.

What they had both seen when they flashed the light to the near side of the crawl space was water. There were puddles of it and they were below his bedroom. There didn't seem to be any water toward the front of the house, but Bobby would have to work his way there to be certain.

"I suggest you call a plumber, Bobby. At least you've discovered this before the ground is frozen around the house."

"I suspect you're right. But I think I'm going to take a further look before I do."

Bobby lowered himself into the crawl space and made his way below the front of the house. He had about three feet of space between the dirt floor and the joists that ran across and above him. They rested on the concrete foundation wall running around the house, supporting it. There had been no sign of water anywhere other than below his bedroom. As he came back underneath the trap door, he saw Donna peering down. He stopped to kiss her, hit his head on a beam, dropped the flashlight and heard a "slurp". He found the flashlight, shined it around the near end to gauge how much water there was and hurried up the hole. As he did, he heard a gurgle.

"I'll call a plumber tomorrow."

That night, Jeff and Melissa came for dinner and joined Fierce and Bobby in creating stories about crawl space monsters that had Donna laughing hysterically, if nervously. There were tales of the Giant Roaring Fork River Rat, the Melancholy Mining Mule and the Silver Swamp Gas Gang. Nonetheless, everyone at one time or another double checked the trap door.

The next morning, a couple of hard working plumber friends of Bobby's came by to investigate. There were no leaks in any pipes that ran below the flooring. They walked the perimeter of the house looking for sinkage that would indicate a broken pipe. The snow from last night had mostly melted, but they found a suspicious spot just outside the back of the house that appeared to be more than mere snow melt. An hour of pick axes and shovels revealed a split in the line that ran out from underneath the concrete foundation. It was another hour before the splice repair had been made and Bobby was as perplexed as he was pleased. The relatively small amount of water that he used day to day could not have flooded the area along his fence. He had already checked his sprinkler system lines, there were no problems and the lines had been drained for the winter. He supposed the split pipe outside could have somehow backed water into his crawl space, but he wasn't as convinced as the plumbers. They told him to listen to the professionals, pay the bill and call them in the spring if the crawl space wasn't dry. They also recommended he have the water pumped out if he didn't want to wait that long. Bobby had other plans. He hoped that it was also among God's plans. He hadn't reconciled the search and acquisition of money with his spiritual evolution as well as he would have liked, yet, but he was willing to go on faith. After all, in the end, he believed, that's all there really was and is.

When he told the dinner guests the night before of his method to unearth the silver he was met with laughter, then disbelief and finally serious encouragement that he needed to exit the house completely for the winter or lose his mind and, probably, his life. Even Donna was concerned enough to urge him not to forsake the raising of the house. Bobby was adamant and single-minded. He had tunnel vision and he would need it.

***

That afternoon Bobby and Donna went looking for ideas for Halloween costumes. The night of trick or treat promised the usual riches of embarrassment. The stores featured the traditional hideous masks of Nixon, Kissinger and (W) Bush for the old guard. For the new wave of resident, there were the Obama and (H) Clinton selections that were sold with the caution that they be worn only at private parties. There were the usual costumes featuring superheroes and super villains, if the masks proved not to be obvious enough.

Donna had brought a costume of sorts from Denver that she heard about from a friend. A rubber chicken hanging from a phone cord pinned to a blue shirt clearly identified her as Chicken Cordon Bleu. Bobby offered to reprise what he considered to be one of his least successful, but most personally satisfying disguises of all time. A pillow stuffed between a shirt and his stomach profiled pregnancy. A pair of oversize white polar bear paws sewn from a fluffy fabric that punned pause. Yes, he was a...pregnant pause. Bobby thought the literary reference was clever and Donna considered it obscure. She was equally unimpressed with his idea of going as a ripcord to a parachute. He would wear ripped corduroy pants and shirt and trail a miniature parachute he had purchased from a toy and fireworks store in Wyoming. He also advanced the idea that he could stuff dollar bills into his pockets and transform himself into D.B. Cooper.

Bobby discarded both simple costumes, deciding to dress as a miner, instead. He owned a functioning headlamp, some tattered clothing, a camp shovel and a pair of ripped boots. He purchased a tin of black make up polish that he would smear on his face, arms, cap and clothing and he would be dressed in an outfit he may as well be donning for his near future. When Donna heard of this, she changed her idea of a costume to something more appropriate, telling Bobby he could wait to see. She was fortunate to procure the necessary items in Aspen's sole remaining drug store. The store had joined the newly traditional practice of stocking Christmas items beginning at Halloween. She had hoped, this one time, that her consumer holiday needs could be met. Otherwise, the practice of Christmas in October quietly enraged her.

As Bobby finished dabbing polish on himself, Donna emerged from the bedroom draped in silver gift wrapping paper with a red bow tied around her waist. He was the miner and she would be his silver nugget. The seeker and the sought for, dressed in warm coats, proceeded to trek to town for the evening's festivities.

They embarked on foot to the shuffling, scratching sound of wrapping paper rubbing Donna's knees raw. Bobby assured her that pain and sacrifice were the lot of a miner's wife, to which she stopped cold in her tracks. She knew she would only get colder and not wanting to lose what heat the abrasive contact insured, asked straightaway, "What did you say?"

Bobby had heard his own slip and hoped the rustling sounds she emitted had muted it. "I said 'life'," he stumbled.

"Is that the truth?"

Bobby turned the miner's head lamp that was blinding Donna away from her eyes, but kept his eyes on hers as they stood in the glow of a streetlamp in the snow. "Well, no it isn't. I did say wife, but it was a slip of the tongue." To which Donna slipped hers into Bobby's mouth.

"I'm sure it was, and all I wanted was for you to admit it. You're cute when you have to admit something that's true. You just can't lie, can you?"

"Hell, yes, I can!" smiled Bobby.

"See? No, you can't. You can't even lie about that."

She put her arm in his and they shuffled together down the sidewalk that Bobby's realigned headlamp lit. Within minutes, they were inside the cowboy swinging doors of The Cebolla Roja. They walked by the man-size gorilla with scary eyes and the accompanying organ grinder, the blow-up pumpkin girl group dancing and bumping into each other and assorted corrupt politicians, military arms suppliers and pyramid schemers. This last was best exemplified by one person of unknown gender who had created a cardboard pyramid covered with dollar bills. At the peak of the pyramid, where it conformed to the mouth, was a drawing of a thousand dollar bill with the words "Thank You" highlighted in jumpsuit orange.

There wasn't much confusion from the patrons about the meaning of Bobby and Donna's getup, but there was general appreciation. They ordered a couple of drinks and fraternized with the costumed clientele. It was early in the evening and the party atmosphere had already lifted off. It appeared the scene came in shifts and sequences of themes. There was the sporting contingent consisting of beach volleyball girls in bikinis, football players in casts, snowboarders with dopey smiles and gold medals and professional baseball players with packages of steroids taped to their uniforms. Part of Halloween was about finding a stereotype and sticking to it. Bobby was relieved to see there were no Colorado Rockies players involved, but he would have to inform his sister, Susan, that, unfortunately, a few San Francisco Giants players were in attendance.

As the 1890's couple, which they were being dubbed, ordered a second drink, the mood morphed from athletics to history. It was slow to reveal itself, beginning with Albert Einstein apparently propositioning Joan of Ark. They offered each other secrets to the universe. Julius Caesar and Cleopatra were in a spat, while George Washington walked about inside the frame of a rowboat. A six foot four inch Napoleon strolled the room howling "Waterloo" to an unfamiliar tune, then falling down.

Gradually, these characters vanished from the room to be replaced by a more sedate gathering of cheerful revelers dressed as werewolves, Draculas, vampires, witches and hospital patients smeared with red and poked with needles. This group was all business and exceedingly polite. Donna erupted in laughter when a ghastly ghoul accidently stepped on one of her feet and continued to profusely apologize, offering to buy her wine for the evening. It may have been he was blinded by her beauty, the silver, or both, Bobby suggested, but an otherwise frightening ghoul begging forgiveness was a humorous sight to them both.

They heard the bartender behind them ask if they wanted another drink, compliments of the ghoul, and they turned around to find it was Fierce Pierce adopting an English accent. In honor of their dinner together the night before, Fierce had spray painted himself silver. He looked over Bobby and Donna and asked Bobby if he was going to put the miner to the metal, winking at Donna. For a reason never completely explained, Fierce continued to speak with the accent. He did say that it made him feel richer, though.

The 1890's couple declined the generous offer from the ghoul several more times before they decided to wander the town some. On their way out the cowboy swinging doors, they were assaulted by Jeff and Melissa dressed as Bobby and Donna. Melissa wore long blonde tresses that sprouted flowers and cascaded over her enhanced bosom, had multiple peace signs hanging from her neck and a mock joint dangling from the corner of her mouth. She wore a flowing, flowery skirt with buckskin fringe wrapped around it. Jeff had judiciously scalped a wig so the top was slightly thinning, the sides and back much fuller than what Bobby could manage in the present day. A full lock of hair, shorn from the wig, had been stretched above his upper lip and around the corners in an exaggeration of what Bobby considered to be his modestly manicured moustache. An especially neon bright Hawaiian shirt dropped loosely beyond the crotch of faded blue jeans that scrunched around his running shoes. If Jeff had worn a red ball on his nose, Bobby thought, he would have looked more like Bozo the Clown. As it was, there was a faint resemblance, Bobby acknowledged. Donna hugged Melissa, asking her why she hadn't come in costume.

After a brief conversation, the four journeyed to the Hotel Jerome, masquerading as the before and further before versions of Bobby and Donna before the present incarnation. They weren't the only escapade artists out that night that had chosen miners and hippies as their themes. But they were the only ones that immediately recognized

225

John and Becky Hamlin's costumes for what they were without any explanation.

When the foursome entered the lobby of the Hotel Jerome, Aspen's most historic, appreciated and famous hotel, they practically bumped into Bobby and Donna, again. John was dressed as a miner with a silver shovel in his hand. On his head he wore a short flat top hat. Situated on the hat was a miniature replica of Bobby's house on stilts. On the front of it was a "Sold" sign. Becky was draped in hippie chick chic. She managed to appear braless while wearing a push-up and not enough makeup to disguise the fact she was still heavily made up. The real estate moguls were regaling friends whose costumes chiefly consisted of masks held to their faces with dainty little sticks.

Melissa and Becky hadn't seen one another since Becky had fired Melissa or Melissa had quit on Becky. It depended upon who was relating the story to whom. When Becky spoke with other real estate companies, Melissa had quit in a snit. When Becky lectured her own employees, of course, Melissa had been fired and let that be a lesson to anyone else considering insubordination. Melissa had committed to the actual version that she quit before she could be fired. The two women just stared at each other until Becky broke the spell by realizing that Bobby was standing nearby. She noted his costume and the woman that stood next to him wrapped in silver. Becky turned to John, whose mouth was agape while his hands reached for his hat.

Donna walked toward Becky, introduced herself, and said, "I take it you are dressed as me. In fact, Melissa here is much closer to the truth from those days."

Bobby quickly slid next to her side and reintroduced Donna to John, while Jeff and Melissa looked on. Donna nodded to John and addressed Becky again.

226

"Nonetheless, I am flattered that you would want to emulate me and," as she nodded toward John, "I'm happy for you, in that you get to hang out with a version of Bobby."

Bobby peered at John, who now held the hat in his hands and suffered a sheepish smile on his face. John shrugged his shoulders, extended the hat with one hand and said, "It was just a joke, Bobby."

Bobby snatched the hat from John's hand and all parties braced in alarm. Bobby rubbed a finger across his own forehead, staining it with dark polish, and spread it over the word "Sold" on the replica of his house. He handed it back to John. "In the interests of accuracy," remarked Bobby, with a tip of his miner's light.

As the four of them walked by John, Becky and their stunned group of friends, Jeff said, "Oh, and by the way, Melissa quit House and Home and is the best employee I've ever had." Melissa and Donna flashed the peace sign to them all and the foursome proceeded to the bar. Bobby was the last to pass and leaned over to Becky's ear to whisper, "I thought for sure that you would be trolling in your trollop outfit tonight."

Becky jumped at the reminder of her costume that caught John attempting to cheat on her at the Halloween ball just before they became married. She glanced hurriedly at John to see if he had overheard. Apparently, he had not, and she briefly revisited her visit to Bobby at his house only a few weeks earlier. She knew that Bobby's comment was intended to also remind her of the visit she had made to his house several days after the discovery of John's planned unfaithfulness years before. She had been rebuffed then, as well. These memories didn't sit well with her self image and she resolved that, after the visit years before and the reprise weeks earlier, the third time would be the charm.

Why it was that people said the third time held charms and changes would continue to remain a mystery to anyone who wondered about it. Sometimes it did and sometimes it didn't, much like everything else in life. That's the way God had planned it. Enough confusion and lack of surety to keep things interesting without convincing anyone completely that they could figure it all out in only one time around. Maybe it took three times. Maybe more. And Bobby thought that was pretty fair. A creator would want some co-creators with experience.

XXI

Donna Deerfield stayed in Aspen with Bobby Early for a couple more days as a snow storm passed through the Rockies. Now that it was November, it was time to talk Christmas plans. Thanksgiving arrangements had already been made. Bobby had long ago committed to visit his sister Susan in San Francisco. Donna was invited to join him in the City by the Bay, but accepted her own sister Laura's invitation to join her and the nieces with their families in New Orleans.

Donna and Bobby had been discussing an extended visit to test their relationship. Things had gone so well, they both concurred, that it was time to consider not only what they meant to each other, but for each other. "In other words," explained Donna, "Should we understand this to be a long distance love affair, or is it to be where I move here, you move to Denver or we decide we should move somewhere else?"

Bobby really didn't mind this discussion. At earlier times in his life, this sort of talk was preliminary to disaster, but it all felt different with Donna. There was something about the timing. He was making a stand with his house, his belief in the silver, and with love, romance and commitment. There was something about love that was good for his soul and great for his search for God. It moved his passion from indulgence to purposefulness. He liked it. Therefore, he liked Donna, and, therefore, he wanted to continue liking Donna. Why shouldn't they find out if a few weeks were as good as or better than a few days? The more he mused along these logical lines of thought, the more intelligence was woven into emotion and the more the blend became the body of his being.

Bobby was ready to pop the question. "Will you agree with me that we should try between two and four weeks with no escape clause?" There, he had said it.

"No less than two and no more than four?" asked Donna. She gave him an investigative, raised eyebrow look-over that she knew would churn consternation through his nerves.

He shifted in his chair, crossed and uncrossed his legs, all the while never taking his eyes off hers. He stopped moving once he had placed his folded hands underneath his chin and rested his elbows on the table. "Unless you think that is too little or too much."

"This isn't going to work if you are going to be mushy about it."

"I know, you want a strong man. You also want a smart man. I'm not sure that I can be both."

"You just convinced me that you can, sweetheart." He had demonstrated his smarts by knowing what she wanted and his strength by knowing that he would always have to be honest and put forth effort. She was pleased.

After all, she thought, I'm being asked by myself and by Bobby to be both things, too. Bobby had told Donna he was ready to dig. He was going to cut another hole in his floor, this time in his living room. He was going to take pick axes and shovels and buckets and wheelbarrows and move dirt from below his house and deposit it outside through the front door. There was no other door. This was going to take most of the winter, he had told her.

When he first told her of his mole mission, and his intent to abandon the raising of his house, she thought him nuts. The relationship was over, the romance buried deeper than the supposed silver that was driving a stake into her heart. But the more they talked it over the better she understood his thinking. Instead of delaying the project into next spring and waiting for the ground to thaw, he could prove the existence of the silver by then. There were many risks inherent with the raising of the house, the excavation beneath it while it was raised, and then the procedure for a safe and secure setting back down. A new foundation may have to be poured or the old one repaired.

Either course of action, the raising or the tunneling, could be devastating to the house. As of yet, nobody had mentioned the possibility that it could be the same for Bobby. Everybody thought of it and worried about it, but nobody talked about it.

He had agreed to begin the project when Donna moved in for the month of December. That way, she told him, she could ascertain whether he was using safe digging practices. What those were, exactly, neither one of them seemed to know.

***

November was the month to gauge the winter. Strong, heavy storms that dropped a couple feet of snow on the mountains encouraged skiers and snowboarders to book their winter vacations in the ski resorts rather than at Mexican beaches. This looked to be one of those winters. By Thanksgiving, every ski mountain that hoped to be open, was.

This didn't matter much to Donna or Bobby, both being out of the state and experiencing completely different family reunions. Donna was in New Orleans, surrounded by the love of a family busy with rediscovering itself in the wake of the tragic loss of Tad. Cajun Jerk Turkey was Laura's specialty and it was served with a mixture of vegetables and sauces that had been in the family's recipe box since around the time of the Louisiana Purchase. Somebody always said this, nobody believed it and everybody enjoyed it. Fortunately, or not, this meal was served early in the day. Those members of the reunion that didn't retire for naps, or sessions with various indigestion remedies, hopped on a trolley for an afternoon of sightseeing and cocktails. When they returned, football games on television and children clamoring for Aunt Donna's attention were the order of the rest of the day. At seven o'clock in the evening, the adults sat around a table in Laura's kitchen taking turns reading from the book entitled "Poems of Tad Johnson". Donna had compiled twenty-four of Tad's poems that she and Laura considered his best and added a few photographs and select art work from Louisiana and Colorado. Throughout the next few days, before everyone returned from whence they had come, these poems were a part of their days and nights. At first, there was wonderment that none of them had ever seen this talent in Tad. At the end, they were simply grateful that he had written them.

Bobby, meanwhile, had endured a late afternoon Tofu Turkey Thanksgiving, followed by a trolley ride through the streets of San Francisco that resulted in a visit to a transvestite nightclub featuring one of his sister Susan's sons. Susan's other three grown children had attended the dinner out of respect and love for their mother and the opportunity to visit with their vague Uncle Bobby. Bobby had sent checks for birthdays, Christmases and graduations, but he rarely had returned to the Bay Area since moving to Aspen. All of Susan's children were still single and it seemed that this, also, was out of love and respect for their mother. Or, so they joked. Actually, they separately confided to Uncle Bobby, it concerned itself more with Susan's propensity to paint everything and everyone in sight. The oldest son, it was understood, evidenced by his nightclub career, would probably never father or mother. The other three were said to be waiting for Susan to promise she wouldn't paint grandchildren with

232

the same frequency she decorated her own children. That promise was stubbornly withheld. Uncle Bobby was asked to intervene on their behalf. When he asked Susan to relent, she readily did so. She told them all she had only refused to acquiesce to delay their parenting until they were older than she had been when she first became a mother. This appeared to be a reasonable reply and answer from their mother and Bobby was delighted. He told Susan that now she could devote herself to her art career in earnest. She replied, "I don't want to move to Earnest, let's go see the show at the club, instead."

Bobby was accustomed to Susan's affection for puns and word play. It ran in the family, but it also ran out the family. The other children confessed they could skip tonight's performance, saying they were all going out to other clubs in San Francisco looking for mates. Knowing the odds for success in this quest, they all agreed to meet tomorrow for lunch.

The transvestite show was fairly predictable. A sizable portion of the audience was terrifically entertained and, indeed, fell in love with some of the stage performers. A significant number of the attendees were confused and were seen to be continually asking questions of their neighbors in the audience. A small contingent, once they had figured it out, got up and left, murmuring disparaging comments about the weirdness they found to be San Francisco.

Bobby was melancholy on these infrequent journeys to San Francisco. There was so much beauty, mystique and personal history here. Every time he returned it was like he had never left. It was also like he could never come back and see it for anything other than what it had been for him. He still saw the Grateful Dead playing on a flatbed truck in Golden Gate Park, the Summer of Love going up in a puff of smoke and the Vietnam War demonstrations around San

Francisco State. Even on a sunny and clear Thanksgiving weekend he felt the Pacific rain and wrapped himself inside the Presidio fog beneath the sculpted Monterey Cypress trees.

If a hillside in Sonoma County that had been previously populated only by old live oak trees was now completely covered by houses he continued to see only the oaks. He looked right through the roofs and walls and saw the green grass and the wildflowers growing in the winter and spring. He saw the tawny hillsides waving in a summer wind and the dark leaves of the oaks shimmering in the sunlight.

He felt the crush of more people, but he wasn't sure if that was them or him. Otherwise, the Bay Area was like a time capsule for the years before Aspen. When he returned to Aspen, he would notice any slight alteration and instinctively long for the way it used to be. Then, he would adjust, judge for himself whether it was for good or ill, and move on. Just like watching his friends and clientele at The Cebolla Roja move Downvalley, being driven out of a lease he could no longer afford, and just like diving with a shovel into the ground below his house. Bobby Early went ahead and took the next step while still arguing with the last step as he kept hoping the steps were going up.

***

And, so it was, that Bobby and Donna met again at the Denver International Airport after experiencing disparate Thanksgiving celebrations. She was emotional and excited and enthused. He was numb. After they exchanged their stories, Donna was dazed and Bobby effervescent. A little while later they were on even keels and sailing the highways covered in snow that fell while they were in milder climes. They spent the night at Donna's, packed in the morning and began the drive to Aspen. Bobby only returned to Donna's house twice to

234

retrieve forgotten items. At the third request, he balked and promised to buy for her whatever she may have forgotten this time.

Spending a month together clearly meant a month together in Bobby's house- turned- mining operation. Or, as Bobby referred to it, thirty days in the hole. When he first used this expression Donna almost slapped him. Then she remembered that as racy and suggestive as Bobby could be at times, he was never crude.

An agreement had been struck that Bobby would not be working all the time Donna was staying with him. He had a weekly column to write, but he would refrain from accepting bookstore or bar work. Donna had no issues with taking time from her job. She was close to retirement and, with thirty years' loyalty, she was encouraged to go off and enjoy herself. It was especially sweet and romantic for her co-workers to think that Donna may have finally found the love of her life. The more she informed them of Bobby's silver the less excited they were, so she neglected to mention that he was beginning his dig soon. The owner and senior partner, in turn, failed to tell Donna that an offer was on the table for him to sell the company.

Donna and Bobby had shaken hands on matters involving the dig. He would dig only when she was at the house and if he should come to a realization that he had made a mistake he would need to admit it. This would be Bobby Early's Second Great Dig. The First Great Dig yielded Caleb Century's journal. He had spent three months digging through the crawl space below The Cebolla Roja to find the source of the sewer gas smell. Everyone had cautioned him with the considerable fact that, as far back as memory served, the repulsive, offensive, vile odor had existed as an entity of its own.

Previous owners of the building, in conjunction with Bobby, had discussed when the foul aroma was most prevalent. There was a common observation that barometric pressures, wind directions and speeds, and radical temperature fluctuations contributed to the increase and decrease of the nauseating fume. Still, the source remained as elusive as the air it drifted on.

Eventually, though, Bobby Early discovered a rusted and broken metal pipe six feet below where he had begun to dig. The strength of the stench had lured him to the point of putrefaction. It was a plumbing pipe laid in the 1940's that had just missed the proper angle that would have assisted in a continuous and safe flow of by-products best moved along from their current destination.

As he dug fresh dirt that covered up the discovery so the smell would be somewhat confined until he could hire a crew to replace the pipe, he uncovered an old steel box that held the journal. He didn't know this for a few weeks, because in the hurried desperation to find a crew that would contract for the job, he misplaced the box. Finding it again, he pried it open and read the words of Caleb Century, sealed for the last hundred years. All of the coincidences helped to convince him of the veracity of his new, and close to sacred, mission in life.

When Bobby had relayed the story of his First Great Dig to Donna she had almost thrown up. Now, with the Second Great Dig, wafted the sweet aroma of success, the silver sheen and substance of certitude for them both.

The first couple of days in Aspen were spent cross country skiing and sawing a trap door in the living room floor of Bobby's house. The skiing was smooth and the sawing was easy. Bobby kept singing "Summertime" as he contemplated how many electric heaters he would want around him while he dug. He was soon to find out the answer was none.

236

XXII

Bobby filled five gallon plastic buckets with dirt that he carved from the crawl space floor below his house. These were known as "pickle buckets," because restaurants would have their pickles delivered in them. Instead of only plain white, they now also came in designer shades of red and green. This seemed appropriate to Bobby as the Christmas season was rapidly approaching. Whatever he finally settled on for Donna's present could be packed into one of these colored buckets in keeping with the motif of the month.

He used a camp shovel and a short pick axe to dig the top layers of dirt, then scooped it up into the buckets. He placed the buckets on a crate, climbed around it to lift himself back up onto the living room floor, and then pulled the buckets up by the metal carrying handle. The first few days he hauled the buckets outside and dumped the dirt into a pile. Soon, it would be *onto* a pile. It was laborious, tedious and, in a routine, rhythmic way, meditative. He could spend a few hours working like this and feel refreshed.

However, within a week, his shoulders ached and his hands brushed along the ground as he walked bent over. Donna offered to buy him a gorilla costume. He gratefully declined her thoughtful gesture. It was this generous and sensitive nature that daily increased his appreciation for Donna. Also during this first week of hard labor, his back began to stiffen and he developed a crick in his neck. Donna proposed to purchase a used traction hospital bed or a medieval torture rack to help him stretch. Endearing qualities such as these only enhanced his adoration of

237

Donna. When he came up gimp one day she volunteered to shoot him. He told her that his love for her had been transformed into pure reverence.

Daily, through the aches, pains, taunts and warnings, the two old lovebirds discovered that their similarities dwarfed their differences. They revealed thoughts and feelings about themselves that they hadn't known they possessed. Part of the reason for this, of course, was that they both were quite the chatterers. The more extensively one speaks, the possibility increases that something, anything, will be said that is unusual, funny or profound. This law contains a caveat, however. If the same subject is repeated continually and then repeated again, it's possible that this could be construed as boring. It could be also be resented as nagging. Neither one of these developments bode well for a relationship of any kind, particularly one that is defined by romance and longevity. In a word, marriage. Therefore, Donna and Bobby resolved they would continue to change, but that they would change together. It hadn't taken them much time to confuse themselves and each other with this kind of chatter, so they gave in and made love again.

Donna's long blonde hair that wasn't really blonde, but looked great perhaps because of that, fell over her shoulders that supported a classy, black negligee. Her smile revealed her delight in the encounter which was to come. Her long and shapely legs personified sexy in his mind and, as they stood kissing in the bedroom, there was a heightening of awareness between them.

They didn't make love every day. In fact, their frequency seemed to have settled into a twice-a-week rhythm. Bobby, being a man who hadn't had a girlfriend in quite a while, would probably have been inclined to a greater number of sexually explicit moments. Donna, being the woman she was, reasonably responded to his more or less constant overtures whenever she felt like it. This was not a cruel or calculating maneuver on her part. She explained that when she was emotionally excited the sexually audacious moments always were better for them both. When Bobby began to reply that it didn't necessarily always have to be better, she cut him off. Not in a sexually erotic sense, but in a speaking sense. She simply asked him to think of what he was going to probably say and to consider the many possible rejoinders. Instead of finishing his thought out loud, Bobby advanced his opinion that when it came to sex, as with so many other things in a worthwhile life, quality always trumped quantity. In fact, Bobby continued, that's how Donald Trumped had taken his name.

"You mean Donald Trump."

"Oh, no," responded Bobby. "There was a fellow a few years back who was charged with building casinos at a faster rate than he could launder the money. His defense was that he was only attempting to emulate his hero, the real Donald Trump. Because his buildings were so poorly designed and built, they were often condemned before he was granted a Certificate of Occupancy. By the time he was sentenced, he had legally changed his name to Donald Trumped."

"Because the quality was so bad?"

"No, he claimed that the bad quality resulted only from too much quantity. Therefore the quantity had been trumped by the quality."

"You know, I don't believe a word of this," said Donna.

"I'd say look it up, but he's in the witness protection program."

"A witness to what?" scoffed Donna.

"Excuse me?" Bobby asked as he adopted a haughty pose of suffering a supreme insult. "Casinos?" he stretched out with his voice and arms.

Donna rolled out of bed chuckling so that Bobby couldn't see her. She thought about how she had fallen in love with this man. It was his caring at the hospital, his humor, his unrelenting pursuit of her, his dedication to his dream, his willingness to visit every subject she introduced with his whole brain. He was also polite, charming and very physically attractive to her. She had hit the jackpot.

"Casinos?" attacked Donna. "Those are probably a lot more legitimate than banks are these days. At least you know the odds are against you in a casino and that they are trying to take your money. A bank is singing a jingle of how they are trying to help you while signing you up for a lifetime of interest payments."

Conversations like this reaffirmed to both of them that they were right for each other and right on the issues. One of them could begin a discourse on a subject such as public schools and the other would finish it with a defense of free education for all forever. They had their differences, of course, like any two human beings that consider themselves almost always infallible do. One of these was the use of space heaters in the crawl space. Donna was infallible this time.

The fire had started behind Bobby, when his electric space heater tipped over on top of a newspaper that rested on a woolen blanket. The first question Donna wanted an answer to was, "Why did you have a paper down there, anyway?"

"Well, I can't be slaving away all the time. There are occasions when I need to read an article that ignites some anger so I can dig hard and deep." Bobby clenched his teeth as he added, "I presume you'll have a problem with the use of the word "ignite" in this situation. That, you might even be "fired up" a little bit about it. "Hot under the collar," perhaps."

"Enough." Donna sat in a chair at the kitchen table with a thermal blanket wrapped around the sweater she wore. The front door, the door that was now differentiated from the two *trap* doors, was open. The window in Bobby's bedroom was open. The windows in the kitchen, the bathroom and the living room were all open, facilitating the fans Bobby had placed to help air circulate. He desperately hoped the smell of smoked, burning wool and slightly charred floor joists wouldn't persist much longer. Soon the sun would be sinking. It was almost three o'clock. In another two weeks would be the winter solstice and daylight had become increasingly a precious commodity.

"I'm sorry, sweetheart." Chagrined, Bobby started over. "It was a mistake."

"You could have burned your house down, Bobby." Donna began softly crying. "I could lose your house. I just don't think I could lose you."

Bobby came to her and hugged her. He put his thought about making love on the back burner, but he snickered inside at his use of the term. Donna need never know. This was one of those times when she may be emotionally excited in a different way, one precluding sexual intimacy. In fact, he castigated himself that he could even joke about the subject in his own mind. In penance, he pulled up a chair next to her and tenderly clasped her shoulders. "You know something, Donna? I could lose the house and I could lose the silver, but if I lost you I would be devastated. I've never loved someone so much. I think I love you more than I love myself."

She smiled and wiped at her tears. "You sure do know how to sweet talk a woman."

"Thank you, ma'am."

"So, you'll quit this digging of yours and hire a crew to do the work for you?"

Donna had been pushing this proposal throughout the week, each day with a little more emphasis to match Bobby's escalating soreness. Bobby knew enough out of work Latinos from his days at The Cebolla Roja to form an entire brigade, however many that might be. And that number would be one. One would know five would know ten. The Latino community was close knit, industrious and reliable. Many were illegal and were taken advantage of by unscrupulous employers. Most would undertake tasks that the children of immigrants several generations deceased would not.

There was an undercurrent of racism in the Roaring Fork Valley between the white and Latino populations. Most of the whites had better educations, more connections, longer work histories and legal documents. Many Mexicans had falsified papers, little education, large extended families and spoke mainly Spanish. But when the influx began, the Mexican stayed hired because he showed up and worked hard. She did maid work and he labored in construction. Soon she learned some English and worked in Housekeeping, a fancier name with higher pay. He moved into kitchens and maintenance. The white worker skipped a shift to go skiing or snowboarding or called in hung over. Bobby was the first restaurant owner in Aspen to hire a Latino, a Mexican, as the manager of his kitchen. He did so because everyone else working in the kitchen was Latino and if Carlos didn't show up for his shift, Rueben did. There was always someone there to do the work and to do it well.

The real rub, though, came with the economics shared among Latinos. Many sent substantial amounts of their earnings back home to the families they had left. Working whites wondered if taxes were being paid and wanted the cash to stay in the community, recycling itself back into their pockets.

No health insurance and hospital bills left unpaid were also a cause of friction between the whites and the browns. It was increasingly a common problem for all workers, but initially not owning health insurance was chiefly a concentrated reality among illegal immigrants. At first, white bitterness about paying for others that were unable to be insured had a basis in fact, but eventually it became just another platform for expressions of racism. Insurance rates weren't rising due to the fact of a few bills left in the hands of debt collectors. They were rising so the insurance companies could reap higher profits.

Gradually, many whites and Latinos began working together. Friendships and business relationships were born and sustained. Yet, culturally, at any party, in any school cafeteria, in any large gathering of socially mixed races, the separation between them was as clear as the color of skin. Assimilation took time and to many whites it seemed as if the Latino did not want to take the time. To many Latinos, it appeared the white man thought himself superior and was intent on perpetuating the classifications he had learned so well while denying the black man equality.

This placed Bobby in an enviable position. Though he had utterly ignored the need to learn the Spanish language, he had dutifully paid complete attention to the humanity of Latinos. He was trusted, liked and respected. Hiring a crew of workers to dig out his crawl space would be quick, easy and cheap. But he had made up his mind to do the work himself and he wasn't going to let one little mishap dissuade him. Much of the experience of uncovering the silver would be missed if he didn't fill each shovel and bucket himself. It was a process for him. His blood would be spilled, his spirit would be tested, his body would be wracked and his mind would become confused,

243

but it would be his ingredients and attributes that would be poured out and transformed. Not any one else's. Well, maybe, Donna's, too.

"As you've asked, Donna, and rightfully so, I have thought through the idea and practicality of hiring a crew. Practically speaking, it makes a lot of sense. It would be quicker, easier and cheaper." Donna gazed at him intently, recognizing the cadence of a practiced speech and already knowing where this dialogue was winding. "But I can't do it. This is my karma. I have to go through this and learn it and earn it."

She was proud of him, afraid for him and in love with him. So, she was happy. She decided right then to never mention it again.

"Are you sure?" she said. She couldn't stop herself. "Suppose you hadn't been able to put the fire out? Suppose you had been at the other end of the house and couldn't make your way back to the trap door to escape?"

Bobby looked at her shivering and said, "Please don't take this the wrong way. I'm shutting the front door, closing the windows and starting a fire. In the fireplace."

Donna leapt out of the chair and exclaimed, "I'll do it!"

Bobby started to laugh, but when he realized she was serious, he simply said "Okay" and nodded his head. "While you do that, honey, I'll go back down into the mine and quadruple check everything."

They had begun calling the crawl space "the mine" in a fun and adventurous way, but Bobby could see that now Donna thought of a mine in terms of disaster. There were plenty of them in the history books, folk songs, blues songs, bluegrass songs, newspapers, books and family histories. Cave-ins, blow-ups, floods, fires and secret monsters from the depths all had parts they played. John

Henry, the steel drivin' man, and Bobby Early, the shovelin' achin' man, had that in common.

Donna darted a look at Bobby to see if he was teasing her and making fun of her insistence he make absolutely certain there was nothing smoldering in the crawl space. He seemed to be legitimate. Donna had informed Bobby earlier that she wasn't fond of enclosed places and she had proved it since arriving for her stay. She had spent a total of one minute in the crawl space and had promised to never return. She wasn't about to inspect his inspection and if he concluded that another examination was necessary, then so be it.

Bobby lowered himself into the mine, put on a pair of knee pads and crawled over to where there were a few black marks on two floor joists. It looked as if charcoal had been smudged on them, nothing more. The blanket had already been removed and placed outside in the snow. When he first smelled the fire, he had rushed to the blanket and wrapped the newspaper in it. This wasn't the best reaction. Quickly, the blanket erupted into a ball of flame that he tossed into the trench he had been digging. He covered the blanket with dirt and waited for the heat to dissipate before retrieving it and showing Donna. It was just a foolish accident that had done very little real harm, but the scare it had thrown into Donna was significant. Bobby would have to work without space heaters while she was in town. He had already discovered that they probably weren't necessary, anyway. The heat from his house and the insulation of the dirt kept the temperature about fifty-five degrees Fahrenheit. When he was digging and sliding buckets of dirt around, he had produced enough body heat to perspire prolifically and a space heater would eventually turn his cool, damp crawl space into a sauna.

In a week he had dug out the width of the house, twenty feet, about two and a half feet deep. This trench was almost three feet wide. He had done good work, he thought. In addition to this feat of earth moving, he had skied with Donna, conversed with Donna, spent time with Donna and paid attention to Donna. As she often said, "It's not about me," but it was wise for Bobby to ignore that statement and sentiment. In truth, it wasn't about her, it was about them. Let's face it, they told each other, it would be a pretty lousy love affair if they didn't yearn for one another. And they were selfish enough and generous enough at this stage of their relationship to want to spend their time and energy together. Everywhere except below the floor at Bobby's house. Fortunately, Donna was entirely comfortable grabbing the handle of a bucket with both hands and carrying it outside. During the second week of excavation she began to envision how wide and high this mound of dirt might become. During a rest period, Bobby suggested that there would be many moons and many mounds.

There were inevitable and much appreciated interruptions throughout these first two weeks. Escapades with Jeff and Melissa, walk-byes in front of House and Home, trips Downvalley to the Glenwood Hot Springs Pool and, most welcome of all, visits with the Drs. Corning. Harriet and Donna had become fast friends, while Bobby suddenly found himself sitting on the edge of a seat listening to the elderly gentleman's musings on life. Frailty and weakness may have overtaken his physical condition, but his mental faculties were a source of encouragement and enchantment for Bobby. They spent hours swapping stories, comparing adventures and reliving romances. Donna and Harriet indulged their passion for indoor gardening during the winter and wondered if the men in the other room had any idea that they would occasionally sneak outside to share a puff of pot.

On this matter, Bobby and Harold only skirted the subject. Harriet's increasing loss of memory was a painful topic for Harold. "I know marijuana can affect short-term memory, Bobby, so it's difficult for me to justify her use of it. Then again, this demon dementia is escalating in an exponential manner and what does it matter anyway? Two years ago I was only suspicious about her recall. Within the last six months she's almost become a different person. Soon enough she won't know who I am, so why should I attempt to limit or define what she enjoys today?" Dr. Corning shifted in his chair at his kitchen table. "Bobby, I hope you don't mind me prying, but if you do, I trust you will educate me."

"What is it, Dr.?"

"I notice, at least here with us, you don't seem to be bothered or upset with the women inhaling the cannabis. Do you partake, as well?"

"Why, Dr. Corning, are you asking me if I can wrangle some from the womenfolk?"

Dr. Harold Corning's face flushed and he was flustered into a paralysis of words. Bobby rose from his chair and searched for Donna and Dr. Harriet Corning. The four of them spent the next two hours discussing topics with a volume of jocularity and insight they were unable to recall the following day. That was when Bobby answered Harold's question.

"I very rarely smoke pot and I don't drink often. Besides not remembering, I am always haunted by the sense that I missed something while I was "gone," so to speak. I just feel as if I should be paying attention in case I actually have a purpose."

"Well, if I may say, Bobby Early, I think you have found a dual purpose to life for yourself. You have the lovely, delightful Donna Deerfield to develop a kinship with and you have the silver. Not many in life have such a combined gift from the gods. The Creator saved Donna for you until you were ready and Caleb Century stored the silver for you until you needed it. You have two gardens growing. Be careful how you reap them."

Harold added that, though he didn't remember many details of his period of "stoniness," he felt the smoking of marijuana with his sister had allowed him a window into her vague states of mind. And into her clouds of happiness, as well.

XXIII

Donna and Bobby had spent three weeks together. It had been almost perfect and close to flawless. Seamless had been their mornings and nights. It was a few days before Christmas and they had both agreed to push their relationship beyond the original boundary. Donna would stay through New Year's Eve.

The holiday season in Aspen was a spectacle featuring public and private displays of affection and wealth. The airport parking problems extended beyond the car lots and limousine stands to the rows of corporate jets and sovereign aircraft. The town's streets, alleys, malls, slopes, stores, restaurants and clubs were busy, had just been busy or were going to become busy. The scene was set for paparazzi, celebrity sightings, scandals and lawsuits. Before the explosion of vast and insatiable markets, famous actors and musicians could come to Aspen and be treated as second-class citizens. Waiting for a drink at the bar might have taken a little longer if one were obviously well-known, just to prove the point that celebrity status alone didn't insure cutting in line. There was a point where Bobby had to warn his bartenders not to deliberately ignore the notorious and forget the famous for the sole reason of demonstrating they didn't play favorites.

There had been a time when John Wayne, Dick Van Dyke or George Harrison would pose with a waiter whose mom was taking the picture. Now, though celebrities decried the violation of their privacy, many of them posed for the legions of cameras and television entertainment show crews until all that was left were the kids with their cell phones beaming pictures back to their friends. There had been a particularly sad afternoon when what formally was known as a starlet, begged and pleaded for more photo shots. She continued entering and emerging from a clothing store in new, quick-change outfits. Even the school of parasites and would-be extortionists carrying cameras were growing weary of the desperate plea for publicity. One remaining photographer, however, captured the prize picture when the starlet neglected to place her famous hair back on her head before she danced out for a final bone-chilling smile. The photographer made money and the starlet experienced a boost to her career. It made pathetic look respectable.

There was a completely different style of power, wealth and good looks that remained anonymous during this cultural feeding frenzy. Private parties with personal chefs that served invited guests who slipped in and out of homes and airports with nary a notice. Classy clientele that showed appreciation for service and discretion with generous bonuses and thoughtful gifts. These types of people were once welcomed and socialized within the places of business and recreation in downtown Aspen. Now, they were banished to the lavish homes on the surrounding mountains. They could use the night life of Aspen primarily as only a backdrop for their outdoor Christmas trees and family photos.

Unless, of course, they were Jewish. In that case, there was little to celebrate about Christmas except the time off. Beside the Latino river of racism, anti-Semitism was a quiet current. Bobby had lost friends among people he thought he knew well who, completely unexpectedly, would throw out an off-hand slur or vile slander against a Jew. Actually, it was more against all Jews. Picking out one was never too easy, because by him or her self, there were only the normal complaints people always have with people. It was more like an entire family came into the restaurant and behaved badly. Therefore, they were obnoxious, arrogant, rich Jew bastards. If the same family was from Minnesota, they were never referred to as mouthy, mongrel, money-hound lying Lutherans. The one group that was spared overt racist treatment was the blacks. This was chiefly due to the fact there were, at any one time, no more than twenty-two black people in Aspen. There were twelve who lived there permanently and ten who rotated in and out on the politician-celebrity-professional athlete circuit. As a curiosity, the black resident was accepted as white with a darker shade of skin. It was bizarre behavior and not many blacks could take it for very long.

Bobby assumed that racism had its beginnings historically when the first group took some of the second group's stuff and wouldn't give it back. Resentment evolved into hatred and hard feelings into killing. Kids grow up in an atmosphere of prejudice and the only way to transcend it is to associate with those they hate, thereby getting to know them. That doesn't happen very often. Instead, the evil force that thrives in the darkness of ignorance and selfishness drinks this up, bloats and burps out more venom to suck into itself. These giants of fallen grace prey on fear and feed greed. They won't vanish into extermination until the Jews lay down with the Lutherans. Or the Semites with the anti-Semites. Or the hippies with the Wall Street investment bankers. Or the skier with the snowboarder, both of them riding on nature's gift with the same spirit of adventure and appreciation for beauty.

In fact, the snow riders had made peace and now shared the mountains. There was hope for mankind, after all. It remained to be seen if Bobby Early would lay down with John Hamlin and Joe Don Burke. In the realm of world peace, this would have to happen, but in the neighborhoods of Aspen, Colorado, it was unlikely.

251

***

On the night before the night before Christmas, all over the town there was a party going on. Credit card machines hummed, reservations were filled and streets were slick from sleighs on snow. In the Aspen Elk Estates, the flakes were still falling and their spirits buoyant and bright when Donna and Bobby returned from dinner with the Drs. Corning.

Earlier in the afternoon, Joe Don Burke had been seen treading through the snow on his lot and Harriet had walked over to greet him. She had wrapped herself warmly and had pulled a knit cap over her ears and halfway down her eyes. She kept her vision focused on the ground as she shuffled across the icy street and then directly toward Joe Don. There were a couple of feet of snow on the ground, but she tried to place her boots in Joe Don's steps so she didn't find herself stuck.

"Who are you?" asked Harriet. She had forgotten for a moment where she was and what she was doing there.

"See, it's Joe Don Burke. Soon to be your neighbor. Aren't you Harriet Corning?"

Harriet lifted the cap above her eyes and squinted through the lightly falling snow at the man with the voice. She faintly recalled a foggy picture of this man from somewhere, but the opaqueness of muddied memory forced her to shake her head. This resulted in Joe Don thinking the trespasser was not his future neighbor.

"Well, then get the hell off my land, old woman. If you're looking for a handout, try over there," Joe Don roared as he pointed to the Corning's house.

Harriet turned and saw the house, remembered it was her house, knew who was yelling at her, bent low, made a snowball and threw it at Joe Don's face. The snow was dry and it flew apart as it approached him. Still, he started to step toward her.

"Leave her alone, Joe Don." It was Bobby Early leaning over his fence and holding a shovel between his hands. He was smiling at the Texan and waving the shovel in a menacing manner. It was difficult for Joe Don to understand to which signal he should give more weight. "Stay right there, both of you. I'll be right over." With that Bobby disappeared behind the fence and reemerged around the corner of it before any further injury was inflicted upon Joe Don by the little old woman. Bobby was covered in dirt and still carried the shovel.

"Whoa there, big fella," said the Texan as he backpedaled, just missing Harriet.

"Oh, don't worry about me, Joe Don. Just doing some excavation work, thanks to the permit you so kindly helped me obtain." Bobby came along side of Joe Don and Harriet and gently put his arm around the elderly professor. "Let me take you back home, Harriet."

"But I thought she was just an old woman," apologized Joe Don.

"She is an old woman, Joe Don. Otherwise she would have squeezed that snowball a little harder."

Harriet stomped a foot and pulled her knit hat from her head. "I know who you are," she accused, as she pointed the hat at Joe Don. "Fuck you!"

"Hey, see here. I'm hopin' to be a good neighbor."

"You're trying to run this nice young man out of his house and home. You're driving him to dig down to China for treasure. Why don't you just move back to Texas where ya'll make each other miserable together?"

Joe Don removed his cowboy hat and for the first time since Bobby had met him looked like an actual human being and not a caricature. "Shit, why does everybody hate us Texans? It's not like we are from New York."

Bobby couldn't argue with that logic, so he escorted sweet Dr. Harriet Corning back across the street, where he accepted Dr. Harold Corning's thanks and an invitation for him and Donna to join them for dinner tonight. He returned to a befuddled Joe Don pretending to brush snow off his suede leather coat. He explained to the oil and gas magnate that Harriet was suffering from early onset Alzheimer's and that she had become quite unpredictably profane. He also invited Joe Don to see the mound of dirt he and Donna had been building. Joe Don declined, but expressed a desire to perhaps drop by sometime after Christmas with his good friend and business partner, John Hamlin.

Bobby returned to the house and was met by Donna on the front porch. Together, they admired the mound of dirt they had been building.

"I guess this is inevitable if the dirt below your house is lessening," observed Donna.

A film of snow covered the sides of the mound, but the top, where the sun had glimmered the snow into what Bobby called "glistens," was now a mix of brown and red sparkles. "It's a beautiful sight, isn't it?" he asked.

"Sweetie, I only wish this didn't need be accomplished with your back-breaking labor." Donna put an arm around his waist and he flinched. She had touched the precise location where he had tripped and fallen on a shovel two days earlier. There really weren't many spots on his body that hadn't been bruised or twisted in the almost three weeks of excavation, but, to Bobby, they were badges of dedication and bruises of progress.

Indeed, the trench was now fifteen feet across and four feet deep. According to his calculations derived from Caleb Century's journal, he would find the silver at a depth of six feet below the surface. He was given a head start in his digging by the crawl space already being three feet below his flooring. His house sat a foot above the ground, so he had dug the requisite six feet by only having to shovel out the four feet of crawl space dirt. Mathematics, kept to simple addition and subtraction, had proven to be a field of expertise for Bobby.

He had managed to compute the inevitability of his Cebolla Roja stewardship sailing into a whirlpool from which he, and possibly the restaurant itself, would never emerge. He had put the figures on graph paper. He marked lines going up and coming down. He added, subtracted and got out before he was broke. He accomplished this by subtracting a fluctuating quantity from his total sums. That portion was love.

Having proven himself a realist, a romantic and an accurate accountant he was quite confident of the depth he needed to dig and the depths of his feelings for Donna. As they sat in front of the fire after returning from dinner at the Drs. Corning, Bobby reminded Donna of his early infatuation with her and spoke of his complete appreciation for all he had discovered about her. She was no longer surprised that in these most endearing moments Bobby had often chosen the oddest music to be playing in the background. Tonight, it was Phil Ochs who serenaded them. The songs were a mix of protest from the 1960's and seductive ballads romancing death. She recalled one time when she thought he might propose marriage to her while the Kingston Trio sang of whaling adventures. She was fairly certain that the Kingston Trio, in whatever incarnation, had never gone whaling, and, in fact, would probably be singing save the whales songs these days.

The Drs. Corning had become, very quickly, great friends and influences upon Donna and Bobby. As they went to bed the talk still circled around tonight's dinner hosts. Harold was concerned about Bobby's plan for removing the silver and Donna was worried about Harriet's health. Harriet wondered if she ran Joe Don over with her car how long it would take for her to forget it. Bobby was

255

preoccupied with Harold's questions for which Bobby didn't have answers.

When Bobby stopped to think about his plans, he invariably confused himself. It was an experience first time novelists encountered. Sometimes it was best just to go with instinct and look back later. He needed to keep his work, plan and goal simple. He had both Donna and the mine in mind.

***

The next morning, Christmas Eve Day, Donna and Bobby went their separate ways to finish their shopping. Actually, for Bobby, this entailed only stopping by the store to pick up and pay for Donna's gift. Donna had developed into a compulsive shopper during her stay in Aspen. She bought nothing, but she certainly shopped. She explained to the retail managers where they had gone wrong in pricing their clothes, accessories and art. In the process, she had failed to purchase anything for Bobby and now was in the classic panic mode of last-minute buyers. Some people thrived on the pressure inherent with this situation. Donna wasn't sure whether she was one of them. After all, Christmas shopping required giving something, anything, for Christmas. Not the day after. Otherwise, why bother before Christmas? She knew Bobby had said all he wanted was her love, but that's what lovers said, even when they meant it.

Now, of course, with the shopper at their mercy, the shops were merciless. The beautiful young blondes with impressive jewelry were given precedence over all others. Second, were the celebrity males who were buying for their seasonal arm adornments. Last and least were the shoppers who, when asked if they needed any help, replied, "No thanks, I'm just looking." Donna rarely made it past the "No thanks" portion of her answer before the inquirer was off in search for a more helpless shopper.

Christmas Eve Day was the day shopping became a professional sport. Many shoppers had seen professional athletes on TV come to the sidelines for a quick break and take a gulp of a refreshing beverage, so they followed the exemplary example. The bars were packed.

Donna finally walked into The Cebolla Roja in desperation for a drink and an idea. She had forced open the cowboy swinging doors to enter because a couple of short women in long fur coats and cowgirl hats wouldn't budge. She was not in a Christmassy mood at the moment. Fortunately, Fierce Pierce noticed her, recognized the look and had a glass of chardonnay waiting for her at the far end of the bar by the time she had shoved her way there.

"Thanks, Fierce. I needed that."

"You haven't even had a sip yet," laughed the bartender.

"No, I mean the pushing people around part."

Fierce laughed again, excused himself and hurried off to service hand-waving patrons with credit cards and cash flashing through their fingers. Donna left a ten dollar bill on the bar beneath a salt shaker and turned around to see if there was any room to find solace. Jeff came elbowing his way through the cowboy swinging doors that bordered the stairs going up to his office, saw Donna and motioned to her to follow.

Inside Jeff's office, they sat down and Donna mapped out her dilemma to Jeff. As he pondered her unfortunate situation, he poured himself a vodka and cranberry juice. From a small reach-in refrigerator where he found the juice, he also produced a bottle of slightly more expensive chardonnay than Donna was presently consuming.

"Are you seriously serious about Bobby?" Jeff knew she was, but he needed to hear her phrase her response.

257

"I've never been more in love or more certain of anything in my life. Everything is a chance and a risk, as you know, Jeff, but I'd gamble it all on the sure thing that is our destiny of being together." Donna lowered her head and a tear came to her eye. "I mean, how lucky, how blessed can we be to have found each other at this time in our lives? And to find each other how we did?" She swept her cheek with a sleeve. "You can call it whatever you like. God, luck, fate, random bumping of entities floating in time and space or sheer accident. Actually, I guess those last two options are the same."

"I call it beautiful and inspirational destiny driven by a universe we have very little clue about." Jeff leaned back in his chair, pulled his center drawer out toward him and lifted up an envelope. "I have an idea what you might give Bobby for a Christmas present. It'll cost you, though." He opened the envelope and presented her two tickets for the Colorado Rockies baseball games at Coors Field. "These are my season tickets that I will never use and nobody knows I even have, except, Melissa, of course. She can't stand baseball."

"Jeff, I don't intend to hurt your feelings and I hope I'm not, but I can't accept these."

"You aren't paying full price, Donna, and you're doing me a favor."

"You don't quite understand, Jeff. I really don't like baseball all that much and I don't want Bobby planning his summers around going to the ballpark. I've got some plans of my own. Traveling around the Rocky Mountains, kayaking and hiking sound better to me than the Rockies baseball team. No offense."

"Before you say no, let me add something to your knowledge of Bobby and baseball. There is hardly anything more enjoyable for Bobby than giving baseball tickets away to kids. When he owned this place, he gave away

258

fifty tickets for every two he kept. Almost every pair of those tickets went to kids who otherwise would never get to a game. It's one of his dreams."

"The gift that keeps on giving?"

"Yep."

"Donna opened her purse and asked, "How much?"

XXIV

Christmas morning had arrived with a thunder boomer from an avalanche crew on the back of Aspen Mountain. Crews deliberately set off controlled slides to avoid the accidental, though predictable, ones that might wipe people and houses off the slopes and bring out the search and rescue teams. Christmas morning was better with a man-made disaster rather than a natural one. It seemed odd, perhaps, in context, but the same feeling was prominent around Easter.

Following the after shocks of smaller avalanche bombs, Donna and Bobby resigned themselves to not sleeping in. Hot coffee, pastries and juice, some Gregorian chants on the turntable, showers, changing of the music to Tony Bennett and they were out the door and up the mountain for some skiing. Donna didn't enjoy downhill skiing very much due to the altitude. One would think she referred to the height and distance from the top to the bottom of the mountain, but she actually was quite uncomfortable on the lifts that gave the skiers a ride uphill. Aspen Mountain had a gondola that was enclosed and speedy, but she could still look down. Bobby tried to correlate her fear of enclosed spaces, such as beneath his house, with her dread of heights. To him, it seemed heights meant an abundance of space, therefore she should relish them. Donna simply replied that this wasn't so and he just let it go.

Nonetheless, once on the snow, Donna's day was glorious. She could still ski well, if a bit slower than in her more youthful period, and certainly exhibited more style and grace than Bobby. He continued to think that pointing the skies downhill and executing as few turns as possible was the most exhilarating and enjoyable experience. And it was. Until he fell. It was inevitable, an inexorable intersection in a day's skiing for Bobby Early. Usually, the crash entailed the loss of at least one ski and the acquisition of two sprains. However, today was special and he stayed skiing with Donna for three runs, top to bottom, before they walked back to the house, carrying their skies and clomping their boots.

They changed into casual clothing and lit a small fire. It was time to exchange presents. Bobby went first, because he was scared, terrified and delirious with anticipation. He went below the floor to the mine and brought up a package the size of an apple box. When Donna unwrapped it, she saw that it *was* an apple box. With help from Bobby, she lifted the top of the box off and discovered another wrapped box inside. Unwrapped, this box indicated it was from the newspaper where Bobby contributed a weekly column. She opened it to find yet another box. At this point, Donna offered Bobby a long look and Bobby prayed that he hadn't gone too far with too many boxes and the present itself.

Donna peeled the paper away from this box, which indicated it was a book from the bookstore where Bobby sometimes, occasionally, every great now and then, worked a four hour shift. It appeared to hold a coffee table collector's size tome on the history of silver mining in the Roaring Fork Valley, starring Aspen in the late nineteenth century. It certainly weighed enough to be a heavy book. As she opened the box, however, she discovered only shredded paper, beneath which she finally came upon two small bars of silver. She was confused and perplexed. Money? No matter how much she wished for Bobby's success finding the silver, how could he think that her love, even scarcely, could include the silver itself?

"They're fake. Keep shuffling the paper," Bobby urged, noticing her disconcerted, even puzzled and embarrassed, countenance. Finally, her fingers came upon a plastic ball, red on one side and green on the other. She shook it, it made no noise and she pried the lip open. Inside was cotton and inside the cotton was a silver ring inlaid with beautiful turquoise. Donna held the ring between the fingers of both hands, rotated it every way possible and stared at Bobby.

"Will you marry me?"

Donna handed him the ring, whispering, "If it fits, I will."

Bobby slipped the ring on her finger effortlessly. "Did you think I was going to take the chance that it wouldn't fit?"

So, Bobby Early gave Donna Deerfield an engagement ring for Christmas and she gave him the answer ,"Yes". Of course, she also presented him with two season tickets to the Colorado Rockies, but only on two conditions. The first was that she didn't have to go along, but would if she truly wanted. The second was that he had to enact his fantasy of giving tickets to children.

They didn't even bother ruminating over the fact they'd known each other four months, they lived in different towns, had never tried this marriage thing before, were both at obviously critical decision points in their lives and had no concept of the contents of each other's bank accounts, or lack thereof.

These minor details just didn't matter. At least, not with any more value than that he ate steak and she didn't. Inherently, they understood the universe had brought them here at this time and space to be together. It was entirely their decision and their effort that would make this another whistle stop or two trains running in the same direction until the tracks fell off the ends of the earth.

***

The week between Christmas and New Year's Eve is the busiest period of the year in many places and Aspen doesn't appreciate being left behind in these sorts of contests. The happy newly engaged older couple rarely went into town during these hectic days and "sardined" nights. This was how Bobby referred to the sensation of squirming and sliding through crowds and it had now become how Donna spoke of any experience relating to the crawl space or the mountain gondola.

One sunny afternoon, after they had returned from cross country skiing throughout a local wetlands area that was conveniently covered in snow, Joe Don Burke and John Hamlin knocked on Bobby's front door. Donna hollered for the knocker to wait for a moment while she dumped a bucket of dirt into the wheelbarrow. Joe Don and John stood transfixed at the sight of Donna and the dirt, the floor and the dirt and Bobby's head poking up from the crawl space, covered in dirt.

Soon, they were all outside admiring the mounds of dirt that had been fashioned, though the visitors were not pleased to receive the news that Bobby had no intention of removing the dirt until it was time to return it to its rightful home, which was below his own. The arguments advanced that property values would be lessened by this decorative display were laughed off by an offended Bobby Early.

"In the first place," thundered Bobby, "The value of living here couldn't be lowered any further than by these obscene castles with driveways for moats that you have built surrounding me. Oh, excuse me, Joe Don, you haven't completed the encirclement, but you will. In the second place, this dirt is mine and if I want to move it from one spot on my land to another, so it shall be. It's got my name on it, it's got my blood on it," here Bobby held up a pinky finger that sported the slightest trace of the most minor cut,

263

"And, it has the labor of the lovely Donna Deerfield, soon to be the beloved wife of yours truly, all over these tire tracks leading in and out of this house."

"Obviously you're a bit agitated today, Bobby, so, perhaps, we'll call ahead first, next time, later this week, hopefully." Clearly, John Hamlin had been surprised at the level of Bobby's adrenaline and was experiencing difficulty formulating his sentence, but he recovered in time to add, "However, I speak for Becky as well, I'm sure, in offering you both congratulations on this welcome announcement."

Joe Don extended his hand to Bobby and propounded, "I know the little missus sure made me a changed man, and by the Lord God that hovers over the Lone Star State shining his light on Mexican, Anglo and Jew alike, I'm as sure as an oil spill that matrimony has saved my sorry ass!"

Donna couldn't help but laugh and offered, "Well, thanks so much for the glowing testimony, though I may never use the word "matrimony" in my life again, and also, of course, for the congratulations."

"Yep, see ya' later," drawled Bobby. Donna shot him a cautioning glance, but after the visitors had departed, the happy couple redoubled their efforts.

***

New Year's Eve was the most hideous night of the year. Feigned romance, expensive dinners that consumed more time than nutrition, a song that few understood past the first line, inevitable and embarrassing lapses of memory and good taste and a colossal mess in and out of doors. In addition, the world apparently stopped for a couple of minutes at midnight around the globe and people kissed or wanted to be kissed by other people they didn't know and didn't want to know.

Nonetheless, inside any artificially beautiful and glamorous affair, there exists a semblance of integrity. In this evening, it resided in the magnificent fireworks. On the Fourth of July, America was proud to celebrate with Made in China sparklers and explosives, and the City of Aspen was no exception when it came to providing a showering of sparks amid constellations of colors inaugurating the little baby new year.

Unfortunately, this year, the City budget had been accidentally stripped of discretionary funds that normally financed the show. Seemingly, these unguarded funds had been exhausted by the City Council's November excursion to Switzerland to discuss whether a three lane highway into town was really feasible.

Heroically, and unabashedly publicly, House and Home had graciously, generously, selflessly, stepped up to the fireworks howitzers that were snuggled into the snow barricades built on Aspen Mountain, and had filled them with a cosmically unchallenged collection of noise and spectrum expanding shoot-'em-offs and blow-'em ups that were guaranteed to kill the old year and imbue the new with a little vigor.

Of course, John Hamlin had solicited the money to bankroll this largess from his high-rolling real estate clients by promising them the first opportunity at his Next Big Thing. He recognized them in a full page ad New Year's Day, perhaps the slowest news day of the year, in small print at the bottom of an otherwise garish promotion of House and Home.

Bobby and Donna enjoyed the fireworks from the front porch of the house, wrapped together in blankets, though the mounds of dirt were in the way of a few of the duds.

***

Donna drove back to Denver on the second morning of January and went to work the following day. She was told then that the business for which she had worked for thirty years had been bought by a conglomerate that nobody who worked in the agency had ever heard of. The agency in Denver was one of sixty-two nationwide that had enjoyed and survived as a loose-knit and usually profitable company. The absorption was an unfriendly takeover unless one happened to be a friend of the conglomerate. Heading the conglomerate was John Hamlin's older brother, Paul.

John had always been in Paul's money tree shadow and it was common knowledge among John's clients that Paul might be reached through John's address. John resented this, had lived with this second-best status all his life, and had finally accepted that Paul was ruthless and that he was only greedy.

Neither Donna nor Bobby had any previous awareness of Paul Hamlin and it was just as well they hadn't. Paul was a plague and if one heard his name it most often indicated the end. Quick research revealed that Paul and his minions sucked up companies and corporations, eviscerated them, bled them to the bone, carved them to the skeleton and then vanished into the vacuum of off-shore accounts. Bobby said he could see the scribbling on the wall. Donna replied that she could not only see the wall, she could see outlines of the unemployment applications, short-sells and foreclosures surrounding her friends and fellow employees as they walked by her. A couple of years, but most likely months, were all they had to scramble away from the sinking ship, the plunging plane that was their former family travel company. The alarm had sounded and the captain had jumped ship with his parachute, leaving Donna to launch the lifeboats.

* * *

January grew colder. It seemed to Bobby that the ground grew harder. Bobby concluded that four feet down, the dirt would be more compacted due to the mere and shear weight of the former dirt that had been above, now removed. This went along with his theory that the earth is becoming bigger and heavier because of the increasing amount of debris that is deposited century after millennia.

A short while after Donna ran into her wall at work, Bobby struck stone in his mine. The first clang of metal on rock sounded and felt like shovel on silver. Alas, though he hadn't found what he was looking for, he was now looking at what he had found. Much the same, he mused, as when he went to the hospital to visit Tad Johnson a few months past and found Donna. He was staring at limestone and as he navigated his shovel he searched for a border, a drop back into dirt, an end to the stone.

The second day the exploration continued he became concerned about the size of the stone he was trying to uncover. It began only a foot below the dirt floor and it went almost wall to wall. He had excavated about fifteen feet from the front of the house, four feet deep and almost the full twenty feet of the width of the house. Donna's help had been invaluable. In fact, he told her he couldn't pay her. Yet.

There remained twenty-five feet to the end of the house. He was leaving a foot and a half near the foundation walls as a possible last recourse to search if these final twenty-five feet didn't produce the result he sought. Now, however, he had dug into what was beginning to take on all the appearances of a boulder. He had always mined from the center of the floor east then west then east. On the west side the rock continued and on the east it seemed to stop three or four feet from the wall. There was no answer to the question as to how deep it went.

The bright side of this dark discovery was that he didn't have to dig rock, just around it. The scary part was that it took up precious real estate that precluded the existence of the silver. Finally, he removed the dirt from the perimeter of the boulder. It rested, still buried below the three feet that Bobby was able to clear away from dirt, about eight feet into the twenty-five he had had left to dig.

Donna was actually quite enthusiastic to hear about Bobby's boulder, for it meant that he would have to spend less time beneath the house while she wasn't there. He didn't tell her how the house occasionally creaked and shifted back and forth in heavy winds. It had probably always done that, he told himself.

***

He also didn't mention that Becky Hamlin had paid him another visit. This would have been the "third time is the charm" visit. Becky had stopped by to assure Bobby that John Hamlin had taken no offense to Bobby's comments about land values having diminished by high end development. She had arrived in her black SUV with opaque windows. She inquired whether Bobby had reconsidered her offer for the roll in the hay, adding that it wasn't a standing offer, but a laying one. She opened the back door of the SUV.

"By golly," said Bobby, "There's a roll of hay."

Becky looked seductively pleased with herself, put her hands on Bobby's pants' pockets and pulled herself closer to him. "I'm taking it to the horses, but we could test it out first."

"I'm glad I caught you during your warm-up act, because now that you're a professional, you're lethal. You'll be the death of poor rich John Hamlin some day." Bobby smiled at her and said, "Oh, what the hay. Hop on in, Becky." She did and Bobby closed the door to the SUV, turned and went into his house and back to work.

He never heard his front door open, but he heard the trap door shut. He heard what he figured was the couch being pulled over the trap door and he heard the front door slam. That was it, until the next morning when he woke up to the sound of the couch being dragged away from the trap door. Bobby pushed the door open from below and first smelled a faint aroma he remembered from the previous afternoon. Clearly, his former heartthrob had been the despicable damsel. His rescuers were readily identifiable, as well. Resting on the couch from the exertion they had expended were the Drs. Corning.

After a shower, Bobby called Donna and explained his unavailability. He then walked to the Corning's house, enjoyed toast and tea and spent the rest of the day chatting plants with Harriet and the universe with Harold.

Bobby decided to take the day off from mining. God had rested on the seventh day, whether it was actually seven days or three billion years. Bobby figured it was all the same to God and if taking a period of rest was good enough for God, it should be good enough for Bobby.

XXV

The obvious question that Donna couldn't help from asking Bobby was, "Why didn't you use the other trap door, the one in your closet?" He had to admit that through his own negligence, a sump pump was blocking access to opening the door from above or below. Plumber friends had been out the day before and pumped the standing water from the crawl space that had not been sucked down by mother earth. In fact, so little had evaporated or vanished from the surface that it was becoming an item of concern. Bobby stated that he would move the earth for Donna, but he had never said anything about mud.

The sump pumpers had returned and, to Bobby's delight, had announced that the water seemed to have practically disappeared overnight. Upon his own investigation, he agreed and he prepared to begin excavating the area between the boulder and the back of his house. By February, he was half way there and the dirt floor had completely dried. Working alone, with no impending deadline, Bobby had grown even more methodical and deliberate about his task.

Admittedly, doubt had begun to sneak in on him. With only a ten foot wide swath of dirt remaining, the possibility that the silver wasn't where he thought it was loomed larger every day. He was aggressive and edgy at these times, arguing out loud with himself and accusing the doubting Bobby of crimes near treason. Donna had noticed the impatience in his voice and reasoned that it was time for a visit.

When she arrived he was uncommunicative, which she had experienced before, but he was also sullen. The weather had been cold and gray and there had not been much snow. Between his time in the mine and the mood of the climate, the atmosphere was slightly charged with an underlying tension. Donna was happy knowing that dynamite wasn't an option for the excavation operation.

She convinced him to get outside and walk, then ski, and then not dig for three consecutive days. She also didn't let him talk about the silver, about the dig, the Hamlins or Joe Don. They spent time with the Drs. Corning, indulged in a few meals at The Cebolla Roja and embarked on a snowmobile adventure one afternoon.

Donna detested the noisy machines from afar and, up close, she grew to loath them. They insured that animals and birds would disappear from observation. A chief reason to wander away in the woods in the middle of winter, then, had been surrendered. It didn't cheer her when they became stuck in a drift part way up Independence Pass and needed to be helped. Bobby had followed tracks through woods and meadows before he had slipped off the trail and overcorrected in his attempt to veer the machine away from a swale. Fortunately, the snowmobile came equipped with rescue equipment, which meant a shovel and set of flares. Donna reminded him that he had established himself recently as an expert in the art of digging, as she encouraged him to scoop a clearing away so they could swivel the machine around and escape. Luckily, Bobby wasn't able to express his gratitude for her support before the monstrous roar of snowmobiles ridden by fur-capped racers drowned him out. The dim, grating sound had begun before she began and by the time she was done with her sentence, six machines had burst through the forest and into the meadow's vale where the machine was stuck.

The fur caps gave the group away as being from out of the area. They were three men and three women from southern California, very friendly in helping Bobby and

271

Donna get the snowmobile turned around and back on track for a safe ride home. It was only as they were leaving that they inquired of Bobby and Donna's place of origin. As Bobby became more specific, the rescuers responded less favorably. The last revelation Bobby or Donna expected was that these fine and fun people were also residents of Aspen Elk Estates.

"So, you're the holdout, eh?" asked the biggest character in a fur cap.

"So, you're the part-time visitors who own huge houses that nobody lives in nine months of the year, eh?" asked Bobby in return.

"We pay our taxes," sneered a petite blonde whose cap perfectly matched her sienna streaked hair.

At this point, Donna stepped forward to proffer peace. "Just a moment ago we were all involved in the same endeavor, which was to help out your fellow human being, and now, because of a small philosophical issue, emotions have gotten the better of us."

"That's easy for you to say, lady," replied another guy in the pack. "It's not a 'small philosophical issue' when it's our property values that are kept down because of some whack-jobs stuck in the '60's."

With that, Donna reached for the snow and screaming, "Here's for Dr. Harriet Corning!", hurled a snowball at her accuser.

The final man of the group pulled out a revolver and shot a bullet at the sky.

"Do you have a permit for that?" asked Bobby kindly.

"Why don't you stop by some time and find out?" He holstered the weapon and motioned to the rest to straddle their machines. "Jeeze, you try to do a good deed these days!" The six riders roared off, scrambling their tracks together so that Bobby would have no clear trail to follow back to the cabin where he was to leave the snowmobile they had rented for the day.

"Do you understand what went wrong here, Bobby?" asked an exasperated Donna.

"Near as I can figure, honey, two things. One, I really should have learned martial arts along the way. I could have disarmed that hombre and tossed his firearm far into the snow. Second, if I was more of a mechanic, I could have disabled their machines and they would be stuck here until we sent out a search party." He stared, almost, but not quite, grinning at Donna. "Actually, though, the most important thing that happened here was that you acted as a peacemaker. It didn't work out, but you did the right thing."

Bobby took her hand and, with the sun behind him, gazed at the light that shone from Donna's face. "If I could paint your picture on the sky, the whole world would look up and smile. There'd be peace on earth, good angels would walk openly with mankind and the music of the spheres would sprinkle down from the clouds as a rain of redemption."

It was pretty hard for Donna, at that moment, to suggest that this was not the answer she had anticipated, so she kissed him, hopped on the snowmobile behind him and they plowed their way across the crisscrossed tracks back to the cabin where they checked the snowmobile back in.

The attendant commented that he had heard there had been an encounter of sorts a few miles back into the glades. He said this with a smile and a tip of his ball cap. Bobby and Donna replied they wouldn't know anything about that with smiles and nods of their heads.

***

Now that Bobby had twisted his way through his crisis of self doubt it was Donna's turn. It would be considered a timely happenstance in the cohabitation of

273

couples if one was up while the other down. That is, if the one who was feeling fine was willing to aid the one who wasn't. Donna had proved her mettle and Bobby would keep the figure eight of spiraling compassion and growth alive.

When they returned to Bobby's house after snowmobiling Donna had a message waiting for her on her cell phone. There would be a change of management at her travel agency and her services would no longer be needed. After thirty years, a phone call from a voice she had never heard before terminated her and her history. Anger was followed by tears and sadness led to depression. Bobby drove his truck behind her VW the next day and she returned to Denver.

There was nothing to discuss in the office of the new boss. He stated the company was moving in a different direction and that Donna should consider herself lucky. When she inquired why that should be the case, he informed her that, apart from the very generous severance package that had already been deposited in her bank account, she was being fired instead of demoted or transferred to another city. The Denver branch would soon be closed entirely and she could file for unemployment insurance.

"But, that's not what I want to do. I'd rather work," offered Donna.

"Well, then go find a job. We'll give you a good reference."

"You don't know me."

The boss held up a disc. "You are right here, Donna Deerfield. Now, who is going to hire a sixty year old travel agency veteran that puts way too much attention on the personal contact instead of letting the computers do the work, I don't know."

Donna rolled up a copy of a local paper, WestWord, and bonked him over the head before she wheeled around in her sneakers and left the office. Bobby had been standing in the waiting area looking through the glass windows.

"Do you think you might know how you could have handled that a little differently?"

Donna started to laugh. "Well, I guess I could have asked him to stand up and then kicked him in the balls, but I didn't have my pointed shoes on." She put her arm in his and said, "Come. Let's go outside where I can tell you how I would like to see your face in a continuous mural across every building in Denver and then throughout the world."

Donna's depression and anger were short-lived. She futilely applied for positions at other travel agencies, not believing she would find employment, nor desiring such. In conversations with Bobby, she decided to spend a couple of months or so catching up on all the things people always say they would love to have time for, but, if given, rarely do. Then, she would decide to stay in Denver or move to Aspen, depending on what she and Bobby did or didn't discover.

***

Bobby dug slowly the following month. Every morning it became a little tougher to get out of bed. Bones, muscles and brain all hurt in a resounding symphony of pain that reverberated from the tip of his shovel, right through him, to the tires on the wheelbarrow. But, he kept on digging, believing, wishing and hoping. There were times he thought Dusty Springfield was singing to him as he worked.

When the Ides of March arrived he was almost to the end of his house. He debated whether he should return to where he began and simply dig another foot or so down all the way across the crawl space, but he knew that was foolhardy. The silver belonged at six foot deep and he had already gone down seven.

To stretch out the agony, anxiety and anticipation, Bobby took to skiing every morning. Before the sun warmed the day too much, the snow was crisp and fast and he skied like he hadn't in years. He took chances through the trees so he would brush against branches and trunks. He tucked on the flats so he would build as much speed as he could before he needed to turn and stop. On the final day of the ski season, when Aspen Mountain closed itself and turned into a mountain of melt and mud for a few weeks, Bobby Early went skiing by himself one last time. The first Sunday in April was already warm and slushy.

It was when he sprayed snow over a couple of conversing onlookers as he skidded to a halt that he renewed his relationship with John Hamlin and Joe Don Burke. Hamlin was sleek and chic in his brand new outfit and Joe Don resembled a slightly burnt oversize marshmallow. His suit was puffy and the falls he had taken had scratched the shoulders and rear end. Bobby was tempted to use his ski pole to poke a hole in the suit and let out Joe Don's hot air.

"Now, see here," began Hamlin, as Bobby lifted his dark goggles atop his helmet.

"Well, I'll be a coyote's bitch if it ain't Bobby Early."

Bobby laughed. "You know, under different circumstances, Joe Don, I might have liked you." He paused and deliberately stoked the corners of his moustache before adding, "No, I guess not. Sorry it took me so long to decide."

"Right back at ya'" retorted Joe Don. "As a matter of record, let it be remembered that the only thing I like about you at this particular point in time is that you'll soon be gone. Speaking of which, this week my bulldozers will be moving the snow off my lot. Sure hope they don't accidentally take down your fence."

John Hamlin skied in between Joe Don and Bobby. He had heard about Bobby's little dust-up with the California contingent and he had begun to think that Bobby may have finally tipped the scales on the side of instability. "It's true, Bobby. Joe Don has all the approval permits and they should be bringing in the backhoes in a few days. I was planning on calling you or stopping by tomorrow."

"I see. Before or after the bulldozers paid their visit?"

John was silent and met Bobby's query with a very faint sheepish smile. Bobby could only detect the upturn on the corners of his lips because he recalled it from the first time Hamlin had informed him Aspen Elk Estates was certified for development.

"I wanted to ask you, Bobby, if you've finished your excavation. I do believe we have an agreement."

"No, I haven't and yes we do."

"See, I sure would like to know when that might be," volunteered Joe Don from behind John.

"Well, Joe Don, I have the feeling that you'll be the first to know." Bobby placed his goggles over his eyes, smiled, kicked his skis and headed down hill.

"Ya' know, John, that sounded a bit ominous to me."

Hamlin bit his lip. If Joe Don wasn't so damn rich and hadn't joined his brother Paul's omnivorous conglomerate he'd tell him to quit whining and shut up. The fat dude had become a burr under his saddle, John thought, and a great relief would come into his life when he was completely finished with Aspen Elk Estates. Between the southern Californians, Texans, New Yorkers and a few mysterious buyers that remained anonymous even to him, the project was almost out of control. These people thought

277

they should still be able to contact him with their complaints about each other. As soon as he divested himself with Bobby's sale he planned to turn the homeowners association over to the petty homeowners and let them fight it out.

"I'll keep an eye on him for you, Joe Don."

"See that ya' do," warned Joe Don.

John could see the speeding speck that was Bobby at the bottom of the hill and suggested to Joe Don that they take the rest of the morning off and have a drink. Joe Don heartily agreed with the idea, began to ski and promptly fell over.

XVI

The bulldozer drivers were careful. They began a berm several feet away from the fence. Bobby could see there wouldn't be a problem and he thanked the operators for their consideration. One of the drivers mentioned that he had worked in Aspen Elks Estate before and he was sorry to see the last lot getting "dozed". He was corrected in that there was actually one more left and it belonged to the man with a shovel in his hands.

Bobby continued to finish the final portion of his dig. When he didn't strike rock, he slumped against the big boulder in the center of what was now almost a basement and contemplated his future. Donna and he had finally discussed finances after she was let go from her job. If Bobby sold the house to John or Joe Don, together Bobby and Donna would have enough of a fund to survive in a friendly fashion. Precisely, this meant they could move somewhere, buy a modest abode, pay bills and, if they managed to find part-time employment, travel a couple times a year. Maybe not far, certainly not in a luxurious style they didn't desire anyway, but they could visit the Grand Tetons, national forests in Maine and spend a few weeks in select villages along the Pacific and Caribbean coasts where most tourists don't frequent.

The deal was done, then. He would call Donna and find out if she was ready. He left a message on her cell phone and then called John Hamlin. He left a message with John's secretary. He visited the Drs. Corning and informed them of the outcome.

The Drs. Corning were sad, though Harriet asked Bobby what he was talking about several times. She would drift in and out, comprehending certain words, remembering some names, but her condition had deteriorated swiftly and dramatically. Harold was melancholic for a few minutes, but readily rallied and cheered Bobby to new adventures in life and love.

"I might caution you to avoid despair and defeat in this matter, Bobby. You've done what you could, what you asked of yourself. Now, let the rest of Caleb Century's story play out."

"Do you know something I don't, Doc? Wait, let me rephrase that. Of all the things that you know that I don't, do any of them include a happy ending to this?"

"Are you happy with Donna?"

"Yes."

"Are you happy that you undertook this challenge for the silver, whether you found it or not?"

"To be honest with you, Doc, I think I'd be happier if I found it, but I know what you mean. Yes, I'm happy I did what I knew I had to do.

"Though you haven't found it, it may still find you."

Bobby thanked Doc and then walked into town to talk with Jeff and Melissa. Jeff and Melissa wanted to host a fundraiser for Bobby so he could bring in machines and finish the dig by raising his house and excavate to the four corners of his property. He declined their offer and reminded them that the reason he had believed in the silver to begin with was because of the journal. If it wasn't where it should have been, Bobby reasoned, it had already been found and carted away. But the metal had been there at one time, Bobby had no doubt.

He heard back from John Hamlin and they agreed to meet tomorrow morning and discuss the paperwork. Bobby requested that Joe Don bring his checkbook.

Donna called Bobby as he was walking back to the house. They talked about his decision and reminded themselves that they knew it could come to this, though they never really had accepted the probability. He told her he would know how long before the deal would close after his conversation with Hamlin and Joe Don tomorrow. Donna planned to drive from Denver in the morning.

***

The meeting took place in Hamlin's office. Becky's perfume was faintly recognizable, but she was nowhere to be found. Bobby hoped she hadn't tried to sneak into his house while the meeting transpired. He was growing suspicious of its stability. Now that Donna was here, he had arranged to have some two by fours dropped off so he could buttress the foundation, narrowed and thinned through all his mining. He would do that right after the papers were signed.

"See, here's the deal, Bobby," began Joe Don. "Remember that sugar I was going to throw on top? Well, I'll still do it, but only if you're outa here by June first."

This would give Bobby a little over a month and a half to move out, to where he didn't know yet. He had assumed it would be to Donna's, but she was now thinking of renting out her house the first of May and spending the month in Aspen with Bobby.

"That's a possibility Joe Don." Bobby gave the impression of a defeated man, finally vanquished by the inextricable forces of a rampaging greed and materialism that continued to slowly consume what couldn't forever defend itself. "I suppose we should discuss what you plan to do with the house."

"Why, we have to keep it for something, that's the agreement with the City. But, that'll be no affair of yours." Joe Don locked his best poker face with a downward motion of his hand, hoping to conceal his plan to

281

accidentally knock the house over and pay a fine. "In fact, you don't even have to bother putting the dirt back underneath that creaky, buckled floor."

"Joe Don, I don't have words to thank you for your generosity."

"He really doesn't," added Donna.

Bobby signed papers, Donna looked sad, Hamlin couldn't conceal the smirk of victory and Joe Don puffed up enough so Bobby took a pencil and gently poked him in the stomach. "I didn't want you to explode, Joe Don."

"From here on out, it's party time, Bobby. Just be gone when you're suppos' to be."

Donna watched Bobby shake hands and noticed a subtle change in him. As they walked through the main office of House and Home, Bobby slipped into a skip, stopping to kiss the cheek of Casey, the receptionist. He pushed open both exquisitely etched doors and escorted Donna onto the mall.

The day was sunny and the weather was warm. Donna looked at Bobby with a cocked head, curious as to what he may or may not have up his sleeve. He motioned her to a bench and sat down beside her.

"Donna, darling, there are times you just have to accept the outcome. Like your job, the way they tossed you without any feeling or respect. It doesn't affect in the least what kind of person you are and it won't change how you treat other people." He turned toward her as much as he could, avoiding falling off the bench, and continued, "And there's nothing else I can do about the silver. I thought it was there and it looks as if I'm wrong. I can't really complain about the result, though, can I? I'll still sell the house and make money. I won't be broke, we'll have enough to do what we need to do, even what we want to do. It's the kids coming up behind us with less of a chance to find a spot like I was able to find, a chance like I had. That's who gets damaged more every day."

"What do you want to do now?

"I thought we'd go see the Drs. Corning and let them know."

***

Dr. Harold Corning answered the door and showed Donna and Bobby to the kitchen. Harriet was reclined in a chair as they walked past, apparently asleep.

"I'm pleased you both stopped by today. I have some news to tell you." Harold coughed, shifted in his hard backed kitchen chair, clasped his hands and said, "It's Harriet. She isn't going to live much longer. In conjunction with the Alzheimer's disease she has a brain tumor. I'm having hospice come in later today."

Donna cried, went over to Harold, leaned down and gave him a hug. She then went in the living room and knelt beside Harriet. Bobby and Harold stood, hugged and sat down again. Harold had become something of a part-time father to Bobby and Harold cherished the affection.

Bobby informed Harold of the earlier meeting at House and Home. Harold replied, "Looks like we will be leaving this neighborhood at the same time. I concluded that one result or another, you would move away, Bobby. Perhaps you and Donna will come visit me. I lived around Mt. Shasta many years ago and I'm going to return. Sure, there's an earthquake coming, but no matter where you choose to go conditions won't be perfect. Aspen proves that, doesn't it?"

"I've been to Mt. Shasta many years ago."

"It hasn't changed much," said Harold with a chuckle. "You know, I thought of leaving the country for Costa Rica, Belize, New Zealand or some other beautiful spot with water at my door step.

283

"I just can't depart this country. I love America. There is no better nation with a prouder history or brighter future. We are still the world's hope. Our history is checkered, but our possibilities are limitless. All you and I can do is hold true to the proposition that all men are created equal by their creator and have a responsibility to their fellow creatures. Nourish life." They moved to the deck above the river and waited for Donna to finish her time alone with Harriet.

"Oh, I meant to ask you if you had heard about what occurred near those homes where the southern Californians live? I believe you've met them," added Harold.

"Um, I may have. Possibly on a snowmobile excursion this winter."

"Yes, I think they mentioned that." Harold grinned, and said, "Not very friendly or accommodating people unless one agrees with them, I discovered."

"Oddly enough, I suffered the same sort of experience."

"Well, yesterday I was walking past their houses when I observed a work crew adjacent to the road. Apparently, there had been a cave in of some sort. The workers had been excavating for an addition foundation." Harold frowned. "How many square feet do two people need to live? More never seems to be plenty. Oh, well, let's don't concern ourselves with the small stuff, not matter how big it seems."

Donna emerged from the house, expressed her sorrow and offered to do whatever she could for Harold. Shortly thereafter, Donna and Bobby walked the long way home so they could take a gander at the cave-in Harold had mentioned. There was a slight depression, but nothing as dramatic as Bobby had hoped to see. Not that he was promoting ill circumstance upon his neighbors, just that the day had already held such large developments he assumed there would be something more to ooh and ahh over.

When they arrived back at the house, Barbara and Hef Bennington were examining the two by four pine planks stacked in Bobby's front yard. There were twenty four of them. Bobby planned on eight each for the sides and four each for the ends. He figured a support every five feet should bolster the foundation concrete so the house wouldn't fall down. Though, he was beginning, for some strange reason, to lose his attachment for the structure. Bobby nodded to the Bennington's and began to walk with Donna toward his front door.

"Excuse me," nearly shouted Barbara.

"You can stand where you are, Barbara. I'm not going to call the cops," said Bobby as Donna smiled and they continued to walk.

"I think we need to talk, Bobby," contributed Hef.

Bobby turned around and approached the Benningtons. "I have no idea what we should talk about, so you begin."

Hef, wearing shorts a little early in the season, arched his back and raised his chin. "Just what do you think you are building here?"

"I guess it's my turn. Excuse me, but what business is it of yours? I can understand Barbara, an esteemed member of our beloved city Council, inquiring of such materials. Barbara?"

"Well, what exactly are you thinking of building here? You need a permit, you know."

"It goes along with my excavation permit. I'd rather leave the house standing when I move. That would complicate Joe Don's life. I know this sounds cruel and spiteful, but, at the moment, I'm enjoying that unanticipated benefit."

The Benningtons gave each other a look of surprise.

"Don't tell me you didn't know?"

"We've been out of town. We just concluded the transaction for the Corning's house over there and thought we would see if he would let us begin touring it before they move out. We drove by here when nobody answered their door and became concerned that you might be setting yourself up for further trouble." Hef looked pleased with his transparent fabric of a fib.

"I honestly can't tell you how that makes me feel, Hef. At least, not without truly landing myself in trouble." Bobby stepped toward Hef, who backed away with alarm. "Hef, I'm a little different than you, that's true. But neither of us has probably hit anyone since middle school. Grow up. Oh, and get off my land." Bobby turned and walked with Donna to the front porch, carrying a couple of the two by fours with him. Barbara and Hef disappeared around the curve where they had parked their car and drove away.

"Aspen is in safe hands when the public officials pay that close attention to detail," offered Donna. When they entered the house, the dust kicked up and sent shafts of spinning light across the room. "That's beautiful," she added.

"And so are you," complimented Bobby. "Speaking of attention to detail, I'll bring in the rest of the planks, you hand them to me down in the mine and then we'll begin discussing our next big move."

***

Bobby felt the foundation was shored up appropriately and, as the evening fell, the cool air brought their bodies closer together. Soon, they were in the bedroom and Donna swore she could feel the earth move.

"No, literally, I felt the earth move. Maybe it was the house, actually."

"I didn't feel anything. I mean, of course, I did, but, well, I didn't feel the earth move. I have to be honest. It was good, but..."

"There! There! Did you hear that?" Donna jumped out of the bed and wrapped a robe around her.

Bobby paused as he climbed out of bed. He felt the minutest of movements and heard a creak. "Yes, I did hear that and I felt an inch of a sway or something."

"The house is falling down!"

"No, no, it isn't," laughed Bobby, as he came to her and hugged her tightly.

Rain had begun to pelt the windows and they could hear the wind howl in the trees. It was true, thought Bobby, that the house was moving a little, but he convinced Donna that it was nothing more than what he had already noticed before she arrived. Still, his own confidence was strengthened by the planks he had just propped between the dirt and the concrete foundation above them.

Gradually, the spring storm blew through and Bobby went down below to look. There was a little water at the far end of the house again, a place that had been dry and disappointing. All the planks were in place, though one or two may have shifted an inch outward from the walls. He wasn't worried and he certainly would be able to honestly assure Donna.

"It's not safe, Bobby," she responded when he presented his report.

"Now, honey, you won't even go below to ascertain if what I'm telling you is true."

"Oh, I believe you think it's true, Bobby, but I feel what I feel and I know what I know."

"Can't argue with that," countered Bobby.

Donna squinted her eyes at him, a sign he had come to know and feel did not portend the most favorable result of this discussion.

287

"I tell you what. Tomorrow morning, I'll get some guys in here to check it out. If they say the foundation is unsafe and we're going to fall in the hole or tip over, we're outta here."

Donna contended she didn't sleep at all that night. Bobby made the unfortunate mistake, in his own sleep-deprived condition, of agreeing that she looked like it.

However, the construction crew that Bobby had found up the street at the southern Californians' abode, confirmed that there was no real danger of the house's foundation failing.

"How about a fake danger, then?" demanded Donna. These workmen seemed rather phony to her, unable to explain the sunken dip by the house to which they were preparing to add an addition.

"Donna, dear, they're construction guys, not geologists."

And with that, Donna and Bobby proceeded to sit at the kitchen table and begin a list of what Bobby would throw away, donate to charity and keep for their happy lives together. Donna's list was considerably shorter than Bobby's, but they kept working in compromise until Bobby's list was as short as Donna's.

XVII

Included in the deal with Joe Don Burke via House and Home was the use of a house on the west end of town for the summer. It allowed him and Donna a summer together before figuring out their next step. Plus, thought Bobby, the house and yard would be a lovely spot for an outdoor wedding and reception.

Donna rented her house, finished placing her items in storage in Denver by the first of May and drove to Aspen with what she considered to be her necessities. These included, among certain pieces of furniture, boxes of clothes and pieces of art including paintings and framed photographs, her own record albums, photo albums, dishes and cookware.

Bobby resented none of these selections, except, perhaps, her record collection. Some of Donna's duplicated his own copies, but, generally speaking across the board, Bobby felt his taste in music was adequate for them both. This proved not to be true.

In fact, as a reward for their 'discussion' about this subject, they promised each other to attend at least forty classical concerts this coming summer as performed by the Aspen Music Festival. They judged themselves equally ignorant of the majority of the master's catalogs and resolved to remedy the void.

As Bobby helped Donna move her furnishings and other needed objects into the summer house, as they took to calling it, they drew a date for the evacuation of Bobby's house. Bobby wrote the numbers fifteen through thirty-one on slips of paper and placed them in a cowboy hat.

He carried the hat through the cowboy swinging door at The Cebolla Roja and together they joined Melissa and Jeff for a few cocktails and the drawing. This took a couple of hours and many songs performed by The Band and the Grateful Dead from their mainly acoustic period. With each number drawn from the hat a sip was taken. The final slip of paper, pulled by Donna, was the number thirty. The previous number had been fifteen, a number that she would have been happier to see, but in the excitement of the event and the accompanying beverages, the result was inarguable.

***

Bobby began moving in the same deliberate and thoughtful manner he had dug out the crawl space. He didn't tell Donna, but she noticed that he seemed to be moving items in an extremely equitable pattern. If one hadn't known better, Bobby may have been accused of removing items by weight, so that no one room bore the brunt of heavy furniture.

He continued to inspect his support system on a regular schedule, morning and night. Though there was no cause for alarm, he found himself growing nervous and suspicious. Nothing should be put past Joe Don or John and Becky Hamlin, he murmured to no one in particular several times a day. Then, his paranoia would creep back into the depths from which it emerged and he would sigh relief. The time was coming closer, as time will, and he found that he was experiencing feelings he never thought were possible.

He actually thought he was going to be happier when the move was finished and he and Donna settled in with each other, absent the drama of his dilemma. She had proved to be a perfect partner in the purging of his thirty year old collection of unneeded, unused and unbearable 'things'. She found no other word adequately described some of the souvenirs he had kept over the seasons. For such a small house, he had been remarkably adept at stashing useless mementos, obsolete and broken gear and out-of-date and style clothes. If the 1970's ever came back, Bobby would be dressed for the occasion.

Donna had been very helpful in directing Bobby as to what should be discarded and what might be appreciated as a donation. He inventoried what remained and suddenly discovered he didn't really have very much to move. Donna was delighted.

***

With only two weeks before the end of May, Dr. Harold Corning and Bobby narrowly avoided driving into each other on the road before Bobby's house. Harold was returning from Harriet's funeral in Boulder. Donna had driven down to join Harold and was now in Denver checking in with her renters.

The two gentlemen climbed from their vehicles and embraced. After relating the events of Harriet's services, Harold asked Bobby if he had recently been on the little road going past the homes of the southern Californians. When Bobby replied that he hadn't, Harold suggested they go together for a walk.

Halfway to their supposed destination, Bobby stopped and said, "What the heck is that?"

"Near as I can comprehend, Bobby, it's a sinkhole."

"What? A sinkhole? I've never seen one, though I've heard of them."

"I actually scuba dived in the one off the coast of Belize many years ago. Of course, they usually only achieve notoriety when houses, bridges or factories are swallowed." Harold stood studying the phenomena, his hand absentmindedly rubbing his whiskered chin.

Bobby approached the hole cautiously, a few feet in front of Harold. The diameter was about five feet and the hole probably not much lower than the same amount from

291

the surrounding terrain. It was eerily circular, almost as if punched out from a cookie cutter. The new green grass still covered the sunken portion and the sides were shades of brown dirt embedded with rock and ripped roots.

"Do you think this is connected with that little depression further on up the road?"

"Oh, I do indeed, Bobby. I don't think you or I are moving any too soon. There's something amiss below this ground. Perhaps an underground river, maybe old mining tunnels or the curse of the Ute Indians finally coming to prophecy."

The two men walked around the sinkhole, listening for some sound that might help them identify a cause. All they heard were the birds in the trees, particularly the mocking crow repetitiously cawing from above. Suddenly, the crow descended into the hole and proceeded to hop about in what both men thought looked like a celebratory dance.

They returned to their vehicles. Bobby went to the house on the west end where he would continue to live with Donna for the next three months. Dr. Harold Corning drove to his house where the movers were beginning to arrive. Virtually all his possessions were being taken for storage in Fort Collins while he spent the summer near Mt. Shasta. He wanted to ascertain if that was where his heart took him before committing to a complete relocation. Donna and Bobby helped Harold remove the last few items from his house over the course of the next week. Bobby had seen Joe Don a couple of times and had asked Joe Don if he wanted Bobby to clean the house before he completely moved out. Joe Don looked at him like Bobby just didn't get it.

***

Joe Don had decided the backhoes and other heavy machinery parked on his lot needed security until Bobby had finally vacated the house. Bobby thought this was amusing, because Joe Don had hired a firm that was owned by Benny the Bookie, Bobby's former financial advisor.

The backhoes were in complete synchronous mode with the dump trucks that hauled away excess dirt and rock from Joe Don's lot. It appeared the crew had been given a deadline, as they hurried to finish excavating for the mansion's basement before the end of May.

Donna, Bobby and Dr. Harold Corning watched the frantic efforts with a certain sense of bemusement, but also concern. Even though Bobby had closed the deal, the legality of the transaction wasn't complete until midnight of May thirty-first. Bobby occasionally expressed a frustration with how close to his fence the crew was dumping rocks and backfill dirt. He was concerned that the fence remained standing until he was gone. It seemed slightly irrational to Donna, quirky to Harold and mildly confusing to even Bobby.

The three of them watched the final moving van drive away from Dr. Corning's house, while the Benningtons arrived for their inspection. All seemed in order and the couple left with nary a hello and goodbye. How the mood of Aspen had changed, mused Bobby.

He and Donna had been planning their upcoming summer with the enthusiasm of tourists visiting Aspen for their first and only time. Bobby had suggested they do all the things that the residents rarely do. Go on every excursion recommended by the tourist board, undertake every hike and nature walk they could find, tour every historic building and house, relax on the lawn outside the music tent to soak in the background sounds of Mozart, Bach and Beethoven, attend the rock and roll and jazz weekend festivals in Aspen and Snowmass, bike to the top of Independence Pass, raft the white water of the Roaring Fork River, play with water balloons on the mall and

293

innocently ask questions of those workers and pedestrians who adopted the self-assured atmosphere of a local.

They were understudying their new roles this morning with a late breakfast at an outdoor café with Harold. He had agreed to stay with them for a week in their west end abode before traveling to California. Donna and Harold proceeded on to the house while Bobby ventured back for one last visit alone with his memories. He climbed down into the crawl space and rested against the smooth limestone boulder. The water had returned, but that was no longer an issue for him. He gazed all around, examining every dirt wall and foot of floor for some shining, gleaming reflection from his flashlight that would signify ore.

There was nothing to see and nothing to hear. The roar of the machines behind his fence had ceased for the worker's lunch break. Gradually, though, he sensed a hum, maybe a growl. A rumble, then a roar. Bobby scrambled as quickly as he could to the open trap door as the house began to shift above him. He clutched the edges of the floor above him and pulled his elbows to the edges. He forced himself up onto the floor as a mighty Whoosh! sucked the air out of him and the house.

The ceiling allowed splintered sunlight through and it shone on his face like a mesmerizing beam. As suddenly as the earth had moved and the ground grumbled, the motion and voice ceased. Bobby stumbled out the front door and looked around the yard. His truck was there, sandwiched between the mounds of dirt he had moved.

He walked around the side and toward the back of his house. He saw crew members perched on the top of their machines looking over the fence and into his back yard. They were pointing, gesturing and yelling to each other. When one spied Bobby, he motioned for Bobby to stop. He looked at the rear corner of his house and saw that it had split apart. Instead of stopping, he rushed to the back of his house and to his back yard. Except that his back yard was gone.

An almost perfectly circular sinkhole had consumed what was once his sanctuary and summer retreat. It was at least twenty-five feet deep. The tall blue spruce that had held his hammock was leaning perilously close to collapsing into the hole. Amazingly, the fence still stretched across the boundary between his once–upon–a–time yard and Joe Don's lot. Bobby presumed that he was a better builder than he had given himself credit.

A few of the workers were making their way cautiously around the corner, while others were climbing into their vehicles and leaving. Bobby inched closer to the edge of the sinkhole and looked down. There was some grass, broken flower pots, branches, flowers, dirt, rock and a small puddle of water in the middle. He glanced around the sides of the hole and, as he came to the portion that was next to the back of his house, he saw a glint that reflected the sunlight behind him. As he bent down to take a closer look, the ground shifted beneath him and he slid back away from the crumbling earth. The remaining workers turned and left.

Alone with the quiet, and still with the absence of wind, Bobby contemplated what he now saw. Here was the silver. Protruding from the dirt wall were three small boulders the size of large soup kettles. Below, mixed in with the debris, Bobby could see reflections from chunks the diameter of dinner plates. He sat down and stared.

"My, my. So, I was a touch off, eh, Caleb?" He spoke out loud to the ghost of the journal keeper. A slight shaking of the ground, however, roused him. Bobby reached into his pocket and called Benny.

Shortly, Benny arrived and together they maneuvered a backhoe around the fence and within proximity of the sinkhole. Carefully, gingerly, they extricated the boulders from the side wall. The highest one almost tumbled into the sinkhole, but bounced off the middle one and into the backhoe bucket. They loaded the silver boulders into the back of Bobby's truck and returned the backhoe.

"You know, I would have taken that bet," Benny finally volunteered.

"What bet?"

"The one that you would have found the woman of your dreams and the silver of your fortune all within a year."

"Truth of the matter, is that it's taken sixty years."

They looked at each other and nodded. "I guess it has," agreed Benny.

***

The next afternoon, the thirty-first of May, Bobby, Donna and Dr. Harold Corning journeyed to Aspen Elk Estates. Joe Don was standing near the sinkhole.

"Well, I guess we figured out where that water was coming from. Lookee down there," Joe Don said and pointed to the bottom. Water was half way up the sinkhole, concealing the chunks of silver at the bottom and the evidence of missing boulders at the sides.

"Leave it to Joe Don to have a bigger sinkhole than everybody else," said Bobby.

Joe Don turned to Bobby. "Well, a deal's a deal. I don't reckon the City will ask me to save your old house now, though."

The four of them eyed the corner coming apart, the roof twisted and the bedroom window swinging in the late spring breeze. Bobby turned and looked beneath his fence, thinking the sinkhole had grown. He wondered, Wouldn't it be odd if Aspen Elk Estates was built on top of a series of sinkholes? If all these huge and high mansions that look down on all else should sink below the ground? Why, it would be like throwing money down a hole.

"What do ya say we go on over as we planned and sign the papers?" Joe Don finished.

Bobby and Donna wrapped their arms around each other while Dr. Corning chuckled.

They walked with Harold to Bobby's truck and climbed in. As they did, Joe Don noted how clean the truck bed was. It practically sparkled, as with specks of silver.

THE END

ADDENDUM

Six selections from "The Poems of Tad Johnson"

The Money Sonnet

From you who have much more is required,
to those in dire need more must be given
in both extremes men's fortunes are mired,
so by circumstance their souls driven.

From you who have much little is taken,
for those with a pittance nothing remains.
by money or spirit do hearts awaken,
reach out to or ignore the people's pains?

Trials and tribulations call us to work
to save ourselves, our next door neighbor.
in this mighty quest yet surges this quirk-
that what you sow you will reap with labor.

Those who have much with little have it all,
you see it in how they answer the call.

The Death Sonnet

I was dead before and I'll die again,
perhaps leaving a legacy someplace.
I have no idea where, how or when,
but one of these lifetimes I'll find a trace.

I'll take a long look and just let it go,
something I could not do this time around.
I'd relive the past and forget to grow,
think more of where I've been than where I'm bound.

'Cause now I'm walking in a waking land
and my future is in the here and now.
it isn't that I really understand,
but to get there I do know this is how.

I was born again, I'll be born some more,
I'll be born again through God's other door.

Nature's Villanelle

The night air is notched by a cold stone breeze
it reaches into our brains and bones
from calm river running to deep wild seas.
its grasp is sure and made with tender ease
like the lover who gives just what she owns
the night air is notched by a cold stone breeze.
we breathe in cool air and speak as we please
listen to the waves that the water moans
from calm river running to deep wild seas.
we murmur in the mist beneath wet trees
in long language of leaves and split pinecones
the night air is notched by a cold stone breeze.
sweet rain where we rest on sore bended knees,
a promise to return what darkness loans
from calm river running to deep wild seas.
before swift winter's ice begins to freeze
against roots and rocks where it aches and groans,
the night air is notched by a cold stone breeze
from calm river running to deep wild seas.

For the Girl I Never Found

While the music sings our thoughts aloud
we dance lightly with the partner we brought,
we twirl as two unaware of the crowd.
we can't remember who asked and who bowed,
who took whose hand first, for it matters not,
while the music sings our thoughts aloud.
this dance together that makes us each proud,
to release a spin and be safely caught,
we twirl as two unaware of the crowd.
heartbeats quicken as we remove the shroud,
recall every step we were never taught,
while the music sings our thoughts aloud.
quick timbre and tempo become endowed
with the music's magic and passion's plot,
we twirl as two unaware of the crowd.
our close caress and soft smile allowed
was never denied, nor was ever sought,
while the music sings our thoughts aloud,
we twirl as two unaware of the crowd.

the map

smooth granite gravestone,
birth and death and final words
hidden in its veins.

decisions

pearls before swine
may be cruel to divide
and unfair to both.

About the Author

Tom Elder lived and worked in Aspen. He also lived Downvalley. He now lives further Downvalley in another valley altogether, with his wife, Mary. He is presently a substitute teacher educating temporary children on permanent subjects. He occasionally visits Aspen, sometimes even with his body.

It's All About the Timing

It's All About the Timing

Made in the USA
Lexington, KY
06 February 2013